Haas

The Medici Hawks

MARTIN WOODHOUSE
and
ROBERT ROSS

E. P. Dutton • New York

First American edition published 1978 by E.P. Dutton, a division of Sequoia-Elsevier Publishing Company, Inc., New York.

For information contact:
E.P. Dutton, 2 Park Avenue
New York, N.Y. 10016

Library of Congress Catalog Card Number: 78-5505-1
ISBN: 0-525-15463-9

10 9 8 7 6 5 4 3 2 1

The Medici Hawks

One

ON AUGUST 11TH, in the year 1480, the invasion fleet of Sultan Mohammed II captured the coastal city of Otranto, and thereby gained a foothold on mainland Italy.

Driven before a scorching easterly wind, forty-six galleys of the mighty Ottoman Empire arrived offshore just before dawn. By early afternoon the town was in the hands of the Sultan's young commander, Shan Khara.

He had expected no other outcome. His force consisted of three thousand Janissaries, the Imperial elite, together with an equal number of supporting troops and twelve heavy cannon. These fired stone shot weighing three hundred pounds apiece, and Shan Khara fired only one round from each of them. He was the finest gunner in all Turkey, and he did not believe in wasting ammunition.

His opponents, the defenders of Otranto, were few in number and low in morale. The garrison contained barely a thousand men-at-arms, about equally divided between exiled Venetians, exiled Neapolitans, and unsuccessful mercenaries. Otranto itself was a pleasant enough city, if somewhat remote and desolate, with a civil population of some twenty thousand or more, but to the common soldier a posting there was considered a prison sentence to be served in the sinkhole of Italy.

It was a sentence richly deserved by its commandant, the aging *condottiero* Sigismondo Malatesta. For him even the most hardened felon in the ranks felt a grudging admiration, mingled with distaste.

Sigismondo Pandolfo di Malstesta had in his youthful days, been called the most barbarous man in the civilised world.

He had poisoned his first wife, and strangled his second.

5

He had committed incest with his own daughter, and had raped the daughters of many others. It may be added that, comprehensive in his sexual tastes, he had also raped their sons. On one notable occasion he had violated the fresh corpse of a young German noblewoman, whom his supporters had accidentally murdered while trying forcibly to abduct her. Excommunicated for these crimes, together with those of forgery, blasphemy, and heresy, he had been burned in effigy by Pope Pius II in Rome.

Mere excommunication, naturally enough, would have been no hindrance to the career of a *condottiero*. A leader of mercenaries is judged by one standard only, which is that of effectiveness in battle. Here, to his misfortune, Sigismondo Malatesta committed a sin far greater than those for which the Church had rejected him. He was a military failure.

During his middle years, therefore, his employers deserted him and his resources dwindled. At forty-seven, he was forced to accept a crusade in Sparta at the pitiful fee of three hundred florins a month. On his return, in a fit of pique, he made the final error of attempting personally to assassinate the successor to Pius, Pope Paul II. Embittered now, at the age of sixty-three, ugly, heavy-set and ravaged by the twin demons of syphilis and gout, he found himself defending a minor Venetian supply depot at the southern heel of Italy. His home town of Rimini had thought him dead for twelve years.

A rapid count of the invading ships told Malatesta, at dawn, that neither he nor Otranto had any hope.

An hour later his handsome and merciless young opponent, Shan Khara, tore a section from the cathedral tower with his first cannon shot by way of demonstration, and knocked a breach in the city's seaward wall with his next eleven. The first wave of howling Janissaries, white-robed and brandishing scimitars, met with only token resistance from the panic-stricken defenders. The second wave met with none at all.

Shan Khara entered Otranto at his leisure. Those parts of the city which he did not need for his own purposes he ordered to be razed to the ground. Before deciding how to dispose of the population, civilian and military, he climbed the stairway to Malatesta's quarters with four lieutenants

6

and, in faultless Italian, requested the defeated mercenary's formal surrender.

'What are your terms?' asked Malatesta. His sword lay on a table in front of him.

Shan Khara appeared puzzled. 'Terms?' he said. 'There are none. Your city has fallen, and is now in the hands of Allah, the Almighty and Merciful.'

'I am aware of it,' replied Malatesta. 'I am asking what ransom you seek for myself, and what price you set on safe conduct for my troops. Their arms and armour are yours. I need supplies for a three-day march to Taranto.'

'I do not understand you,' said Shan Khara. 'Neither you, nor they, will march anywhere.'

'What then?' asked the *condottiero*. 'You do not propose, surely, to slaughter us?'

'Why not?'

'Because,' Malatesta said, 'to do so would be both wasteful and uncivilised. Moreover it will certainly bring Rome, Venice, and Naples down upon you like a swarm of hornets. If you deal with us fairly, then the city-states will see you as a man worth bargaining with. Is that not your ultimate aim? And besides, ' he added shrewdly, 'it will buy you several weeks of delay, which you may use to refortify Otranto.'

An unpleasant smile fleeted across the Turk's features. 'I will promise you, if you like, that your men will not be killed at once,' he said. 'I have need of labour, and therefore of slaves. They will build what fortifications I require, and you will work alongside them until you drop, as befits an infidel and a coward.'

At this, Malatesta reached across the table and picked up his sword. He turned it over once or twice, as though examining its blade.

'What is this?' demanded Shan Khara.

'It seems we have been speaking at cross purposes,' replied Malatesta. 'I am a mercenary, and fight for hire. If I am defeated, I seek to negotiate fairly with my opponent. I thought you would understand that.' He straightened up, and looked at the young Turkish commander. 'I am too old to be a digger of ditches, and I do not take kindly to being called cowardly by any dog of a heathen. Defend yourself.'

7

Shan Khara shrugged indifferently.

'Take him,' he ordered.

Malatesta killed two of his lieutenants before their scimitars were free of their scabbards. As they rounded the table, he chopped viciously to right and left, the edge of his blade biting deeply into their necks. They fell, but the white linen robes they wore entangled him as they did so, and he was able to only wound the third in the shoulder before he was overcome. Moments later, he was on his back with Shan Khara's foot across his throat.

'I withdraw it,' said the Turk shortly. 'You are not, at least, a coward.' He swung his heavy steel crescent downwards, and Malatesta's head rolled clear of his body, which convulsed once and then lay still.

The loss of two of his officers put Shan Khara into a mood of suppressed irritation all afternoon. When he saw the golden satin canopy of Sultan Mohammed's personal galley arrive among the fleet that lay in the harbour mouth, he went aboard it and prostrated himself.

'Lord,' he told his ruler simply, 'they will treat us like merchants if we do not teach them otherwise.'

Sultan Mohammed II considered this opinion for a while. He was reclining against the back of an ebony divan, and wore a cloak made from the skins of Persian gazelles draped around his massive shoulders. Though in his late fifties and dogged by recurrent fever, his eyes were still piercing and he ruled his empire as he had done ever since his accession as a young man, offering swift personal justice to his subjects and an implacably barbaric cruelty to his enemies. He had two sons, both of whom he regarded as worthless; therefore he looked upon his youthful commander as once he had hoped to look upon them.

'What would you do?' he asked.

'Lord, I would teach them,' Shan Khara replied. 'And in doing so, instruct all Italy.'

'Then make an example of them,' said the Sultan, 'remembering only that the Koran enjoins us to offer them salvation, if they will accept it.'

Shan Khara went ashore again at sunset, and vented his annoyance with swift and terrible efficiency. The Arch-

8

bishop of Otranto, who throughout the brief battle had remained at his altar imploring the help of God, was sawn in two before the cathedral doors. The civil governor suffered the same fate, after his wife and two sons were disembowelled in front of his eyes. To the rest of the city's inhabitants Shan Khara offered a straightforward choice; conversion to Islam, or death. Those who renounced their faith were enslaved as manual labourers or in the Turkish galleys. The younger and more presentable of the women were rounded up to await shipment to Constantinople; the elderly or infirm were set free in the surrounding barren countryside, where most of them perished from hunger.

Those who refused conversion were taken to the top of a low hill overlooking the town. There were about twelve thousand of them, and all were slaughtered. Some were used as living targets for Shan Khara's bowmen. Some were dismembered piecemeal, or drawn and quartered, or torn apart for sport by teams of horses. Others were soaked in oil and burned alive, the flames that shrivelled them in screaming agony illuminating the sky far into the night. The bodies of all were left to the dogs.

Having thus purged Otranto, and while the stink of charred human flesh still hung over it like a pall, Shan Khara set about refortifying the town, particularly its landward side. He had more than five thousand slaves with which to undertake this task, and if the time at his disposal for its completion worried him at all, he did not show it.

Four hundred miles from the scene of these events, a man and a young woman were sitting in the tiny walled garden of a villa in the Tuscan hills, a day's journey from Florence. The scent of vines sweetened the fading twilight, and the night promised to be hot and dry.

The young woman was Bianca Maria Visconti. She was seventeen, and her family had once ruled the powerful northern city of Milan; but the Visconti were now scattered in exile through France and the Low Countries, and her cousin Lodovico Sforza had made her a ward at the court of Florence. She was Countess of Abbiategrasso, though her title had been all but forgotten by others and meant little to Bianca herself.

9

She was of medium height, slender, and beautiful. Her hair was long and fair, and her golden skin lightly freckled. Her mouth was considered appealingly generous by those who admired her, and her mind and movements were those of a dragonfly.

She was, at the moment, wearing fewer clothes than her Florentine guardian, Lorenzo de' Medici, would have thought proper. Indeed, since the evening air was sultry and she had recently been posing as a model for her lover, she was sitting naked upon a silken scarf. She had a smudge of charcoal above the nipple of her left breast.

Her companion wore a linen shirt open to the waist and russet-coloured hose. He stood a little over six feet tall, broad chested and narrow in the waist. At a distance he appeared to be lightly built, but he could straighten horseshoes with his bare hands and had been known, for a wager, to stop a cantering stallion by catching its bridle as it passed him. He was clean-shaven, and had reddish-golden hair. His eyes were pale blue—the blue of ice, some said—and were deeply set beneath heavy blond brows. He was twenty-eight years old.

He was squatting tailor fashion beside a small oval pond scattered with the pads and blooms of water lilies. On a stone by his side rested an open lantern, and in one hand he held, gently and delicately, a bat. The creature moved its head from side to side and chittered at such presumption; but, dazzled by the nearby light, it made no attempt to fly away to rejoin the squadron of its fellows that swooped and dived for gnats above the ebony waters of the pool.

'Isn't he pretty?' said Bianca, leaning forward. 'Look at his ears!'

'She.'

'I beg your pardon?'

'*She* is pretty. I agree with your judgement, but this is a female bat,' explained Leonardo da Vinci.

'And how do you know that?' asked Bianca suspiciously.

'Through long and patient study of bats. That is how.'

'I don't believe you. You may know a great deal, but you are always *saying* you have the answers to questions about which you know nothing at all. Admit it.'

'Certainly not,' Leonardo said. 'After all, I have been

studying you for a long while too, and I have no difficulty whatever—'

'But I am not a bat.' Bianca raised her arms and stretched luxuriously. 'And those things about me which prove my sex are easily seen. Aren't they easily seen, Leonardo?'

'And beautiful beyond comparison,' said Leonardo. 'Yet, on the other hand . . . '

'On the other hand, what?'

'Since we cannot inquire, we do not know whether they would be equally obvious to a bat. You perceive the difficulty?'

'I perceive that you are about to win another argument.'

'Out of doors I always win arguments,' Leonardo said. 'In bed, never. It's an excellent arrangement. Here.'

'Yes,' said Bianca. 'Give him to me, poor little thing. You are mistreating him. Or her.' She held out her hand, and felt the bat's claws grip the ends of her fingers. 'What is your interest in bats?'

'They fly.'

'This one does not seem to wish to.'

'She will, when I close the lantern. She is a flying mouse. And if a mouse can fly, why not a man?'

'Because a man is too heavy, even if he could make himself a pair of wings.'

'And not strong enough to move them. Yes.' Leonardo smiled at her. 'As a matter of fact, I believe you're quite right, my darling.'

'Close the lantern,' Bianca said. 'She's frightened of us.'

'She knows we mean her no harm. What does she remind you of?'

Bianca bent her head and studied the bat carefully. 'A gargoyle, perhaps?' she suggested. 'I suppose that is why stupid people are afraid of bats; they look like the devil, or one of his imps. Close the lantern, Leonardo.'

He obeyed. The bat slithered across Bianca's palm; and spread its leathery wings. Squeaking, it launched itself, and was gone.

'Personally,' said Leonardo, half to himself, 'I imagine Satan—if I imagine him at all—as looking somewhat like the Count of Imola. Handsome on the outside and yet rotten within, so that you can look at his eyes and see

11

through them the very pit of hell.'

Bianca shivered. 'Don't speak of him!' she begged. 'it will bring you ill fortune. Come inside.'

If to speak of the devil is to summon him, as many believe, then Girolamo Riario, Count of Imola and Captain-General to the armies of Rome, resembled him in more respects than Leonardo had suggested. Two days later, old Jacopo toiled up the hill from the village and knocked at their villa door.

'Rome is about to disturb your love-making,' he announced.

Leonardo gave him a florin and a cup of wine. 'In whose person?' he asked.

'The Count,' said Jacopo, and spat.

'Has he an escort with him?'

'A company of Florentines, sir. It amazes me that they haven't slit his throat before now.'

'He must have a safe conduct from Lorenzo de' Medici,' said Leonardo. 'I thank you for being my ears, friend Jacopo.' He went to find Bianca, who was brushing her hair by the garden pool.

'When will I learn to trust your intuition, my heart?' he asked. 'Riario is here in the village.'

At once Bianca rose to her feet in alarm.

'Then we must leave at once!'

'No,' said Leonardo. 'I think we are safe enough.'

'Safe? From that Roman carrion? How many times has he tried to murder you, Leonardo?' Bianca covered her eyes with her hands. 'I am sorry,' she went on more quitely. 'I shouldn't behave like a hysterical child, but somehow the mere thought of Girolamo Riario makes me shake with horror. Others have tried to kill you, but he seems to make even death itself fouler and more loathsome than it already is.'

Leonardo took gently hold of her wrists. 'I am not over-fond of the Count myself,' he admitted. 'But this time it seems he's accompanied by a party from Florence.'

'But how could that be?'

'It is simple, I think,' Leonardo explained. 'The Turks have landed on Italian soil. I predicted last year that they

12

would do so, didn't I? Rome, therefore, must put together a patchwork of allies as best she can, and has accordingly forgiven Florence our terrible offences against the Church —such offences, you know, as our having routed Riario at Castelmonte, and not having permitted Rome's agents to murder Lorenzo de' Medici as well as his brother. That kind of offence. Take heart, my love. If you'd care to dress a little less provocatively than usual, you might even offer Rome's Captain-General some refreshment.'

'Not I! I would spit in his face first,' declared Bianca. 'I care nothing for political friendships and alliances, which are as filthy as he is. Be careful!'

Leonardo kissed her. 'Since he has half Florence with him,' he told her, 'I am likely to survive this meeting with him, at least.'

He received his guest at noon, in the spacious hall of the villa. Girolamo Riario, black-haired and wearing a breast-plate of fluted steel with a cross at one shoulder, was accompanied by a Papal Nuncio, three pages, and his personal bodyguard. The latter was a tall man of about forty, with deeply hooded eyes.

Behind these six were ranged some fifteen or so Florentine soldiers under a captain of infantry, and the resulting atmosphere was very far from cordial. Girolamo Riario, indeed, saw no reason to be courteous. He was, after all, the acknowledged nephew of Pope Sixtus IV himself—though there were more than a few who went further than this, and said openly that he was the Supreme Pontiff's unacknowledged bastard.

'You are to accompany me to Rome,' he announced. 'Now.'

'Oh?' said Leonardo. 'By whose orders?'

'Those of your ruler, Lorenzo de' Medici.'

'I see. It may surprise you to learn,' Leonardo said, 'that although Lorenzo de' Medici is Florence's ruler and mine, I do not always obey his orders.'

'It does not surprise me in the least,' sneered the Count, 'seeing that you keep his ward as your whore.'

'My lord,' said Leonardo gently, 'let me make things still plainer to you, since you must have them so. I imagine you

13

have a piece of paper somewhere which grants you safe passage throughout our republic? You have? I thought so. Well, Count, if you do not keep a civil tongue in your head, I will ram your safe-conduct between your teeth and kick you all the way down the hill which you have just climbed at such pains. Do I make myself clear enough?'

'And we'll help you do it,' muttered a low and unidentifiable voice from among the ranked Florentines, all of whom were gazing innocently towards the ceiling when Riario turned to glare in their direction. He turned back again. There was laughter, and the Count set his teeth.

'Show me your orders,' suggested Leonardo.

Riario handed over a parchment scroll, which the artist scanned minutely before giving it back.

'I will follow you in about four days,' he said shortly.

'That is not what your orders tell you to do. They instruct you to accompany me. Today.'

'I know that,' replied Leonardo. 'Must I explain once more? I do not obey orders blindly, but only to the extent I agree with them. You will oblige me by returning to Florence forthwith—it will not take you far out of your way—there seeking out three of Captain Rigo Leone's gunners. You have cause to be familiar with the Medici Gunners, have you not? I see from your face that you have. Well, I care not which three of them Captain Leone can spare me, but he is to send them here in order to escort the lady Bianca Visconti safely back to the city. When they arrive I will leave this villa, and not before. Nor do I propose to ride anywhere in your company, Girolamo, since my back is a broad target for stray knives and I prefer to travel with an easy mind. And now be on your way. I will meet you in Rome.'

'His Holiness shall hear of your insolence,' said Riario.

'I am sure he will,' replied Leonardo equably, 'and as you see, the thought makes me tremble in my boots. However, I have no need of Sixtus. It is Sixtus who apparently has need of me. In this, for once, he shows the stirring of wisdom, since it's likely that I am the only man who can save Italy from the Turks. Good day.'

'A self-confident fellow,' said the man with the hooded

eyes, as he rode alongside Riario down the dusty road to Florence. 'And to some extent impressive.'

His name was Antonio da Narni, though he was sometimes known —as his grandfather had been known— by the nickname of Gattamelata, the Honeyed Cat. Three generations of the Narni family had served Venice as mercenaries, but the services offered that city by Antonio were of a more specialised nature than those of his father or his grandfather. For the time being, for reasons of her own, Venice had placed those services at the disposal of Girolamo Riario.

'He is the bastard son of a provincial notary and a serving girl,' said Riario. 'That is all. I will admit that he has become a thorn in Rome's side.'

'But it is improbable that he can save Italy from the Turks.'

'He is vainglorious. Of course he cannot.'

'And yet it was his cannon that drove you out of Castelmonte two years ago,' continued Antonio da Narni with deliberate persistence. 'Was that mere vainglory?'

Riario made no immediate reply to this, and Narni reined his horse closer. Glancing across at his employer, he saw on the Count's face a look so malevolent, so coldly evil that he recoiled and allowed his mount to fall back a few paces.

'It was a surprise attack,' said Girolamo Riario after a while. His voice seemed deceptively calm. 'Well executed, one must grant, but nothing more than that.'

'Was it?' replied Narni. 'Well. We shall see what we shall see. I serve Venice, and Venice believes Leonardo da Vinci to be a dangerous man. A man, perhaps, who would be better dead.'

Two

'WHAT IS THE Turkish intent?' fluted Pope Sixtus IV. His
fingers worked nervously on the arms of his inlaid chair.
'What is their ultimate purpose, and is it possible for them
to achieve it? Do they imagine they can subject all Europe
to their heathen dominion? We believe they do. We have
therefore brought you together, in brotherhood and in
peace, to determine what must be done to prevent them *at
whatever cost.*'

He subsided. His bulbous eyes roamed here and there,
fearful yet calculating.

The commercial and military might of all Italy seemed to
have gathered in the library of the Papal Palace in Rome.
And not of Italy alone; the ambassador of King Louis XI of
France was present, as were the envoys of the King of
Hungary and Maximilian of Austria. Spain's Legate-
General sat beside Cardinal Rodrigo Borgia, himself of
Spanish descent; they looked bored, as was the manner of
Spaniards, but their expressions belied their true feelings.

From the Italian peninsula itself, the city-states of Milan,
Florence, Genoa, Ferrara, Siena, Bologna, Lucca, Mantua
and Montferrat were represented. Ferrante of Naples, in
whose territory the city of Otranto lay, had come to Rome
in person, and as a gesture towards Florence had
withdrawn his son Alfonso the Terrible from Tuscany.
Between Rome and Naples there was little love lost.
Neither would have supported the other if their common
foe had not been the long awaited, and long feared, Sultan of
the Ottoman Empire. So it was between many of the cities
whose delegates were present; each had been rudely
astounded by the invasion and collapse of Otranto, each
sought co-operation from his fellows, and all sought, in
addition, their own advantage.

Or perhaps not quite all. Of the assembly, two men alone were above the fray, considering only what was best, and not what was most expedient for this interest or that. One was Leonardo da Vinci, and the other was the careworn and greying man of fifty who sat beside him—Rome's Apostolic Chancellor, the Cardinal Domenico della Palla. These two, artist and prelate, had known each other for barely thirty-six months, and yet they were probably the only people in the room who had achieved true friendship with one another. It was a precarious friendship, perhaps, and one whose warmth was for the most part carefully concealed by both of them; but it existed and it was growing.

They sat at the back of the assembly, as befitted those who had no axe to grind. Leonardo was sketching in his notebook. By his side Cardinal della Palla registered disapproval of this informality by remaining bolt upright and listening with apparent attention to the Supreme Pontiff's renewed flow of words.

'If the faithful wish to preserve their lands,' intoned Sixtus IV, 'their houses, their wives, their children, their liberty, and their lives, if they wish to maintain that faith into which we have all been baptised and through which we are regenerated, then let them at last trust in our word. Let them take up their arms, and fight.'

'And let them, also, take care to look over their shoulders while they are doing so,' murmured Leonardo, inaudibly except to Cardinal Domenico della Palla. 'My lord, I am a penniless scholar, and faint with hunger. I crave the boon of supper with you tonight.'

'We are a long way from supper yet,' whispered Cardinal della Palla severely, 'but you may indeed take it with me at my apartments—if you will grant *me* the boon of your silence for the present.'

Some hours later, Pope Sixtus IV led the way into a small private salon, where he addressed Leonardo and Count Girolamo Riario.

'Leonardo da Vinci,' he said, 'you are our well beloved son in Christ, no matter what sins you may have committed against the Church in times past. We have summoned you

17

to Rome in God's own work. Take the hand, then, of the most excellent Captain-General of our Armies, Girolamo Riario, Count of Bosco and of Imola. Promise us that all enmity between you is finished. For you have a most formidable task to accomplish, which is that of dislodging the heathen from their hold on that Kingdom granted us on earth by Almighty God, and we cannot allow you to seek each other's harm while you accomplish it.'

Riario's smile was broad and like a steel trap.

'My life upon it,' he said, and held out his gloved right hand. Leonardo took it in his own.

'I wish no man harm,' he said, and knelt briefly to kiss the Papal ring before departing.

'A penniless scholar, indeed!' said Cardinal Domenico della Palla. 'I know very well that Lorenzo de' Medici gave you thirty thousand florins for taking Castelmonte. And he gave you the Tuscan estate in exchange for that jewelled clock you presented to him last year.'

'My lord, you are wrong,' Leonardo said, smiling. 'I have merely borrowed the estate and its villa. It is true that they were offered to me as a gift, but I cannot carry an estate with me when I travel, and anchors make me uneasy.'

The Apostolic Chancellor glanced at him shrewdly. 'Well,' he said, 'at all events I dare venture he paid you nothing for your escapade in Venice, whether you rescued his ward or no. Am I right?'

'You are, my lord. He abused me somewhat for it, but that was all. He has a tongue that cuts like a whip, but he means nothing by it.'

They were in the Cardinal's apartments in the Lateran Palace, overlooking the Piazza San Giovanni. The room was neat and austere, most of its walls taken up by rows of leather bound books.

Della Palla laughed. 'Do you drink wine, Leonardo?' he enquired, with his hand on a bell rope. 'I confess that I don't, but as host to a starving scholar I daresay I can find some.'

'I thank your Eminence,' Leonardo replied, 'but I am indifferent to wine. When I am in the company of Captain

18

Leone and his gunners I drink it, since it would be an affectation not to do so. Here, I can do without.'

'And in the company of the lady Bianca Visconti?'

'My lord,' said Leonardo simply, 'when she is with me, we need no wine to bring us happiness.'

A servant brought in a cold supper on several trays. When the Apostolic Chancellor had filled their two platters he returned to his argument.

'Do not suppose that you will persuade me to approve of your liaison with her, my son,' he said. 'How old is she?'

'She is seventeen, my lord, and therefore a grown woman. She has a mind of her own, I might add.'

'So I hear from her tutors in Florence. Of whom she has seen little this summer, but that is by the way. Do you talk with her, then? On matters apart from love and passion, I mean?'

'Of course.'

'And what do you discuss?'

Leonardo smiled. 'Most recently? Bats.'

'*Bats?* Why bats?' della Palla raised his hand hastily. 'I withdraw the question,' he said, 'since I already know the answer to it, and I did not invite you to share my supper in order to hear more of your fantastic opinions concerning flight. Why don't you marry the child?'

'By whose permission?' said Leonardo. 'It is most unlikely that we should ever be allowed to wed, as your Eminence knows full well.'

'And do stop addressing me as "Your Eminence",' said Cardinal della Palla testily. 'The name given me when I was received by God is Domenico.'

'Sir . . . my lord . . .' replied Leonardo in some confusion, 'I do not know that I should feel—'

'On second thought,' said the Chancellor, 'let us leave things as they stand. I was going to suggest that you use my title whenever your conversation was likely to be offensive, heretical, subversive, challenging, or otherwise annoying to me. To return to your lamentable affair with the lady Bianca . . . you are aware that Maximilian of Austria is seeking her hand in marriage, I expect?'

Leonardo pushed his platter from him slowly.

'No, I did *not* know that,' he said. 'Are you sure?'

'I never say anything of which I am not sure. It is true. I offer you the information as a gift, since to be forewarned is also to be forearmed. And now,' said Cardinal della Palla, 'to Rome, and the Turks. His Holiness will receive a great many flowery promises for today's work, but very little practical help. My net is extensive, as you know. I hear things, and have been known upon occasion to write them down.'

'Which is why the power of your Office is greater than that of the Papacy,' said Leonardo. 'Well, my lord?'

'Naples, who is directly concerned, cannot help herself,' said della Palla. 'She must fight with all the material at her disposal. Florence will provide fifteen galleys. Genoa, five. Venice, none. Ferrara, perhaps four. Siena, three. Bologna will promise two, but will deliver only one. Lucca, Mantua, and Montferrat are good for a single ship from each, if that. The same tally will hold for men and for money. Nothing will arrive in time for any assault on the Turks at Otranto. Thus, if you intend to do anything useful, I must point out that you'll probably find yourself alone. Would you care for an apple?'

'Thank you. Are they afraid?' Leonardo asked him.

'Who? The city-states? They are confused, I dare say. As time wears on and nothing happens—and nothing will happen, since Sultan Mohammed will be quite content to remain where he is for the present—they will relax their vigilance and begin to carry on their normal business, which is fighting with each other.'

Leonardo bit into the fruit offered him by the Cardinal.

'You are certain that the Sultan will do nothing?' he said.

'Reasonably so, reasonably so. Why should he? Let us grant that he has achieved one aim, which is to throw Italy and half Europe into a flutter. What then? He has chosen his first blow well, since the occupation of Otranto gives him command of both sides of the Adriatic. But—does he have territorial ambitions in Europe? We cannot tell. What is certain is that he has strategic problems. The Ottoman Empire is vast. Long supply lines, delay in transmission of orders and information, things of that nature. If he fortifies Otranto and stays where he is, he invites Italy to strike a return blow. If that blow fails, as he may well be confident it will fail, then he'll know our strength or our weakness, how long it takes us to organise, and how many of our cities will finally agree to move against him. After that it will be time enough for him to decide his European policy.'

'Sir,' said Leonardo, 'it is a great pity that you do not command Rome and her armies.'

'Is it? Perhaps it is,' said Cardinal della Palla. 'His Holiness, at all events, is badly frightened. Of that I can assure you. My correspondent in Avignon tells me that the Papal Court there is being made ready to receive our Holy Father should he decide to flee Rome.'

'And Girolamo Riario?' asked Leonardo.

'He seems unworried. I wonder why. Of course,' said the Chancellor, 'you know he wants your death. An obsession, no doubt. I think he is pleased to have you near.'

'Then . . . Domenico . . .'

'Yes, Leonardo?'

'Of your kindness, give me what protection you can,' said Leonardo. 'I do not ask for miracles. I can retake Otranto in one fashion or another, but I cannot at the same time be in Rome, and Florence, and Venice. I need a wall at my back.'

'I will be your wall,' said Cardinal della Palla.

Leonardo returned to his modest lodgings in Rome's outskirts a little before midnight; he went to bed with the hilt of his sword resting conveniently to hand, having little faith in Papal assurances and Girolamo Riario's protestations of goodwill. The night air was hot and sticky, and smelled slightly of decay. The plague was overdue in Rome this year, he thought. A bright harvest moon shone outside the arched window at the foot of his pallet. Leonardo lay on his back, impatient for sleep and yet driven to consider the Apostolic Chancellor's words.

There had been, he realised, a notable absence from the audience which had listened to the rhetoric of Pope Sixtus IV. Venice had not been represented. Yet Venice was the city which had most to lose from the Turkish presence in Otranto. For Venice's lifeline to the foreign trade that made her rich lay through the Adriatic, the Strait of Otranto, and so out into the wide Mediterranean.

It was always possible, of course, that Venice was already seeking some treaty of accommodation with the Sultan for this very reason. She might, for instance, accept a levy upon each of her ships allowed passage through the Strait. But why should this keep her from Rome? He must discuss the matter with Cardinal della Palla in the morning, he thought as he fell into a light and dreamless sleep.

He was not at first aware of what it was that woke him. He lay quite still, on his back, with his eyes half closed. A man who has reason to fear assassination does well not to move immediately, when awakened; not unless some instinct forces him into blind reaction.

Leonardo kept his head motionless, therefore, and looked about the room as best as he could. His mind retained the half unconscious imprint of a small sound, perhaps the soft thump of a piece of heavy cloth dropped to the floor.

He saw the pale moon-lit outline of the window at his feet. His first thought was that someone was lowering a knotted rope from the floor above, and that it was dangling and swaying slightly in the arch.

At once he perceived that this impression was wrong. A soft hiss penetrated the room, like the gentle rattling exhalation of a dying man, and he caught sight of the glint of eyes in the moonlight as the monstrous snake coiled on the sill turned its bulbous head towards him. No adder, he told himself, could be that big, nor would it possess the flaps of skin at either side of the neck that gave this creature the appearance of some huge and deadly fruit upon a writhing stem. It was a cobra, he thought, though he had never seen one; that sacred killer of the Orient and Arabia, the legendary horror whose bite was instant death and which spat its venom at its victim's eyes.

Its own eyes now seemed to lock upon him; the gaping mouth hissed again.

Slowly, Leonardo drew his feet up the bed toward his chin. The thing was immense; it stood tall as a man, it was thicker than an anchor cable. It could reach his legs with a single lightening strike from where its coiled base rested on the stone ledge of the window. What would happen if he reached for his sword? He decided against the attempt. As

22

though reading his thoughts, the snake leaned forward.

The tales of travellers insisted that the cobra could paralyse its prey by staring at it. Leonardo's pulse slowed and steadied, and he knew what he must do. He gripped the upper edge of his blanket, pulled it loose from the foot of the pallet, and flapped it at the animal. The cobra reared, and struck swiftly at the moving blanket; a drop of tepid moisture splashed against Leonardo's cheek, burning slightly as it made contact with his skin. He jerked at the blanket with all the force and speed he could muster, and felt the bony snap he had hoped for as the poison fangs broke out of the serpent's jaws. It thrashed like a bullwhip, still tangled in the rough woollen cloth. He rolled from the bed, seized his rapier and hacked at the giant cobra again and again, until he was sure that the remaining convulsive movements of its body were those of death.

Then he went to the basin and ewer which stood on a marble stand at the far side of the room, drank a scooped handful of water, and washed his face with care.

On the following morning Leonardo obtained a large sack from the tavern keeper and put the body of the cobra into it. Slinging this burden over his shoulder, he made his way once more to the Lateran Palace, and sought admission to Cardinal Domenico della Palla's suite.

Here, he laid the snake out on the carpet.

'A fearsome and deadly beast indeed,' said the Chancellor. 'I have never seen a serpent so large.'

'Nor I, until last night,' said Leonardo. 'But it is one of God's creatures, and was no doubt as alarmed as I was. The question is: where did Count Girolamo Riario obtain it? I'm assuming for the purposes of argument that it did not fly all the way from Arabia and enter my window of its own will.'

'I think,' said della Palla. 'that this is not the Count's work, or at least not directly. I cannot believe him subtle enough to deal in murder by snake bite. An ambush in a back alley I could credit. But not this.'

'I think I agree with you,' Leonardo said.

'The idea, of course, may have been his,' said the Chancellor. 'I am sure you are right in that. Which is likely

to make Otranto an interesting place for you, my son.'
'Why?'
'Because Girolamo Riario is leaving for Otranto to-morrow, with two thousand men and four heavy artillery pieces, and I cannot protect you there. Not, it seems, that I can do so even in Rome. Go with God, Leonardo.'

'A serpent?' said Cardinal Rodrigo Borgia. 'My dear Chancellor, how interestingly original. Tell me more.'
They were dining on Borgia's terrace. The two Cardinals were neither friends nor enemies, but felt for each other a certain cautious and neutral respect. It was Cardinal Rodrigo Borgia's intention to become Pope one day, a fact of which Cardinal della Palla was quite aware. For his part, Borgia was one of the few men in Rome who appreciated the Apostolic Chancellor's intelligence system and the considerable acreage of files he kept beneath the Lateran Palace.
Both men were vastly more capable intellectually than any of their fellows in the College of Cardinals, and this gave them something in common.
'Riario is bent upon destroying him,' said the Chancellor, 'and it would be a great pity if he succeeded.'
'So you keep reminding me,' Borgia said. 'I concede that one of them is likely, eventually, to kill the other. What of it?'
'You have no interest in the outcome?'
'Well,' said Cardinal Borgia, 'little practical interest. You will not persuade me to choose sides, Domenico. You know that. Where is your artist now, by the way?'
'He has returned to Florence, at my instructions.'
'For what purpose?'
'To collect together several of his friends, who are gunners.'
'Ah,' said Borgia. 'Leonardo da Vinci's famous small cannon again. Is he bringing these friends of his back to Rome?'
'No,' said Cardinal della Palla, faintly surprised. 'Why should he?'
'In order to take his cannon with him to Otranto.'

'What are you talking about?' demanded the Chancellor. 'His guns are in Florence, not here.'

Cardinal Borgia drank deeply, and wiped his lips with a satin napkin.

'The *new* ones are here,' he said. Then he looked closely at the Apostolic Chancellor. 'Or perhaps they are not his? They are being cast to his design, are they not?'

'Here? There are some new cannon being made in Rome?'

'My dear Domenico,' said Cardinal Borgia with barely concealed delight, 'I assumed that you already knew about these weapons. As a matter of fact, since it was to yourself that Leonardo da Vinci originally gave the designs, I thought they were being made on your orders. They're at the foundry of Messer Andrea Spoleto, you know. You *didn't* know? Domenico, do not tell me that I have at last got hold of a piece of news of which you're ignorant? How very unusual.'

'Unusual indeed,' replied Cardinal della Palla. 'So unusual, your Eminence, that I think I shall have to look into the matter.'

Three

LEONARDO DA VINCI travelled back to Florence by way of the small village of Pistrola, some fifteen miles from the city and now the informal headquarters of the Medici Gunners. They had adopted it for recreation and repair during the campaign against Rome at Castelmonte three years before, and had stayed there ever since. The rolling countryside which surrounded it was well suited to artillery practice; and Captain Rigo Leone preferred his men to spend their time and money in Pistrola rather than in Florence itself, wisely holding that the village provided better ale and wine, and fewer opportunities for mayhem.

The villagers on their part accepted Lorenzo de' Medici's now famous corps of troops with pride, the more readily once they had found out that the gunners paid handsomely for the lighthearted damage they frequently inflicted upon Pistrola's tavern and market square.

It was in this tavern—aptly re-named The Sign of the Gun—that Leonardo found the squat and powerfully barrel-chested figure of Florence's Captain-Gunner in his accustomed corner. Rigo greeted him with a wave of the split gunmetal hook that served him for a right forearm. Leonardo himself had designed and built this contrivance for the gunner who was his closest friend, and had in addition fashioned him a very lifelike gloved hand with flexible joints to improve its appearance. But Rigo seldom wore this, preferring to display the strength and precision of the bare metal device he now used to pass a tankard of ale across the table.

'Wash the taste of Rome from your throat,' he advised, 'and tell me what is afoot.'

'We are going to dislodge the Turks from Otranto,' Leonardo said.

'Are we, by Christ? That's excellent news. How?'

'I have no idea. But I've assured everyone that the Medici Gunners can do so.'

'Of course you have,' said Rigo. 'Did you see your friend Girolamo while you were down there giving these assurances?'

'I did. We shook hands in the presence of the Pope himself, and vowed that we would on no account seek each other's harm.'

'Did you, by God? And what then?'

'Oh, then he tried to kill me by putting a cobra in my bed,' replied Leonardo airily.

'What the devil is a cobra?'

'It's rather like a viper,' Leonardo told him, 'only larger.'

'How large?'

'Well, I thought this one could have swallowed me at a mouthful. But perhaps I was a little overwrought at the time. In any case, as you gather, it was an ordinary commonplace trip to Rome. In Rome they always try to kill me.'

Rigo Leone raised his tankard. When he set it down he was scowling. 'Be serious,' he said. 'It is long past time for Girolamo Riario to die. The next time I cross his path I shall break his back.'

'Not this year. The Count, like ourselves, will be fighting the heathen. Rome and Florence are now allies, Rigo.'

'Rome and Florence may kiss each other's backsides,' announced the gunner, 'but that doesn't mean I have to set aside my trifling wish to snap Girolamo's spine like a carrot.' He squinted across the table at Leonardo. 'He is going to be at Otranto, then?'

'Rigo,' explained Leonardo with patience, 'he is, after all, Rome's Captain-General. I expect he will be sitting outside the walls of Otranto by the middle of next week. And you and I will lighten his life by telling him what he's doing wrong. It's simple enough. And now, where are your gunners?'

The gunners were in a field half a mile from the outskirts

27

of the village. As Rigo and Leonardo approached them, they seemed to be engaged in manoeuvres, and arguing heatedly among themselves.

At one corner of the meadow, by a clump of willows, stood a rugged wooden shelter roofed with shingles, beneath which were ranged five of the Medici Guns. A sixth gun was in pieces in the centre of the field. Its carriage and wheels stood apart from the gesticulating gunners, four of whom were holding the barrel by means of the paired handles cast into its sides, while the others gathered around them. Since rapid stripping down and re-assembly of the weapon was a regular exercise for all six crews under Rigo's command, there appeared to be nothing unusual about this scene. It was only when Leonardo and Rigo came closer that Leonardo became suddenly alarmed.

He saw at once that the gun barrel was loaded; the rolled fuse of gummed paper, packed with a mixture of gunpowder and varnish, was protruding from the touch-hole in its breech. Moreover Tesoro di Veluti, the youngest of the gunners, was carrying in his hand a smouldering length of slow-match.

Leonardo broke into a trot, and reached the group a moment or two ahead of Rigo, who was roaring in outrage.

'What in hell do you think you're doing?'

Tesoro obligingly moved aside, to allow Leonardo and Rigo a clear view of the four gunners holding the gleaming bronze barrel. They were, Leonardo observed, probably the four least responsible and most foolhardy of the entire troop of fifty-odd men.

'It's a wager,' said Scudo, who was the largest of the four. He was a mountain of a man, standing six feet seven inches in his boots and weighing well over two hundred and fifty pounds, all of it bone and muscle. 'We are going to fire our little gun with the four of us holding it, as you see, rather than resting on its carriage. Agnolo says it cannot be done. I say it can.'

'It is, after all, a *portable* cannon,' said the man opposite Scudo. This was Cipriano di Lucca, a handsome, dandyish gunner with a broken nose. Cipriano was at least nominally, third in command of the troop, after Rigo and Agnolo Fulvio. It was immediately clear to Leonardo that this dangerous experiment had been proposed by Cipriano, which caused him little surprise.

'Put the gun down,' ordered Leonardo, 'and think.'

'What is there to think about?' asked Tomasello Cennini, who was grasping one of the forward handles. Leonardo knew him for a man who would do anything which smacked of risk, purely out of bravado. The fourth member of this misguided group was a large and amiable buffoon called Balestraccio, who said nothing. No one made a move to set down the gun barrel.

Leonardo surveyed the other gunners. Those at the fore were presumably holding the other side of this wager. Nearest to him was Agnolo Fulvio, in his forties and second in command of the troop. Close to him stood Guccio Berotti, Marco di Carona and Giunta di Lenzo, all of whom were good marksmen and crew leaders. The horses against the donkeys, Leonardo thought.

'Let them try it,' said Guccio Berotti. 'Fools must learn.'

Scudo turned his head and addressed Guccio over his shoulder. 'Close your mouth,' he instructed, 'and open your purse. There is nothing foolish here. This is not one of the monsters we used to handle. It is a small cannon. How much recoil can it produce? Very little.'

His description, at least, was accurate. The barrel they were supporting was barely four and a half feet long, and slender. Leonardo, who had designed the original Medici Guns, had improved them over the course of the past year, casting these later versions in bronze and winding each of them with three layers of tempered Damascus steel wire before annealing them. Accordingly, each barrel weighed a mere two hundred and forty pounds, a fact which Scudo now emphasised by signalling his comrades to let go of their handles. He then hefted the gun chin high, almost without effort.

'You see? he said. 'Tesoro, where are you? Light the fuse, infant, and let us collect our winnings.'

'*Wait!*' Leonardo said. 'I promise you that Guccio is right, and you are wrong. Remember Castelmonte, and the Casa Albano in Venice? These guns will smash a heavy oaken gate to splinters, and batter through a brick wall.' He picked up one of the small polished cannon balls. It lay in the palm of his hand, a steel sphere about three inches across and four pounds in weight. 'This may seem a toy,' he went on, 'but it leaves the muzzle with such force that it will break down walls and gates. And I assure you that the gun which fires it recoils with an exactly equivalent force, no matter how it may seem to you.'

'Is this more of your mathematics, then?' demanded Cipriano de Lucca rudely. 'Can you prove it?'

'Not exactly,' admitted Leonardo. 'But I know it to be true.'

'How do you know?' pursued Cipriano.

'It is in the nature of force,' said Leonardo. 'The mathematics I will leave until later.'

'Good,' said Cipriano. 'In the meantime, we are but following your own methods, which are those of experiment. Truth is found only by experiment, as you have told us many times. Stand aside.'

'Rigo?' said Leonardo.

'What do I care?' replied the Captain-Gunner.

Scudo grinned. 'Very well,' he said. 'Light the fuse, and let us see.'

Leonardo retreated to a safe distance, at which Scudo grinned more widely still. Tesoro di Veluti blew on the end of the slow-match until it glowed, held it against the quill in the touch-hole, and prudently stepped back out of the line of recoil. Leonardo's arguments had impressed him, even if they had made no dent upon the minds of Scudo, Cipriano Tomasello or Balestraccio.

The fuse spurted and flared. Its flame vanished into the bronze, and a second later the cannon boomed deafeningly, kicking backwards with the force of a mule team and hurtling from the grip of the four stunned gunners. It flew several yards before thudding heavily to the grass, where it lay smoking gently. Tomasello sucked his fingers, two of which were broken. Fortunately, this was the extent of the personal damage caused, though even Scudo was hugging a badly wrenched shoulder.

Leonardo said nothing.

'Well,' said Cipriano di Lucca, unabashed, 'it seems you are right after all. For so tiny a weapon, it has a surprising recoil.'

30

'And now that you have done,' said Rigo ominously, 'perhaps you'll settle your debts with those who have more sense than yourselves. Now gather round and listen. We have *real* work to do.'

'How many do you want to take with you?' asked Lorenzo de' Medici.

'Two only, apart from Captain Leone,' replied Leonardo. 'I need Scudo, who has enough strength for six ordinary men, and young Tesoro di Veluti, who needs experience and—I hope—is likely to do as he is told.'

Lorenzo de' Medici stared from the narrow window of his private conference chamber on the upper floor of the Medici Palace. The room was small, sparsely furnished, and monastic in appearance, with walls whitewashed for summer coolness. The street noises of Florence formed a busy and reassuring background to the cooing of doves in the garden beneath and the meadow beyond its walls. In the meadow itself some urchins were splashing one another with the waters of a stream, risking their ruler's anger with happy confidence; as did all the children of Florence. Lorenzo had barely turned thirty, but to his people he seemed middle aged, or rather ageless and unchanging. His face was stern, ugly, and powerful, and he seldom raised his voice in wrath. He had no need to do so.

'Very well,' he said, without turning from the window. 'You may take them. Leonardo?'

'Yes, sir?'

'Rome must fight the Turks, since they have invaded Christendom; the Pope cannot afford to stand by and do nothing to oppose them. Naples has no choice, either, because it is upon the territory of Naples that the Turks have set foot. But Florence has no need to fight them. Do you understand that?'

'I do,' replied Leonardo. 'If one looks at if from a certain angle, Sultan Mohammed has done you a favour, since if Rome and Naples were not distracted by his action they might both be at Florence's throat this autumn.'

'Quite true. And yet Florence represents all that is most admirable in Italy,' said Lorenzo. 'It is Florence who is the

31

guardian of Italy's free soul, and not Rome. If the Sultan strikes at any part of Italy, he strikes at us. We can easily perceive Rome's intentions. If Rome can defeat the Turks, and if she is plainly seen to have done so, then she is well placed to pursue her own aim, which is the control and leadership of Italy. Do you understand that, too?'

'Yes.'

'Do you agree with me?'

'Yes,' said Leonardo.

'Then do not let Otranto fall to Girolamo Riario. I want no songs of triumph sung for that foul carrion. Otranto must be retaken—but Italy must know that Florence, and *not* Rome, made victory possible. God knows this will be a hard task, the more so since I cannot spare you an army. And there are other things which you must bear in mind as well.'

'What things, sir?'

'I have no wish to quarrel openly with the Ottoman Empire, nor with its Sultan. I have a large and expanding trade in alum with the east, and I want eventually to open a branch of the Medici bank in Constantinople. I cannot achieve this by wiping my boots all over Sultan Mohammed's face. So you see,' said Lorenzo, turning at last with a faint smile, 'I have laid a heavy burden on your shoulders. I would not do so unless I believed them broad enough to carry it. We have something in common, you and I, which is confidence in our own respective abilities. Few can claim as much. Do what you think fit, and keep me informed. That is all.'

As Leonardo was already aware, Count Girolamo Riario had left Rome late in August. Since his army must cross the central mountains to reach Otranto, with siege cannon weighing upwards of eight tons apiece, he could not be expected to arrive at the extreme south eastern tip of the Italian peninsula before the end of September. Leonardo, therefore, saw no urgent need to rush.

He spent a week, then, in bidding a loving and reluctant farewell to Bianca Visconti. They stayed, as before, on Leonardo's borrowed hillside estate, a day's ride from the turmoil of the city. If Lorenzo de' Medici knew what they were doing, he was wise enough to keep his disapproval to himself.

Cipriano di Lucca, who was to take Bianca back to Florence when the time came for Leonardo to depart, stayed with them at the villa during the daytime. In the evenings he joined Rigo, Scudo, and Tesoro in the village below, pursuing his own pleasures.

'The Cardinal,' said Leonardo, 'believes that we should marry.'

'Does he?' said Bianca. 'Let him mind his own business. I am not ready for marriage yet. It's quite likely I never shall be.'

It was the night before they were due to part, and they were lying companionably entwined in bed. Two bats— possibly emboldened by Leonardo's gentle study of their habits—fluttered and dipped in and out of the casements like small ghosts. The sound of their wings thrummed in the vaults of the ceiling overhead.

'It is said in Florence that Lorenzo is negotiating your wedding with Maximilian of Austria. He has seen your portrait and is apparently madly in love with you,' Leonardo pointed out.

Bianca pinched him. 'I have no need to marry you just in order to discourage Maximilian,' she said. 'Nobody will ever negotiate *me* into marriage, though I suppose they'll keep on trying . . . don't do that.'

'What?'

'What you're doing now. It's lovely, but it stops me from thinking properly. In any case,' she added, kissing him, 'you are probably the only man who'd have me.'

'Why?'

'Because my face is scarred, though it can't be in the portrait they're showing around to people like Maximilian, I suppose,' Bianca said.

'So it is.' Leonardo ran his finger down the faint hairline scar upon her cheek and jaw. 'In a good light, if one is truly searching for it, one can almost see the mark of it. Do not be so vain.'

'That is not what Cipriano tells me. He says it makes me look mysterious and romantic. Anyway,' Bianca said, 'I see no need whatever for us to marry. I shall never love anyone

33

else, and nor will you; let that be enough for us. And now tell me what you have been doing in your studio downstairs these past days?'

Leonardo rolled to the side of the bed and stood up. 'Why, I had almost forgotten,' he said. 'I have made you a gift.' He went to a closet, and after a few moments came back with his hands cupped around a curious and fragile object built of silk, feathers, and slivers of wood. It was like nothing Bianca had ever seen before. Leonardo parted his hands, and the little contrivance soared into the air, whirring noisily, as it drifted across the room, impelled by a pair of flapping parchment wings.

Bianca jumped from the bed in high excitement and brought back the toy from the corner where it had come to rest. 'It *flies*, Leonardo! How marvellous! Oh please—tell me how you did it?'

Leonardo lit a paper on the bedside table, and demonstrated its delicate mechanism to her. 'Its wings are driven by these little cranks,' he said. 'Thus. You see? And the power comes from these strands of twisted leather, and from this spring here, which is made of bone.'

'Do it again, then.'

Leonardo, kneeling by her side, set the mechanism with care. From the gardens below the slightly drunken voice of Cipriano di Lucca, singing off-key, broke into the silence of the room. Bianca at once got to her feet and wrapped a sheet around her body. 'Give it to me,' she said. 'That's Cipriano, and I want to show him. How must I hold it?'

Leonardo put the tiny flying machine in her hands. Bianca went to the window that overlooked the garden.

'Cipriano! Cipriano, look!' she called.

Cipriano, weaving slightly, clapped his hand to his sword hilt and looked blearily about him until he saw where her voice was coming from. Recognising her at the window in the bright moonlight he bowed deeply and nearly fell into the fish-pond.

'My lady,' he said.

'Watch,' cried Bianca.

In order to launch the machine, she leaned well out of the window. At once, the satin sheet slid from her shoulders and its folds tumbled to the sill about her knees.

34

It must, regrettably, be recorded that the Lady Bianca did not immediately see fit to retrieve her lost modesty, as was proper. It may have been pure mischief on her part, of course. However, Bianca simply leaned forward, tossed the machine lightly into the air above Cipriano's head, and only then retired in search of the sheet's protection.

Cipriano, bemused, did not even catch a glimpse of the toy until several seconds after it had landed at his feet. To this extent, then, the first public exhibition of powered flight in history was a total failure. As for Cipriano, he blinked and shook his head as he picked the device up, laid it on top of a sundial, and sounded a long, low and very evocative whistle.

Bianca returned to the bed, the sheet trailing, to find Leonardo helpless with laughter.

'I'm sorry,' she said. 'But what was I to do?'

Leonardo made no answer. Bianca began to grow pink. 'Cipriano is like a brother to me, as you well know,' she observed. 'And furthermore, he has just spent all evening down in the village, and we both know what he's been doing there. So that by the time he came back here he can hardly have been thinking about . . . well, you know what I mean.'

Leonardo pulled her down beside him and kissed her soundly.

'Madonna,' he said, 'you are innocent beyond belief. Or possibly you're not. To take your points one by one; firstly, because Cipriano treats you as a sister, it doesn't actually follow that if he sees your naked body he will pretend you are a statue. Secondly, I take it you're implying that by this time of night he will have satisfied all of his sexual appetites. My sweet, I must tell you that I've known Cipriano for a long time, and I've never known his exploits with women to tire him in the slightest degree. And thirdly, even if he were so exhausted sexually as to make it necessary to carry him on a stretcher, the sight of your body in the moonlight would resurrect him at once. The trouble is, darling, that you simply don't know Cipriano. Though I'm delighted,' Leonardo added, 'to hear that his devotion to you is brotherly, or at least that he has told you it is.'

The following day dawned bright and clear. Leonardo saddled his stallion, kissed Bianca long and soundly, and rode down the steep hill to join Rigo, Scudo and Tesoro di Veluti.

Within the hour, they had left the village and turned their horses' heads southwards, towards the high passes of the Arno valley.

At noon, Bianca set out with Cipriano for Florence. She had cried briefly during the course of the morning. Her companion was suspiciously light of heart.

'We shall see them again sooner than we imagine,' he said. As it happened, he was right.

Bianca, after glancing across at him several times, spoke with a diffidence unusual in her.

'Cipriano?'

'Yes, madonna?'

'Last night . . .' Bianca began, and then stopped. Cipriano who had anticipated a conversation of this kind, became elaborate.

'I pray you to think nothing more of it, my lady,' he said. 'Let us think of it as a rare instant of beauty and truth, a moonlit glow which brought momentary radiance into the grey life of a poor soldier of fortune, and leave it at that. How else could one comprehend it?'

This piece of transparent hypocrisy nevertheless restored Bianca's spirits.

'As a dream, perhaps,' she replied tartly. 'What about a dream?'

'Of course. It was a dazzling dream.'

'Is that why you are screwing your face up?' asked Bianca. 'I thought you had a headache.'

'I have. By the way,' said Cipriano, 'what *was* that contrivance?'

'A flying machine,' Bianca said.

'Oh,' said Cipriano. They rode on towards the city in silence.

Four

CROSSING THE PENNINE Mountains by way of Campobasso,
Leonardo and his three companions reached the be-
leaguered city of Otranto on the thirtieth of September.
They approached it from the north west, after riding down
the Adriatic coast. Lying at the eastern-most tip of Italy's
heel, Otranto is surrounded by a plain, and much of the
terrain through which they spurred their horses was
marshy and desolate. Long before they came within view of
its walls they caught sight of many plumes of smoke rising
to the sullen skies.

'This is not the place I would choose to fight a war,' said
Rigo Leone. 'It smells of the fever, and despair.'

Six miles north of the town they detoured cautiously
inland, taking advantage of such hilly ground as they could
find. Below them lay the encampment of the Roman army,
its baggage trains and picket lines divided by a stream
whose sluggish waters were already fouled. The camp, the
plain, and the grey walls of the city formed a dispiriting
vision, even when briefly illuminated by the hazed autumn
sunlight. If he were given charge of the campaign,
Leonardo thought, he would allow Sultan Mohammed to
keep Otranto and the whole of Italy's heel. If he were held
at bay across the base of the peninsula between Taranto and
Brindisi, one could wait for him to overextend himself. But
no Roman commander, he realised, would take such a long
term view.

They reined in at the crest of a low ridge, and Scudo spat.

'All wrong,' said Tesoro di Veluti knowledgeably. 'See
where he has placed his guns? Foolish. He holds the nearest
bump of high ground simply because his gunnery

commander could not be bothered to look for a better position. What does he imagine he is firing at? The walls are thirty feet thick where he has chosen his aim.'

Rigo laughed. 'A fair summary, infant, though I do not recall anybody asking for your opinion. Proceed. What would you do in Riario's place?'

'Me? Build redoubts. And I would look carefully before I did so.'

On the plain below them, one of the siege guns puffed smoke like a toy, and its report echoed about them a few seconds later.

'Stone shot,' Scudo announced.

'Where did it strike?' asked Rigo. 'I did not see.'

'It flew high,' Leonardo put in. 'Come.' And without more ado he urged his horse southward, and the others followed him.

Late in the afternoon they made their own camp in a secluded glen where a spring bubbled up from beneath a moss-covered rock. They were four miles from the outposts of the Roman army, and if they were not totally concealed they were at least out of immediate view from Count Girolamo Riario's headquarters.

'We'll ride over and pay our respects when it gets dark,' Leonardo decided. 'For now, let's eat and make ourselves comfortable. Something tells me this is going to be a long and unprofitable task.'

'They have arrived,' announced Antonio da Narni, the Honeyed Cat. 'Four of them. I saw them ride past us to the west.'

'Damn their souls,' said Riario. 'Though in point of fact I could do with Captain Leone's advice. My own gunner is a fool.'

'And Leonardo da Vinci?'

'I would not take advice from him,' Riario spat, 'if he and I were the last men left alive on earth.'

Antonio da Narni looked keenly at him, but kept silent. The Count pushed his food away, and cuffed his page for being too slow with the fingerbowl. He rose and led the way out of the pavilion, taking his companion's elbow in a confidential manner.

'Gattamelata,' he said softly, 'how many men have you killed?'

'A sufficent number,' replied Narni. 'I keep no tally, since it would be wearisome. What matters from your point of view, my dear Count, is that no one else has been able to keep my tally either. My trade—perhaps I might say the speciality of my trade—is death by misadventure.'

'Such misadventure as poison?'

Narni shook his head. 'I know of only three people in Italy who are competent poisoners, and one of them is a woman. There is a great deal of stupid rumour concerning the efficacy of poisons. Few of them work. You may kill an old man or a sick one that way, but of ten people who are said to have died because of some poison in their food or drink, the truth is that nine die of ague or a fever or a suffusion, or of some other quite natural illness. Such stories serve the poisoners, I dare say since it increases their reputation at no cost to themselves, but that is all. White arsenic is fatal of course, but if one were to put sufficient white arsenic into a man's drink to kill him, he would spit out the first mouthful.'

'I am pleased to find you so expert in your craft,' said Riario. 'What of our problem here?'

'Poison would be of no use to you,' replied Narni. 'Did you not tell me that no breath of suspicion must blow in your direction? If a man falls dead at your table it will hardly serve your purpose, will it? No. Fortunately, we have other tools at hand.'

'Tools?'

'My dear Count, we are in the middle of a war, are we not? Men die in war. They can even be seen clearly to have died in war. Witnesses can attest to the fact.'

'In battle, perhaps,' rejoined the Count. 'But with less certainty in a siege, to my mind. Sieges do not often bring our enemy close enough to kill by hand.'

'Yet, it may be arranged,' said Antonio da Narni.

During their conversation they had been walking toward the fringe of the encampment. They climbed a low rise, and at its summit came upon a huge siege cannon. Its four wheels, each the height of a man, rested in shallow trenches lined with brushwood.

To one of these wheels a man was trussed, his belly against the axle spike, his arms spreadeagled and lashed to the rim.

It was almost dark, but in the twilight the cross-hatching of weals across his shoulders contrasted with the pallor of his skin. Black trickles of blood had coursed down his back, and were now dried.

Riario went to him and twined his fingers in the man's hair, wrenching his head backwards.

'Well?'

'My lord,' gasped the man, 'give me water, I pray you!'

'No.'

'Sir, sir! In the name of God, why do you treat me like this? Did I not come to you of my own free will? I risked my life!'

'You were captured by one of my patrols.'

'They did not capture me! I called to them! My lord, have I not said that I am Milanese by birth? I am no Christian, it is true, since I had to save my life when the Turks seized my ship! For this God will punish me. But I seek no harm to Italy. She is my mother country! Give me water!'

Antonio da Narni came up beside the Count. He looked at the beaten man with mild interest.

'His appearance is Italian,' he pointed out. 'What is his story?'

'Why,' Riario replied, 'it is simple enough. He was found wandering between here and the city by some of our outriders and brought in for questioning. In order to buy his worthless life he has produced some counterfeit tale of traitors in our camp, claiming that he deserted from the Turks in order to bring us this piece of nonsense.' He released the man's hair and forced his head against the wheel, so that his temple began to seep blood. 'Of course,' Riario continued, 'it is most likely that the reverse is true. He was probably sent here as a spy himself, which accounts for his appearance.'

'My lord,' cried the bound man, 'it is not so! Have I not told you everything I know? I am not even a soldier, but a steward. My position allows me to overhear things. I swear by the Virgin that what I say is true! Sultan Mohammed himself talked of his spy!'

'If you are not a Christian,' said Riario dispassionately, 'Then do not take the name of God's Holy Mother in vain.' He picked up a bloodstained leather whip and sliced it viciously against the man's back. 'Tell us who this traitor is.'

His victim groaned. 'I heard no name.'

Riario beckoned a man-at-arms.

'Twenty more lashes, and let us see if that will loosen his tongue.'

At the fourth blow the man began to scream thinly.

Two men rode up to the gun and dismounted. Leonardo walked swiftly to the soldier who wielded the whip, took it from him, and threw it aside.

'Enough,' he said.

The soldier would have turned on him, but found Rigo's hook at his chest and subsided. Leonardo slipped his knife from its sheath and began to cut at the cords which held the man's wrists to the rim of the wheel. Riario made no protest; he stood beside Antonio da Narni with a sardonic look.

'That,' he said conversationally to the Venetian, 'is Master Leonardo da Vinci, whose humanity is well known to one and all.'

'I hope I am also known for my common sense,' said Leonardo. 'What is his crime?'

'He is a spy.'

'And doubtless you were asking him questions.'

'It is the usual procedure, with spies.'

'And one which achieves nothing,' Leonardo replied. He was now supporting the beaten man, who clung to the spokes of the wheel against which he had been crucified. 'This man would have been flogged to death, which is merely brutal, or else he would have invented whatever lies he thought you would like to hear, which is useless. Useless brutality is your whole stock in trade, my lord. But you will not indulge in it while I am present.'

'You see?' said Riario to Narni. 'Did I not tell you he was a humanitarian?' He turned to Leonardo. 'What now?'

41

'Imprison him, or set him free,' replied Leonardo. 'Both are permissible in war.'

'And if we imprison him, I dare say you will make a better job of questioning him?'

'I could not make a worse one,' replied Leonardo. 'What is his name?'

There was no immediate answer to this. Leonardo turned to the man, who was rubbing his wrists. 'What is your name?' he asked.

'Stefano Morelli, sir.'

'Where are you from?'

'I was born in Milan.'

'You are a Milanese? They are famous gun makers there,' said Leonardo.

'The best,' said Stefano Morelli.

'Who was the greatest of them, when you lived there?'

'Vittorio Monforti, until he died. His workshops were taken over by another, who went to Florence, I think.'

'Rigo Leone,' said Leonardo. 'He stands yonder, before you.'

'That was the name.'

'I am amazed that it did not spring instantly to your lips,' said Rigo, coming forward with a grin. 'Well met, friend.'

'I am honoured, sir,' Stefano said. He worked his shoulders painfully, and the beginnings of a smile came to his face. 'Milan rings with your fame, I am sure; but it is a long time since I was in the city of my birth.'

'What happened to you?'

'I was taken off Ancona twelve years ago,' Stefano replied. 'Three Turkish galleys attacked our ship and took us prisoner. They offered us the choice of becoming Mohammedans on the spot, or dying. They always do this, or nearly always. I renounced Christianity, and became a steward in the service of the Sultan. It is not a bad life.'

'Are there many such as yourself with the Turks?' asked Leonardo.

'Very many. Have you not heard of the Janissaries? All are foreigners, not Turks. If a man is good at his trade, the Sultan would rather use him than kill him.'

From several paces away, Antonio da Narni came towards the gun.

'All of this is fascinating, no doubt,' he said. 'But what is its purpose?'

'Its purpose is to show you that there are better means of conversing with a man than flogging him half to death,' said Leonardo. 'You did not even know his name when we arrived upon the scene.'

'Your point is taken,' said Narni, a hand to his chin. 'Let him go.' He turned to Riario for confirmation. Riario said nothing. 'You are free, then,' he told Stefano Morelli.

'Thank you,'

'What will you do?' Leonardo asked the Milanese.

'Who knows?' answered Stefano. 'Sir, I thank you also for your mercy. Perhaps we shall meet again. For now,' his smile became a little more certain, 'I need my shirt.'

'In the name of God,' said Riario, 'give the fellow his shirt, and some wine and let him find his own way to perdition.' He turned on his heel, and was about to walk away when Rigo called to him.

'My lord Count!'

'What is it?'

'You should move this gun,' Rigo told him. 'It is serving no purpose here. What cannon has the Sultan?'

'I have no idea, Captain. He has fired none in this direction.'

'Then bring your own nearer the walls of Otranto, and half a mile northward,' said Rigo. Riario stared at him coldy for a minute, but made no reply.

As they rode back towards their own camp, Leonardo whistled merrily. Rigo was somewhat depressed and demanded to know why he was so cheerful.

'It was an interesting meeting,' said Leonardo. 'Stimulating to the mind, you know.'

'I found very little stimulating about it. I felt a powerful urge to break his neck, but that was all. Where is your interest?'

'When a man steps out of character, it's always interesting. Riario kills as naturally as he breathes. Then why did he let the man go, I wonder?'

43

Five

CARDINAL DOMENICO DELLA PALLA, Apostolic Chancellor
to the Holy Church at Rome, rode into Florence only a
few days after Leonardo had departed for Otranto; he was
disappointed to find him gone.

Ostensibly, the Cardinal had come to persuade Lorenzo
de' Medici that it would be politically prudent to make a
gesture of formal submission to the Pope. In fact, ever the
realist, he did not expect to persuade Lorenzo of any such
thing. In any case, della Palla did not care greatly whether
this aspect of his mission was crowned with success or not.
The Apostolic Chancellor held no brief for political
gestures. Had he done so, he might himself have been
Supreme Pontiff in place of Sixtus IV. Few men were as
clear-sighted concerning the realities and the trappings of
power as Cardinal della Palla.

He arrived at the Medici Palace accompanied by a
secretary and riding a mountain pony. Rome had often
pointed out that to travel without at least a page or two was
an offence against protocol. Cardinal della Palla's answer to
this was that he could dress himself tolerably well and had
often managed to take a bath unaided, and that protocol was
the final refuge of the incompetent. In this, at least, Lorenzo
de' Medici agreed with him, and this gave them some
narrow ground in common.

'The eloquence of Your Eminence is famed throughout
Italy,' said Lorenzo in the upper floor conference
chamber, 'and likewise the purity of your intentions.
Nevertheless, my answer is no. Are you hungry, my
lord?'

'I thank you, but I have eaten,' said Cardinal della Palla.
'No, you do not believe such an act of symbolic submission

44

to be in the interests of Florence? Or no, you will not in any case make it?'

'Let us suppose that I were to comply; to kneel three times to kiss the papal foot; to rise and kiss the papal hand. My countrymen would call me craven, and rightly so. They know, you know, the *world* knows that Rome slew my brother and came within an inch of slaying me. Abase myself to Rome? Plead submission? Let the Holy Father extend his apology to *me*, Eminence, if it is a symbolic gesture you seek. Beyond which, Rome needs me more than I need her,' replied Lorenzo. 'Tokens of submission are for children tussling in the streets.'

'You have not quite answered my question.'

'Nor do I propose to. My lord, let us have done with this play with words. You and I are grown men. What brings you to Florence?'

The Cardinal rose, gathered his robes about him, and crossed to the small window that overlooked the walled garden and the meadow beyond. After a moment or two he spoke without turning his head.

'Who is that?' he asked. 'Is it not the lady Bianca Visconti?'

'If you mean the young woman in the pale green cloak,' Lorenzo replied, 'yes. Is she on the bridge crossing the stream to the field yonder?'

'She is indeed.'

'She will be there until dusk, if your Eminence wishes to speak with her,' said Lorenzo somewhat drily. 'At least, such is her habit of late.'

'Why so?'

'Because she is young, and in love. Two conditions which provide their own answers for everything under the sun—or the moon. Her lover being elsewhere—'

'At Otranto.'

'I did not know, my lord, that you were concerned with the personal affairs of Leonardo da Vinci.'

The Cardinal turned. 'Are we not both concerned with them?' he asked mildly.

'Perhaps so. The lady Bianca is my ward, after all.'

'And you disapprove of their relationship.'

'I did not say so.'

45

'Your tone implies that you do.'

'Let us say, then,' said Lorenzo, 'that any relationship which binds Leonardo da Vinci to Florence—and to myself—cannot be merely a matter for approval or disapproval. He is not a man who can be held by a chain.'

'Unless the chain is one of his own making. Why not let them marry?' asked della Palla.

Lorenzo de' Medici allowed himself a shadow of a smile. 'The House of Visconti,' he murmured, 'is a prominent one, if a little decayed in these times. We must also consider the view of her cousin Ludovico Sforza, the Regent of Milan. I am sure . . .'

'And who is playing children's games now? Give Leonardo a city or two, a title, a province, and where is your argument? Has he not deserved as much? You cannot suggest, surely, that his manners and breeding make him unfit for life at court? I will name you six dukes whose pretensions flicker like expiring candles in his company. My lord, are you a hypocrite?'

'I am a practical man,' Lorenzo rejoined, undisturbed by this shaft. 'I have come to know Leonardo, a little at least. I assure you that he would not welcome a dukedom. Since it does not suit me to find him one, things are well enough as they stand. And I think I know my ward as well. I would venture a guess that the lady Bianca is not longing for a wedding ring either. She would prefer to stand on a footbridge and sigh, which at her age is entirely proper.'

'You do not see that she may come to resent you?'

'Of course she will not resent me,' said Lorenzo, much amused. 'Love, particularly romantic love, requires obstacles. I am Bianca's obstacle. If I were to remove myself from her path, she would have one matter the less to sigh over. Ask her, if you do not believe me. She has a quicker and more honest mind than one might suppose for a girl of her age.'

Later that evening, the Cardinal found Bianca Visconti no less amused than her guardian.

'Did he really say that?' she asked, delighted. 'I didn't think he knew anything about love.'

'Well now, Lorenzo de' Medici has barely turned thirty

years of age. I realise that he must seem as old as Methuselah to you, my lady, but I assure you that he is not exactly creaking in every joint,' della Palla replied.

He looked about him. They were in Leonardo da Vinci's attic studio in the Medici Palace, a long, raftered chamber whose windows faced north. The room was littered with sheets of paper in portfolios and out of them, with pieces of machinery, glue pots, bolts of cambric and silk, easels, stuffed animals under glass domes, paintbrushes, odd lengths of timber and coils of rope. From a central beam was suspended a four-foot model of a bat's wing, varnished and gleaming, the bones represented by split canes and the membrane made of tautly stretched parchment. An enamelling furnace stood in a corner beside a brass armature that would some day be an equestrian statue, and beneath a table was a mouse-trap of curious design with a weighted and finely balanced door. Whatever bait it had once held had disappeared, but the trap remained unsprung. It must have been invaded by a mouse of singular inventiveness and enterprise; a Leonardo da Vinci among mice, perhaps, thought the Cardinal.

He was seated on a window ledge with his robes gathered about his knees. A lesser man, properly mindful of his position as Rome's emissary, would have sent a clerk to find the lady Bianca and bring her to him. Not so the Apostolic Chancellor, who had learned long since that informality made friends, and felt the need of this young woman's trust. Bianca was at the table, with an open leather notebook in front of her. She surveyed Cardinal della Palla gravely, prepared to like him.

'Tell me,' said the Cardinal. 'Do you write letters to Leonardo da Vinci?'

'My lord?'

'Forgive me. I do not mean to pry into your personal life,' the Cardinal went on. 'It is merely that I hoped to find him here, and must now communicate with him urgently. If anyone knew how to reach him, I felt it might be you.'

'Ah. No, my lord, I cannot help you. If one of the gunners were to ride for Otranto, I dare say that I would ask him to take a letter with him,' Bianca said.

'That had occurred to me as well. In fact, I was thinking

47

of asking a man called Cipriano di Lucca to carry my own message. Do you know him, my lady?'

'Why yes,' Bianca replied. 'I know him very well indeed. He is capable, loyal, and responsible.'

Cardinal della Palla coughed behind his hand. For a moment or two he appeared to be on the verge of choking.

'Your feelings do you credit,' he said when he had recovered, 'but I already know him to be thoroughly irresponsible, and if he has any loyalties—as you now say—they lie with yourself and Leonardo da Vinci rather than with Florence. I understand that you were placed in his care last year. To escort you to a nunnery in Pisa, was it? And behold! Both of you subsequently arrived in Malta in most improper circumstances. I was not asking you to give him a character, my lady, but only to tell me whether he would make a good messenger. I am sorry if I misled you.'

'If your Eminence gives him a letter to carry,' said Bianca sweetly, 'he will neither drop it in the mud nor lose it at a wayside tavern.'

'Thank you,' said Cardinal della Palla. 'What are you studying there, my child?'

He rose from the window and came across to look at the leather bound portfolio before her.

'They are casting-patterns for guns,' Bianca said. She swivelled the portfolio so that della Palla could examine the drawings, and laughed when she saw his expression. 'Are you surprised, my lord? Were you expecting kittens, or flowers?'

'Something of the sort,' the Cardinal confessed. 'Guns are a harsh subject for study, wouldn't you say?'

'These are the Medici Guns. I owe my life to them, and Florence owes them her freedom. And are they not beautiful?'

'They are, I admit.' The Cardinal turned a few pages, then reached inside his robes to bring out a folded manuscript. He opened this and smoothed it on the table top, and Bianca saw that it, too, bore diagrams—though clearly not by Leonardo's hand. Yet, they were similar to those in the portfolio. 'Forgive me,' the Cardinal said, 'but it happens that these guns of yours are the chief concern of

48

my visit here, and the reason I must contact Leonardo. Fifty of them are at present being cast in Rome, and I am curious to know why.'

'To take Otranto from the Turks?' suggested Bianca. 'Rome and Florence are allies in this, if in little else. Perhaps Rome's foundries are bigger than ours?'

'Perhaps. Perhaps that is it.' The Cardinal paused. 'My child, you continue to surprise me, I confess. An interest in casting and foundries rather than needlework and music? Well. It must be that I am old fashioned. How old are you?'

'I am nearly eighteen, my lord.'

Della Palla laughed. 'Old enough to be an apprentice engineer, then. Have you fired a cannon, my lady?'

'Not yet.'

'Let us give thanks for small mercies. What is the matter?'

Bianca was now studying both drawings the Cardinal had brought with him and those in Leonardo's portfolio. 'These are not the same,' she said. 'The carriages and the aiming mechanisms are similar, but the . . . the bores are different. These you bring from Rome are somewhat larger.' She pointed . . . 'You see, my lord?'

'Why—so they are,' said della Palla. 'I had not observed it, but you are right.Well, you see my difficulty. It is that I would like to know whether it is Leonardo himself who has ordered these cannon built, and who is paying for them, and suchlike matters. I am sorry to have intruded upon you, my lady. I did not really intend to discuss gunnery with you, even though your knowledge of it clearly exceeds my own.'

Shortly thereafter, the Apostolic Chancellor gave Bianca his blessing and took his leave. After he had gone, Bianca sat with the portfolio, studying it by candlelight and very deep in thought. The Cardinal might appear as casual as he wished, but she did not think he had journeyed all the way from Rome to Florence in order to find out who was to pay for the casting of fifty cannon.

Finally she took quill in hand, to write a letter of her own.

Three days later, at mid-morning, Cipriano di Lucca was

saddling his horse in the stables of the inn at Pistrola and
checking his supplies for a journey southward. As always,
his fellow gunners were at practice in the field outside the
village. Cipriano had been given another mission, and one
to which he looked forward with pleasure. Practice was one
thing; the prospect of action at Otranto quite another. As
he packed his saddle bags, Cipriano hummed cheerfully.

Burdened now with bedroll, sword and buckler he
walked from the inn to the stable to find a youth standing
by one of the stalls, patting the neck of a gelding.

'Good morrow, boy,' said Cipriano.

'Good day, sir. Are you not Master Cipriano di Lucca,
the famous gunner?'

'I am Cipriano di Lucca, certainly. I was not aware that
fame had yet descended upon me. Why?'

'Sir,' said the youth, 'I wish to be a gunner.'

Cipriano smiled sympathetically. 'Out of my way, boy,'
he said, not unkindly, fastening the bedroll to his horse's
crupper. 'We are not recruiting gunners, and certainly not
among those whose voices have barely cracked. Come back
when you have reached sixteen.'

'Sir,' persisted the youth, 'I would like to ride with you.
They tell me at the inn that you are to join Captain Rigo
Leone.'

'So I am,' replied Cipriano. 'And if you imagine that
Captain Leone will do anything other than eat you alive,
you are sadly mistaken.' He leaned his arms on the saddle.
'Listen to me, lad. We have twenty good men begging to
join our company every month. And you do not even begin
to look like a gunner to me. You are too delicate. Where are
you from? The city? It seems to me that I have seen you
there. Go back and learn to be a tailor. It is a useful trade.'

'I do not wish to be a tailor,' said the youth sulkily, 'but a
gunner.'

'So you keep saying. And I would like to be the King of
Naples. Look at me, boy. You see my nose?' Cipriano laid a
finger alongside this feature, which was somewhat crooked.
'I was once a handsome fellow just like yourself. That was
before I became a gunner, and before I was forced to fight
every man in the troop when they seemed to find my looks
amusing. They did not do so for long, because I broke open

50

several of their heads; but that is a different tale. Are you a fighter? I hardly think so. Do you want a nose like mine? No. Go away, lad.'

'I think it's a very nice nose,' said the youth, laughing. 'I have often admired it.'

'Why, you impudent young devil!' shouted Cipriano. And then, striking his forehead. 'Oh, dear Jesus! I might have known it! *What have you done to yourself?*'

'I have cut my hair,' said Bianca Visconti demurely. 'Don't you find it becoming?'

'My lady,' replied Cipriano earnestly, 'I do not know what scandalous plot unwinds inside that pretty head of yours, but I promise you most faithfully that I am *not* going to take you with me to Otranto. Do you understand that?'

'And why not?'

'Disguised as a *boy*? Lorenzo will have my guts. And Leonardo . . .'

'You didn't recognise me,' said Bianca.

'That is because . . .'

'Yes?' inquired Bianca innocently.

'Never mind why.'

'My pony is just along the street.'

'Then get on him, Madonna, and ride back to Florence. Florence is over there,' said Cipriano, pointing.

'Listen, Cipriano,' Bianca said. 'You have two choices. You can take me with you, quietly and amicably . . .'

'Or?'

'Or I ride behind you with tears in my eyes, imploring you not to abandon me. I am not quite sure what that will do to your reputation with women, but it will doubtless entertain everyone vastly.'

Cipriano closed his eyes. 'You have a truly terrible, *terrible* mind.'

'Yes,' agreed Bianca. 'Would you like to see me weep? I can do it very well. Watch.'

'I believe you,' Cipriano said hurriedly, 'and I beg you to spare me your tears. I may shed a few myself if you persist in this nonsense. Lorenzo . . .'

'You are not afraid of Lorenzo. We already know that.'

'And Leonardo?'

'He will be overjoyed to see me. Rigo will fume and

51

growl, and bring me wine. As a matter of fact, you begin to like the idea a little yourself. Will you fetch my pony, please?'

'Fetch it yourself, lad,' said Cipriano, surrendering. 'And I trust you can cook over a campfire.'

On the night of October the second, at Otranto, the rains poured down. Squalls drove across the surrounding plain from the west, trailing hissing banners of spray that beat on the tents of the Roman encampment. In the light of scattered lanterns the raindrops turned to golden needles and tattooed branching patterns of rivulets into the muddy ground. Those who could shelter, Christian and Moham-medan alike, did so; those who could not cursed fitfully and paced the nightwatch as best they could.

Among those who were out of the rain were Leonardo da Vinci and Rigo, although they were in fact wetter than most. In a sewer beneath the wall of Otranto, with the rising water foaming about their waists, they clung to an ancient iron grid which barred their passage. Their faces were dimly lit by their flickering oil lamp, now suspended from its topmost rail.

'Give me your arm,' Leonardo said, his voice echoing eerily in the tunnel.

Rigo held out his left hand, eyes round with puzzlement.

'Not that one. Your right hand. Take it off.'

'What for?'

'Because it has your hook and pulley, and I will need them both if we are to wrench this dammed thing aside.'

Awkwardly, Rigo shrugged his way out of his sodden leather jerkin and proffered his artificial hand to his companion. Leonardo swiftly dismantled the limb, slipping the hook from its wooden socket and unthreading the narrow cords that actuated it from the pulley above Rigo's elbow. From about his own waist he unwound a twenty foot length of woven silk line. He tied one end of this to the base of the hook, and then waded back down the sewer for a short distance until he found a projecting bolt in the stone wall of the tunnel.

To this he fastened the pulley, taking a turn with the line around it. He came back to the grill with the hook in one hand and the end of the line in the other, dived below the water's surface, and searched for a vantage point. The bottom of the grill was set into the masonry at either side of the tunnel, but years of immersion in running water had weakened and rusted it. Leonardo clipped the hook under the lowest bar, and took in the slack. He braced his feet against the wall and heaved at the silken line. It stretched, began to give . . . and the bottom of the grill came free. Stooping once more, Leonardo wrenched the entire piece of meshwork upwards.

'I have probably damaged it a little,' he said, giving the reassembled arm back to Rigo a few minutes later, 'but I dare say I can fashion you another.'

They ducked underneath the raised grid and waded onwards, Leonardo holding the oil lamp above his head. Within sixty paces they came to a dead end; a domed chamber, into which the mouths of several drains were discharging cataracts of water from the streets of the city above them. In the centre of the ceiling was a circular slab. Leonardo climbed to Rigo's shoulders and pushed at it tentatively. It gave, and moments later he was helping Rigo into the open air.

They left the slab slightly ajar and looked around.

They stood now at a corner of two right-angled lanes, one of which, as they had expected, ran along the back of the city's southern wall. Two-storied houses, once inhabited but now blind and deserted, seemed to lean over them at either hand. Behind one of these rows of dwellings rose the ramparts that had fallen so quickly to the Turkish invaders. Repaired and reinforced, they were now Sultan Mohammed's bulwarks against recapture. Here and there they caught sight of patrolling figures on the battlements, though the driving rain obscured everything beyond fifty paces.

Cautiously, they set about their task. They were looking for guns.

Few men in Italy knew anything of Turkish artillery except by rumour and repute. The gunners of the Ottoman Empire were legendary in their skill, and their weapons were said to be of prodigious size and magical construction. Magic aside, Leonardo was prepared to grant the rest, but he intended to reach no conclusions until he had seen both the guns and gunners for himself.

Since they were in no way disguised and neither had more than a smattering of their enemies' language, they floated through Otranto like shadows, passing unseen from one dark doorway to another.

Their survey did not take them very long; two hours, perhaps, at most. The Turkish defences were brutally efficient. Shan Khara, who had charge of the Sultan's artillery, had set up some twelve cannon of varying kinds about the city. To give each weapon a clear line of fire he had simply razed every church, every monument and every home that stood in their way. He had thereby destroyed more than half of the entire town, and Rigo and Leonardo had little difficulty in spotting every gun, often from a distance.

In the small hours of the morning, then, they made their way back towards the alley beneath whose cobbles they had forced their entry. The rain had slackened, lessening their discomfort but increasing the chances of their being seen by a patrol. Rigo was visibly disconcerted when Leonardo proposed that they now take a closer look at one of the Turkish emplacements.

'The rain has soaked your brain,' he said. 'We came to find their guns. We've *found* their guns. In Christ's name, enough is enough!'

Leonardo took out his notebook from the folds of his cloak. Its cover and most of its pages were sodden.

'I need measurements,' he explained patiently. 'What is the bore of these weapons? If we know that, we can calculate the weight of the shot they throw, and we can even make a guess at their range.'

'I can make a guess at all three without taking a measure to them,' said Rigo. 'Their length is about eight feet. Their bore, twelve inches. If they fire iron shot, that gives us about two hundred and fifty pounds for each ball. If stone, say two hundred pounds. Their range will be a little less than a mile, and they look devilish accurate. How is that?'

'Excellent guesswork,' replied Leonardo, 'but guesswork is guesswork and we need to be sure. Come.'

They chose the nearest emplacement as their point of entry. It was about a quarter of a mile from the corner of the alley, at one side of a square, and they approached it from overhead by climbing the stairway of a vacant building nearby, making their way to a front window. Three men were by the cannon, two of them deep in sleep. Leonardo made several careful drawings of the cannon, its mounting and aiming mechanism, and the redoubt that had been built around it.

'Now for a closer view,' he said, and led the way down the main stairway of the empty house. Pausing for an instant in the doorway behind the unsuspecting gun-crew, they launched themselves across the few yards of paving that separated them from the redoubt. The guard who was on his feet turned too late to ward off the pommel of Leonardo's sword, which took him in the side of the head. He fell, dazed, and Leonardo locked an arm around his neck, pressing hard on the arteries at either side until he sagged limply. As for the two sleepers, they awoke only after several hours had passed. Rigo saw to that.

Unhurriedly, Leonardo measured the barrel of the gun. He recorded the thickness of metal at its breech and muzzle, its bore, its length from touch-hole to mouth; probed the touch-hole itself with an inquiring finger, and tested the bronze with the edge of his knife.

He was performing this last task when Shan Khara saw him at work. The young Turkish commander, on his customary nightly rounds, was a hundred paces away and perceived only that something seemed amiss at the redoubt. At such a distance, unfortunately for him, he could not decide exactly what it was, and made the mistake of shouting to summon the archers twenty yards behind him.

Leonardo and Rigo ran.

Seeing the direction in which they were headed, Shan Khara rapped out brisk orders to head them off.

'They have scaled the wall!' he shouted. 'Follow them to their ladder, and cut the dogs down!'

Leonardo and Rigo reached the right-angled alley by the same route they had used to leave it earlier. They emerged half way down one of its arms, by way of the back window of what had once been a cobbler's shop. Leonardo was in the lead as they approached the partially raised slab that led down into the sewer; he looked up the other arm of the alleyway, to see two arbalestiers with their weapons raised. As he turned to make certain that Rigo was at his heels, a bolt struck him a glancing blow on the temple.

He fell as though pole-axed, and lay still.

Rigo wasted no time whatever to see if he was alive or dead. He drove the claw of his hook beneath the edge of the circular slab that would give them escape, heaved it aside, and pulled Leonardo after him. Dropping through the opening himself, he eased his friend down into the domed chamber as best he could. Speed, not care, drove him at his task. Water was now thundering from the mouths of all the drains leading into the chamber, and the outgoing stream was now a raging torrent. Rigo put his left arm around Leonardo's chest, let go of the projections he was holding, and allowed the water to sweep both of them away. His sleeve caught once, on the twisted iron grill as they passed under it, and Rigo tore himself free, choking. He surfaced a few yards further on, tried to grab a handhold at the tunnel's side to give them a moment's respite, and failed. Seconds later, the sewer spewed both of them outside Otranto's wall and into the swollen river that ran through the Roman encampment before surging past the city to the sea.

Rigo fought his way to land, and rolled Leonardo up onto the bank ahead of him. He grabbed a branch, pulled himself from the river, and set to work to get some of the water from Leonardo's lungs. In this he succeeded, though the artist did not regain consciousness; Rigo listened for his heartbeat, and was relieved to find it strong and steady.

For a moment he considered doing the obvious thing, which was to run for the camp of the besiegers and seek help. Instead, he heaved Leonardo to one shoulder, and set off towards the southwest.

Scudo and Tesoro found both of them shortly before dawn, half a mile from the glen in which they had made their temporary headquarters. Rigo was exhausted, and Leonardo looked quite dead. He lay on his back without moving, his hair caked with blood.

'Get blankets,' said Rigo shortly, and the gunners obeyed. Tesoro supported his commander, and Scudo carried Leonardo as though he were a leaf. Safe in the small

56

valley once more, they waited for the coming of day. The rain had lifted, and a light mist filled the glen.

Leonardo opened his eyes to sunlight, It seemed to him that he had been dreaming of—what? Floating? Flying? He could not quite remember. He stayed as he was, motionless, and while the recognition of where he was slowly returned. The side of his head throbbed, but he paid it no attention.

Beneath him was a blanket, its sides folded over him. Beyond the blanket, at either side, damp grass stretched out across a gentle slope; to his right a stream gushed noisily from under a rock. Rain. It had rained heavily during the night. He had been out in the rain, with Rigo. What had they been doing? He pieced it together, sending his mind back into Otranto to wander through the rubble strewn lanes and squares. *Guns*. That was it. What had happened to his head? He didn't know. He would, in fact, never know. Memory returns slowly and almost completely, but seldom recalls the blow that caused its loss.

Meanwhile, the need to sleep flowed over him. He stared towards the sky, across which the rearguard banners of the night's storm were still drifting. Two hawks circled immediately above him, gliding, their wings tilting a little this way and that as they sought and found upcurrents of air from the warming earth. Male and female, he thought; they hunted in pairs, mated for life, were faithful each to the other until the death that parted them; as death must part all lovers. Suddenly, one of the pair swooped, dropping like a small thunderbolt behind the valley's rim; the other circled serenely, its pinions spread like delicate fingers. Leonardo recalled a dream of his youth, or perhaps a vision. He had been lying on his back, as now, and a hawk descended upon him from the sky, beating him about the lips with its tail. Had he been asleep, or awake? Or between sleep and waking, as perhaps he was at this instant? As a boy he had told his dream to few, and all had laughed. What did dreams mean, or visions? He knew what his own had meant. The bird had been commanding him to be faithful to truth and to tell it wherever he saw it and in whatever fashion he saw it; a command which had caused

57

him no little trouble and which he saw would continue to trouble him until his death.

And these birds—for the second of the pair was climbing back to join his mate in the sky's vault—were telling him something. It was not until he had fully recovered and had eaten a meal cooked by Tesoro di Veluti that he lifted his head suddenly and stared up to the clouds that floated high above him, and then the message was at once clear.

Six

'IT WAS WELL done,' purred Girolamo Riario. 'To penetrate the infidel's stronghold in such a daring fashion, and to such good purpose? Excellent! Tell me, then, what you think of our chances.'

Leonardo's head wound had been stitched—by Tesoro di Veluti, under the artist's personal instruction—and was well on the way to healing. All four Florentine gunners were sitting together in carved chairs in the sunshine outside Riario's pavilion, though Scudo showed his discomfort in a frown. The Count himself, with the Venetian, Antonio da Narni, at his side, was affable in the extreme; suspiciously affable, so Rigo thought.

'You will never retake Otranto, my lord, with the men and material at your disposal here,' Leonardo said. 'If your Captain-Gunner will allow Rigo Leone to choose fresh positions for your heavy guns, you may in time breach the walls. But if you succeed in this, the Turkish fire power inside the city itself will decimate your assault force before they can do more than reach the breach itself. Have you any reinforcements planned?'

Riario took a draught of wine.

'Not at present,' he admitted. 'My intention is to stay where I am until next spring. I cannot feed an additional ten thousand troops through the winter, even if I could obtain them at short notice. The report you have brought back to me, and your excellent drawings, confirm that I am right in this.'

'Next spring?' said Rigo. 'A long way off, my lord.'

'I know. But the Turk is far from home and time is on our side.' Riario turned to Antonio da Narni. 'Do you not agree?'

'In the circumstances, yes,' replied Narni.

'Sir,' asked Leonardo, 'will you permit me to ask you a question? Are you not in the service of Venice, as your father was and his father before him?'

'I am a Venetian,' said Antonia da Narni. 'Why?'

'I had heard that Venice was on the point of signing a treaty with the Ottoman Empire,' said Leonardo mildly.

'She is,' admitted Narni. 'But it does not affect my presence here. Venice, Master Leonardo, lives by her sea trade, and must have passage through the Adriatic to survive. The Turks can deny us that passage, at some cost to themselves. Our treaty affects only the safe passage of our ships at sea. That is all. Invasion of the Italian mainland by Turkey is another matter. Your suspicions are understandable. I hope I have answered them.'

'So you have,' said Leonardo, 'and I thank you.'

'Supposing we were to bring the Medici Guns into this campaign,' said Rigo, returning to his theme. 'We might save your winter.'

'I think not,' Riario said. 'I have every respect for your weapons, Captain—'

'And rightly,' grunted Rigo.

'Rightly, as you say. But I have no plans for more artillery here. Even your guns cannot breach Otranto's wall, and I assume you are not proposing to take them through that drain of yours.'

'We could,' put in Tesoro di Veluti.

'Keep silent, infant,' growled Rigo. 'Listen. That is what you are here for. No, I don't think we can drag cannon through a sewer. Leonardo?'

The artist smiled. 'I might consider it, except that the Turkish commander by now knows how we entered his city. There will be no more unguarded drains for our use. My lord, I see that your baggage train is being made ready. Are you moving your headquarters?'

'Yes,' said Riario. 'There is a small castle four miles north of here which has been disused for several years—the Castello del Mar. My servants are making it habitable. If I must spend the winter here, I see no reason for sinking knee-deep in mud every time I set foot outside my bedroom door. It is not unreasonably far from Otranto, after all. In fact, I was about to suggest that all of you join me as my guests there for dinner. Over wine we may have a more detailed conference, perhaps. I am sure your own quarters are comfortable, but I can offer you wine and music. What do you say?'

'That we accept with gratitude, my lord,' said Leonardo. 'When?'

'Shall we say five days from now? You will be fully recovered from your wound by then, no doubt.'

'No doubt,' smiled Leonardo, and a little later they took their leave.

'He's a poor commander,' Rigo said that evening when they had returned to their camp. 'He will allow his troops to stagger through the winter as best they may, while he retires four miles away from them; and if the Turks make a sortie, there will be fewer Christian soldiers to feed, I swear.'

'He is a nobleman,' pointed out Leonardo da Vinci, as he watched over a plump chicken roasting over a glowing fire. 'Would you have him live in a tent like a commoner?'

'And there are his tactical conferences to be considered,' added Tesoro.

'My tactical arse,' said Rigo inelegantly. 'Which, incidentally, I mean to keep intact.'

'Do you, indeed?' Leonardo asked.

'I do. Sooner or later Riario will try to kill us. At his little dinner, for example. Have you charred that bird to your satisfaction? I'm hungry.'

'The food will be better, no doubt, at Castello del Mar.'

'It will also, no doubt, be poisoned,' said the Captain-Gunner. 'I have survived your cooking. I don't propose to see whether I shall survive his. Though I expect I shall now have to listen while you produce fourteen good reasons why I should.'

'We'll be safe enough, I imagine,' Leonardo said, breaking a portion from the chicken and passing it to Rigo. 'He'll have all his field commanders there. He cannot, therefore, seek our harm without openly breaking Rome's safe conduct, and even Riario would have to think twice before doing that.'

'You cannot be serious. *Rome's* safe conduct? Have you seen it?'

'I have a copy of it here,' said Leonardo, laughing. He reached into his tunic. Rigo turned in amazement to Tesoro and Scudo.

'Marvellous, by all the saints!' he said. 'He has a copy of it! A piece of paper issued by none other than His Holiness the most excellent son of a pox-ridden Ligurian whore! Give it to me.'

Leonardo held out the folded document. Rigo sniffed at the parchment with exaggerated awe. 'By Christ,' he said, 'it reeks of sanctity! Why am I such a miserable unbeliever?' He got up, marched to the fire, and thrust the safe conduct into the flames, which at once consumed it merrily. 'And now let us talk sense for a change. Scudo, do you want to dine with Count Girolamo Riario?'

'I go where I'm told,' said Scudo with his mouth full. He perceived, though dimly, that he was being asked to choose sides, and had no intention of doing so.

'Tesoro?'

'I take my orders too,' the young gunner replied. 'The question is, from whom do I take them?'

'From me,' said Leonardo.

'From him, from him,' said Rigo, waving his arm in dismissal. 'Much good may it do us all.'

'Dinner at the Castello del Mar,' said Leonardo. 'Five days from now. One cannot make gains without accepting risk, which is our chief reason for going there. Unlike Riario, I am not prepared to sit here all winter staring at Otranto's walls.'

On the evening of October the eighth, then, the gunners rode up to Castello del Mar and dismounted in the light of a splendid array of torches, giving their horses into the charge of a pair of ostlers in green livery.

The castle was isolated, being in the middle of its own somewhat dilapidated estate at the edge of the sea. Much work must have been done, Leonardo reflected, to make it fit for living during the space of a mere week or so; but then Count Girolamo Riario had a retinue of nearly a hundred men whose only function was to assure his comfort. By daylight its frontage was bleak, Leonardo remembered; he and Rigo had scouted the surrounding countryside several times as a matter of simple military precaution. Behind the Castello about half a mile away rose a watchtower, a century old or more, which must from time to time have been used to warn of ships sailing the Adriatic. Formal gardens, now fallen into disrepair, surrounded the castle itself. But the driveways had been weeded, and a fountain played before the shallow, curving steps which led to the arched front doorway.

They climbed this stairway and were received by a footman at its head. The man had some difficulty in persuading Scudo to relinquish his leather cloak, and he looked at it with a Roman's icy disdain when he had succeeded. Rigo kept his left hand ostentatiously on his sword hilt.

'A hard life indeed,' he said, looking around. 'Had I known, I would have taken a bath before I set out.'

The main hall was a blaze of light. Save that there were hardly any women present, they might have been attending some occasion of state in Florence, Venice, or Rome. Laden tables lined the walls, replenished by a bustle of servants. In a gallery at the far end of the room a group of musicians played lutes, tambour, and viols. Girolamo Riario himself, dressed as always in black with a light and fluted breastplate of mail, walked the length of the floor to greet them. At his shoulder was a small cross of diamonds, set in gold. He raised his hands in welcome.

'Well met, friends,' he said. 'Rome is honoured to receive Florence! If there have been differences between us in the past, let us set them aside tonight and rejoice.'

He touched Leonardo's fingers, and bowed to the others. In this he was wise, since Tesoro di Veluti, for one, would not have taken his hand had he offered it. Riario had killed the young gunner's brother Andrea two years before on the battlements of Castelmonte, and had done so brutally; he had packed Andrea's mouth and throat with gunpowder and then blown his head off. Sensing Tesoro's rage at the remembrance of this, Leonardo took his arm firmly and propelled him in the direction of the upper table, where all of them took their seats.

It was a somewhat awkward repast, as the Count recognised with ironic amusement. Leonardo had countered his friends' suggestions of poison by telling them to drink nothing except water, and to eat only those dishes of which others at the table had already partaken. He himself was capable of managing this with sufficient grace to pass unnoticed, and Rigo could carry it off in a pinch. Tesoro, however, refused to eat at all; he was, perhaps, more mindful of his brother's murder than of poison. Scudo solved his own problems by dourly appropriating his neighbour's platter, and scowling at the resulting protests.

None the less, their first hour at Castello del Mar passed amicably enough, and without incident. It was a state of affairs that was not to last long.

Cipriano di Lucca, accompanied by his youthful protégé, had arrived in the Roman encampment shortly after sundown. They had driven their horses very hard since early morning, when they left Lecce, thiry miles to the north. Cipriano sought out a Captain of infantry, to ask him where they might find Leonardo da Vinci and his companions.

'The Florentines?' said the Captain. He pointed. 'Their camp is up in those low hills yonder. Do not ask me why they choose not to join us here. Who knows why Florentines do anything?'

'I am a Florentine,' said Cipriano.

'It does not surprise me in the least,' the Captain said. 'You look like one.'

'And what is that supposed to mean?'

'Florentines,' the Captain explained, 'are usually overdressed, and nearly always too big for their boots. Romans are quiet, industrious, courageous, and sober. That is the difference.'

Cipriano bristled at once and would have pursued this discussion further, but was restrained by his young friend. He promised the Captain that they would meet again. The Roman grinned. Foreseeing a tedious winter ahead, he was already bored.

'They are not at their camp,' the Captain said. 'Save yourselves the ride.'

'Where are they?' asked Cipriano.

'At Castello del Mar. You must have passed it on your journey here.'

'And what are they doing there?'

'They are the guests of the Count of Imola, Rome's Captain-General, Girolamo Riario.'

He was about to ask them to stay and take some wine with him, since he was a good-hearted man, Roman or not; but he found himself addressing their backs as they ran for their horses.

'Florentines,' he said to himself and to the empty air. 'They are all the same. One of those is a dandy, and the other a boy with eyelashes pretty enough for a filly.' It was well that Cipriano did not hear his other comments. Remarks like the Captain's about his virility and sexual preference had followed Cipriano for half the length of Italy. He was growing extremely tired of them.

An hour or so later, the Count's major-domo crossed the hall to the high table and bent to murmur in his master's ear. Riario lifted one eyebrow fractionally as he heard him out.

'Have them brought in,' he said, and turned to Leonardo. 'Two more of your friends have arrived, it seems. Were you expecting them?'

'No,' said Leonardo. A moment later Cipriano entered and led his companion to the Count of Imola's seat. Leonardo, eyes wide, rose suddenly from his seat, knocking a water goblet over in his sudden agitation.

'I am Cipriano di Lucca, my lord, and this is Angelino Muselli, a young friend of mine.' Cipriano bowed smoothly.

'You are both welcome,' said Riario. He surveyed the youth narrowly: a handsome lad and delicately dressed in a loose white shirt, lace fronted, beneath a doublet and hose of maroon satin. 'And are you, too, a gunner?' he asked.

'He is hoping to become one,' replied Cipriano before his companion could speak. 'In fact, that is why I am here.' He turned. 'Captain Leone,' he went on, 'Master Angelino has insisted on riding with me from Florence, and seeks entry to our troop. One must say at least that he is tenacious though I have told him that the decision is yours.'

'He looks to me,' Rigo said, 'as though he would make a better page than a powder boy. Have you lost your wits?'

Leonardo, who had recognised 'Angelino' as Bianca from thirty paces away, at last recovered his voice. 'Well, let us not be too hasty about this, Rigo,' he suggested. 'As Cipriano says, to ride all the way from Florence is no mean feat. Appearances may be against . . . Angelino Muselli, did you say, Cipriano? But at least let us talk to him now he is here.'

'Very wise,' said Cipriano. 'Why don't you talk to him yourself, Leonardo? It might prove rewarding.'

'Then I will do so, by all means.' Leonardo fixed Cipriano with a gaze that would have wilted any other man. 'And perhaps I should have a few words with you as well, later on.' He excused himself to Riario, and took the youth into a corner of the hall beneath the minstrels' gallery. Rigo rose and followed them, cup in hand. He tapped Leonardo on the shoulder.

'You are wasting your time,' he said firmly. 'For one thing, I choose my gunners, not you. For another . . .'

The cup fell from his left hand and rolled across the flags chiming metallically.

'Yes, I know,' said Leonardo. 'Please, Rigo, go quietly back to your seat. Say nothing, and keep your hand near your sword. Do you understand?'

'Quite clearly,' said Rigo. He retrieved his cup, and walked away.

'And now, Madonna,' said Leonardo softly, 'since I do not know at this moment whether to laugh or cry, I must fall back on questions. All else can wait until we are safely out of here. You have something to tell us, or you would not have taken this risk, my darling. What is it?'

'They are building fifty guns in Rome,' answered Bianca steadily. 'Fifty Medici Guns.'

'Riario?'

'It *must* be Riario. Cardinal della Palla travelled all the way from Rome to Florence to tell you—but he did not know who was having them cast. And if *he* did not know, then their casting is a secret indeed! At first I thought the answer was easy: they were being made for use here at Otranto. But in that case, why shouldn't Cardinal della

Palla know of it? And why, having found out, should he come to Florence with the news? Do you see, Leonardo?'

'I do indeed.'

'And there's something else, These new guns are being made to your design — *but their bore has been changed.* Well,' Bianca went on a little defiantly, 'was I right to come?'

'Yes, you were right. As always. And Riario told us plainly that he was expecting no artillery here.'

'Then you are in danger. Which is why I dared not wait, but made Cipriano bring me directly to you.'

'We are all in greater danger now, Madonna.'

'I know.'

'Well,' said Leonardo, looking around, 'you have not been recognised yet. So let us get through the rest of this evening as best we can, and leave as soon as possible.'

'He is coming this way,' Bianca said urgently. She tried to lower her voice by several tones. 'What difference, pray, is there between an arquebus and a cannon? I am a good shot with an arquebus. There's no difference.'

'None at all,' said Riario, moving smoothly to her side. 'one is a little larger and more dangerous than the other, but that is common everywhere and in all things. Are you truly a good shot, Master Angelino, or was that an idle boast?'

'I am quite fair, my lord.'

'Excellent. Come and sit with me, then, and let us discuss the practice of gunnery. And afterwards I will tell Master Leonardo and Captain Leone whether or not they should make you an apprentice. Come.' He bowed to Leonardo, and ushered Bianca firmly away.

Leonardo took his own seat again, clapping Cipriano on the back as he did so.

'Life is full of surprises,' said Cipriano. 'Don't you agree?'

'Yes, indeed. One day,' said Leonardo, with a broad and pleasant smile on his face, 'I am going to take your head, Cipriano, and pound it against the nearest and most convenient stone wall until your brains drip out through your ears.' He hammered Cipriano's spine again with apparent good humour, causing the gunner to stagger slightly. 'Through your ears,' he repeated. 'That will be one of life's surprises, won't it?'

'You weren't there,' said Cipriano defensively. 'You didn't hear what she threatened to do.' He glanced in the direction of the Count. 'He suspects nothing,' he added hopefully.

'At least she knows more about gunnery than Riario will learn in a lifetime,' Leonardo said. 'But he knows more about trickery. Or perhaps he does not, now that I come to think of it.'

Five paces away, Girolamo Riario was at his most charming.

'You do not look over strong, Angelino,' he said. 'Are you sure that you have not allowed admiration for Leonardo da Vinci to overcome your good sense? He is famous, and so is Captain Leone.'

'I will become stronger as I grow older, my lord,' said Bianca, 'and I am very quick.'

'Are you? Come then, and let us try you.' Riario took his stiletto from its sheath and held its blade between his fingers, the haft stretched out in front of him horizontally. He flicked it a few inches into the air, catching it by the handle when it had described a semi-circle. Then he offered it to Bianca, who repeated the simple trick.

The Count took back the dagger, held it as before, and flicked it again, this time allowing it to turn through one and a half circles before he caught the haft. He gave it to her once more.

By now, Leonardo and the three gunners were watching this performance closely. They saw Bianca toss the knife lightly in front of her, catch it, and return it to the Count, who laughed.

'Very good,' he said. 'Let us make it a little harder. Two complete turns, and a half turn more. Remember—the blade is sharp! Watch.' He balanced the dagger again, and cleverly flicked his fingers upwards. The knife became a spinning arc of steel as it rose and fell, its handle smacking neatly into Riario's extended palm.

'Two and a half,' he said softly. 'Have a care, Angelino. We are not half way done yet—but then you are younger than I am, and faster of eye. Here.'

Bianca glanced quickly over her shoulder at Leonardo, as she took the dagger. What she was doing could hardly be important, she knew, but none the less her fingers were suddenly damp with sweat. She poised the blade between them spun the knife in the air, and saw at once that she had misjudged her throw. Sensibly, she withdrew her hand as it fell, and it clattered to the floor.

'Aha,' breathed Riario, suavely. 'I win.'

Bianca stooped hastily to pick the dagger up, but the Count was too quick for her. He reached beneath his chair, grasped the weapon, and brought it up between them; his hand moving swift as a chameleon's tongue. The tip of the blade, razor sharp, sliced through the ties of Bianca's doublet and slit open the entire front of her silken shirt. Riario grinned like a wild dog as he reached forward, seized the edges of the cut material and pulled them apart.

'And, being the winner,' he said, 'I seem to have gained a prize! What have we here, *Angelina*? You will never make a gunner, my sweet; somehow I feel quite sure of it.'

Bianca swung her hand at his face. He caught her wrist easily and set the point of his stiletto with deft and cruel precision between her breasts. 'And now,' he said, looking past her at the rising figures of Leonardo da Vinci and the gunners, 'let nobody move until I have the answers to one or two questions.'

Leonardo whirled and clamped his hand over Rigo's before the gunner could draw his sword. 'Be still,' he commanded. 'You too, Cipriano. Scudo, Tesoro, do nothing rash. Nothing at all.'

'Good,' said Riario approvingly. He half turned and addressed the remainder of those present in the hall. 'Continue. Florence and Rome are merely having a small discussion here. There is no cause for concern.' His startled guests began to murmour among themselves. Few of them could see clearly what was happening at the high table. Riario beckoned, and a group of his personal guards came forward. 'Take them all away,' said the Count. He sighed with pleasure. 'I have not yet considered what questions to ask them.'

Seven

LEONARDO STRETCHED HIS arms in front of him and examined the length of chain that linked his fettered wrists.

'All that comforts me,' he said, 'is the thought that wherever she may be, Cipriano is still with her. It is small enough comfort, God knows, but it is something.'

'Cipriano may be dead,' said Scudo stolidly. Rigo, who could perceive the depth of Leonardo's anguish, kicked the big gunner hard on the shin.

'I doubt it,' Leonardo said. 'That wolf from hell would murder him—or her—without a second thought, if it suited his purpose. But his purpose is not clear yet.' He raised his hands again, and dashed his fetters against the wall. 'By God,' he cried, 'but it was plain enough for anyone with the wit to see it! That Milanese deserter he was flogging told him there was a traitor somewhere, and Riario was quick enough to let the man go. And why? Because he was afraid *we* might question him, and so discover that the traitor was Riario himself.'

'Then get us out of here,' Rigo said calmly.

'I am not a magician.'

'And I am not seeking a miracle. I am asking you to take thought,' said the Captain-Gunner. 'You have the quickest wit among us, my friend. Do not use it merely to torment yourself. We are not yet dead.'

Leonardo looked at his friend steadily. 'I know that you are right. I know it. And yet, however desperate our situation may have been in times past, we have never been taken all together. Not until now.'

'None the less,' repeated Rigo, 'we are still alive. But if you surrender, we may as well be dead. Think it over.'

★

70

'You cannot kill them out of hand,' said Antonio da Narni. 'My lord, I must tell you that you were over hasty in seizing them at all. Did I not warn you to be careful in this matter?'

'I cannot let them go either,' said Riario.

'Precisely. Well, if they must die, they must. But let me talk to Leonardo da Vinci first.'

'Why?'

'Because,' said Narni, 'I must find out exactly what he knows.'

'And how will you persuade him to tell you?'

'I shall offer him a bargain,' said the Venetian. 'What else?'

The days inched by, broken only by miserly portions of food and drink—and much silence. No sunlight found its way to their windowless prison, while the three men waited. And then, at last, the lock on the cell door clanged and four guards entered. Without a word they seized Leonardo, and hustled him into the passage way outside. They led him upstairs, and five minutes later he found himself in the presence of Antonio da Narni.

'You know who I am,' the Venetian said. 'I am called Gattamelata, as my grandfather was called by those he served. You are the prisoner of my lord Girolamo Riario, but I have some influence with him. Do you understand me?'

'Yes,' said Leonardo.

'Very well. I need information from you which I am sure you are unwilling to give me. It is a common enough situation, and one which the Count and myself approach in different fashions. His procedure is to sever hands, or heads, until he is told what he needs to know; but as you observed not many days ago and in my presence, such methods do not always extract the truth. I am a servant of Venice, and therefore a trader. I offer you a trade, Master Leonardo.'

'I am listening.'

'Good. Now the lady Bianca Visconti brought you a message of some importance, which I believe confirmed certain suspicions you may have already formed concerning the Count of Imola. I want to know what those suspicions are, what she told you, and who else knows anything of the matter in hand. I trust I am not being too oblique for you.'

'No. I understand you perfectly. What do you offer me in exchange?'

'I will tell you,' said Antonio da Narni, 'what has happened to the lady Bianca.'

Leonardo folded his arms. The chain at his wrists rattled softly.

'Do you offer me her life?' he asked.

'I did not say that. I offered to tell you, truthfully, what her fate is. That is all. Others might say that my offer is a mean one, but I fancy that you would not agree. Am I right?'

'Yes. Yes, you are right. My reason tells me that your trade is of no substance whatever, but my heart tells me otherwise. Do you swear to tell me the truth, if I do likewise?'

'I am a merchant, not a cheat. Besides, you will recognise the truth—as will I.'

'I agree, then,' said Leonardo. 'Here is what I know. Venice, you told me, has signed a treaty with the Turks—a treaty which you rightly interpreted as of little importance in this war. But you are going beyond that treaty. You intend to betray Rome, and Italy. In this you are joined by Girolamo Riario, Rome's Captain-General, though without the knowledge of anyone else in Rome. You are selling Otranto—and more than Otranto—to the Ottoman Empire.'

Antonio da Narni nodded encouragingly.

'How much more?' he asked.

'You are selling fifty cannon to the Sultan. They are weapons designed by me. Men have called them the Medici Guns, and I gave the plans for them to Cardinal Domenico della Palla, Rome's Chancellor and archivist, in fulfilment of a promise I made him. They are the finest artillery pieces in the world. I do not know what the Sultan offers you in exchange. Nor do I care. But I know what you have offered him.'

'And what of the lady Bianca's message to you?'

'She confirmed the truth of what I have said. Fifty

72

cannon are being cast in Rome, and none knows their true purpose. Their bore is different from that of the Medici Guns, no doubt in order to suit the calibre of shot already used by the Ottoman Empire.'

Antonio da Narni shifted in his chair.

'Sir,' he said, 'I admire your powers of reasoning. Who else suspects any of this?'

'Nobody outside these walls,' Leonardo replied. 'The Cardinal is puzzled by the fact that fifty guns are being cast in Rome, but he has no other facts to go on, as I have.'

'Yes,' said Antonio da Narni, 'you and your friends. I think you will have to die. Your removal, you see, will also remove your suspicions, all of which are true.'

'And the Lady Bianca . . .?'

'Of course,' Narni said. 'I must complete my side of our bargain.' An expression of evil satisfaction spread across his features. 'First, then,' he said, 'she is not dead. However, it's always possible that you might prefer that she were. She has been taken to Constantinople. The galley which carried her left some days ago. I cannot, of course, be responsible for what may happen to her when she gets there. She is a remarkably beautiful woman . . .'

'Enough,' interrupted Leonardo levelly. He studied Narni's face for a very long moment and turned. The guards fell in beside him, leaving Antonio da Narni with his heart—unaccountably—racing in an unreasoning panic.

'I do not understand you,' said Bianca impatiently. 'Take these . . . things off me at once.'

'No,' said Shan Khara. 'And I would advise you to stop addressing me in the tone of voice you have been using thus far. Do they cause you any discomfort?'

'That is not the point,' Bianca said. She was seated on a cushion in the sumptuous after-cabin of a Turkish galley, and in front of her was a low table of rosewood and ebony. Sweetmeats in silver and crystal dishes were scattered on its surface, and opposite her the young Turkish commander was squatting comfortably. Bianca laid her outstretched hands on the table. Her wrists, like those of her lover Leonardo, now more than a hundred miles away, were joined in fetters; but hers were light in weight and

73

fashioned of delicate links of alloy gold. The wristbands themselves were padded with blue silk so that they would not chafe her skin. None the less, they were fetters.

'But you are a prisoner,' said Shan Khara, with a charming smile.

'In that case,' pointed out Bianca with devastating logic, 'why is my companion Cipriano di Lucca over there not chained also? There is nowhere for us to escape to, anyway.'

'Because he is not a gift to my lord and master, the Sultan,' replied Shan Khara, 'and you are.' He turned to look at Cipriano who was lying on his back across several pillows of satin, examining the ceiling. 'You will go to work in Constantinople, gunner,' said the Turk cheerfully, 'while you, my lady, will not. You are a golden morsel. You will find it very pleasant, once you have learned a certain gentleness of speech which at present seems foreign to you. Persuade her, Cipriano di Lucca, if you will. Eh?'

'Sir,' said the gunner negligently, 'when you have known her as long as I have, you will learn that the lady Bianca is not easily persuaded.' He reached out his left hand, took a sugared morsel and placed it in his mouth.

The young Turk rose, bowed deeply to Bianca, and took his leave. 'My lady,' he advised, 'do not fret. If you have any complaints concerning your treatment on this ship— aside from the golden chain which burdens you so lightly—I beg you to tell me of them. Meanwhile, your friend yonder will sleep across the threshold of your door, so that none may molest your sleep. Good night.'

'He is a good fellow,' said Cipriano when Shan Khara had departed.

'He is certainly exceedingly handsome,' replied Bianca. 'Cipriano, you amaze me. What on earth do you imagine you're doing?'

'Enjoying life. I have never been a prisoner before,' explained Cipriano. 'It is not a bad life after all.'

'It may cease to be so when we reach Constantinople. For the present, kindly take your station outside my door. I want to sleep.'

As Cipriano reached the doorway, however, Bianca's equanimity wavered.

'Cipriano?' she said.

'Yes, madonna?'

'What do you suppose has happened to Leonardo?'

'Madonna, I have no idea,' said Cipriano, 'but I do know Leonardo and I am not unduly worried.' In this, of course, he was lying and Bianca knew it; but she was grateful to him just the same.

'My dear Antonio,' said Girolamo Riario, 'the affair presents no difficulties. They must die. You agree that it is necessary.'

'And what of Rome's safe conduct?' said Narni. 'We are not ready yet to defy His Holiness so openly.'

'Then let them die in war,' Riario replied. 'The suggestion was yours. The means for following it are mine. Moreover, we can arrange for their departure from this world to be very unpleasant indeed.'

'I care not whether it is pleasant or unpleasant,' said Narni.

'I know,' said Girolamo Riario. 'But I care.'

An hour before sundown, a priest came to the cell where Leonardo and his three companions were held. He was bald, and pompous.

'My sons,' he said sorrowfully, 'you are about to die. When today's sun sets, it will do so upon your lives; yet this is no matter for despair, since by God's Grace and through the prayers and ministrations of our Mother the Church, you shall pass to a better place than this world, even as did the Penitent Thief upon the Cross. Make confession, therefore, of those grievous sins you have committed, and receive absolution for them.'

'Are you a Roman?' asked Rigo Leone.

'I am, my son. I am chaplain to the Count of Imola.'

'Then I thank you,' Rigo said, 'but I will make my own peace with God.'

Tesoro di Veluti, however—who had lived barely long enough to sin other than trivially—did not share his Captain's more robust views on God's mercy.

'Bless me, father,' he began, 'for I have sinned . . .'

'Hold,' interrupted Leonardo, stepping forward from

beneath the cell's single barred window. 'Tesoro, you have no need of blessing.'

'What, sir!' demanded the priest, outraged. 'Would you deny a man his last absolution? This is sacrilege!'

'It might be,' replied Leonardo gently, 'if he were on the point of death. But he is not.'

'You are all at death's threshold,' said the priest.

'Not quite,' Leonardo said. 'We are perhaps a mere few paces from it, but we are not there yet.' He turned to Tesoro again. 'I would not deny you your comfort,' he went on, 'but once you have made your final confession and composed your soul for death, you have surrendered upon this earth. It may be necessary to do so, but the time for surrender has not yet come.'

'Fool!' cried the priest. 'Where is your hope? You have none save in God's mercy.'

'In which we trust, as all men,' replied Leonardo. 'Attend us later, father, if you please—perhaps when our heads are upon the block.'

'Where you are being taken,' said the priest somberly, 'no priest can follow you. Do you still refuse me?'

'Yes,' said Leonardo.

When the cleric had gone, Tesoro began to weep. 'I am not afraid to die,' he said, 'but to die outside God's Grace is a terrible thing.'

Leonardo crouched by the boy and raised his chin with one manacled hand. 'Tesoro,' he said, 'God's Grace is where we find it. No man can give it, or take it away, and least of all a man such as that one. Did you not hear him say who he was? Chaplain to Girolamo Riario, and a hypocrite to boot. He is farther from God than you or I. Did he bless your brother, do you suppose, when the Count murdered him foully before your eyes? Or the lady Carla d'Avalos, who died with him? What horrors must he have watched, daily and without protest? Dry your tears, lad. Life has not done with us yet awhile, and if it had I would not ask to be cawed over by a carrion crow such as him.'

Half an hour later a platoon of twenty armed men dragged them from their prison. Scudo spat at the feet of their leader, and was at once knocked senseless with a pike. Six men fetched a litter, and on it bore the unconscious

76

giant up the narrow stairway and out through a side door of the Castello del Mar.

Most of the Count's retinue gathered to watch the gunners' progress to their execution. Perhaps there were some among them who felt sympathy for the doomed Florentines, though they would hardly have dared to show it. It was even possible that one or two of those present wondered ironically why an escort of twenty was needed for three men walking with chained hands and a fourth who must be carried.

The procession made its way seawards, in the direction of an abandoned watchtower overlooking the Adriatic. The sun was sinking behind a low range of hills at the gunners' backs. Its last rays picked out the gaunt and forbidding pillar whose sheer walls soared from a rocky base and tapered slightly to the narrow battlements that topped it like a crown. At the tower's foot Riario and Antonio da Narni waited on horseback, shading their eyes to look at the advancing column of men.

'I confess,' said Narni, 'that this is admirably conceived, I can find no fault in it.'

'Thank you,' said Riario . . .

The vanguard of the procession reached them.

'What is the matter with him?' asked the Count, pointing to Scudo.

'He tried to resist,' said the leader of the escort party. 'And besides, he has the appearance of being three men in strength. Things are easier this way.'

'They will not be easier when you are carrying him up the stairway,' said Riario. 'Have a care that he does not knock you off it. Take him first.'

The six men who were carrying Scudo set the litter down, grasped his head, his arms, and his feet, and staggered with him through the narrow entrance door to the tower.

'They tell me,' said Riario, addressing Leonardo da Vinci, 'that you are a heretic. I believe it. Behold your stake and your funeral pyre.'

'Unchain us,' said Leonardo. 'We have no wish to die in shackles.'

'You must take me for a fool. Wear them until your bones are burned and broken. Or in your case, Captain,'

77

Riario added, addressing Rigo, 'if it gets too hot for comfort, you can always drive that hook of yours into your brain and die painlessly.'

Rigo made no reply. Of the three who stood there, he was the only one who could have released himself at any time he chose, by removing and dismantling his false right arm. Since there would have been no point whatever in doing so, he had refrained, though he now measured his distance from the Count with a baleful glance.

Beside the doorway stood a pile of stone blocks, and a plank laden with mortar. It was easy to guess the purpose of these materials. Through the open door itself Leonardo could see a pile of loose timber, whose top was beyond his view. Riario's intention was clear, deadly and cruel.

The soldiers who had been carrying Scudo emerged into the open again, and the rest of the Count's men began to push Leonardo, Rigo and Tesoro into the base of the tower. Inside, the pile of firewood was stacked to three times the height of a man, and covered almost the whole of the floor area. Apart from this timber the tower was empty. A narrow stair climbed spirally around its inner circumference. There was no handrail, and its wooden treads were socketed into recesses in the wall. Overhead was a rough ceiling of pine, supported by rafters.

They were driven up the stairway by their escort with no chance for attack or escape. Above the first ceiling was another cylindrical room, likewise bare; the stairway entered this by way of stout trapdoors. They continued to climb, urged onward by the pikes of their captors, and passed through another two levels before emerging onto an open roof above the fourth storey. This roof space was surrounded by the battlements, and at one side lay Scudo, still unconscious and on his back.

Riario's soldiers retreated down the precarious stairway, closing the last trapdoor behind them and bolting it. A faint breeze was blowing through the notches in the embrasures of the low wall around them. The sky gathered darkly in the early dusk. Leonardo walked to the western side of the rooftop to look down. If he had hoped to find a means of descent outside the tower, there was none; so much was absolutely clear.

Riario raised his hand and called upwards. 'Farewell.' He took a burning torch from the hand of a soldier standing by.

Leonardo retreated from the battlements and turned his attention to Scudo.

At the foot of the tower, Riario settled into his saddle and watched four of his men cement the last few blocks of masonry into position to fill the doorway. Behind them he could see the heavy oak of the door itself, now bolted tightly shut. When the last stone was in place, he tossed the blazing torch through a ventilation slit, standing in his stirrups to peer into the base of the tower until he was sure it had fired the stack of dried timber. He turned to da Narni.

'An act of war,' he said softly. 'The Turks were bound to attack this outpost sooner or later, wouldn't you say? It overlooks their waters, after all. I am afraid that it will be difficult to tell whether the ashes and bones that remain are Roman or Florentine, but that cannot be helped. When we find out who the gallant defenders were, we'll send their remains back with full military honours. Eh, Gattamelata?'

The escort column, dismissed, was already beginning to make its way back in the direction of the castle. Antonio da Narni and Riario waited in the deepening twilight until the first great plume of smoke burst from the top of the tower, and then pulled their horses' heads about and rode away.

'And may they roast in hell,' murmured Riario. After which, he remained silent until they reached the Castello del Mar.

Eight

THE SMOKE WHICH Count Girolamo Riario had observed with such satisfaction was pouring through cracks in the roof timbers beneath their feet, and would soon be followed by flame. Looking around them, Leonardo and Rigo found their situation desperate; so desperate, indeed, that Tesoro di Veluti seemed to have abandoned hope, and was sitting with his head on his knees by the side of the still unconscious Scudo.

A swift circle of the notched wall around the top of the watchtower was enough to show them plainly that there existed no prospect of descent. The masonry everywhere was smooth and almost seamless. Below them and far beyond their reach, it was pierced here and there by narrow embrasures, through which smoky wisps were already drifting outward to rise and mingle with the vapours that curled about their feet.

At least, Leonardo thought grimly, their passing would not go unnoticed, either by friend or foe. The tower—a giant flue—would soon become a raging column of fire, a hundred-foot torch, a signal visible for leagues across the Adriatic and the plains of Otranto. Here die four gunners of Florence, he intoned silently to himself, and in a true blaze of glory. Seared or suffocated according to the whim of providence, their skins would flake and their blood boil, the fat of their bodies would add fuel to the beacon which consumed them, and their bones would turn to glowing twigs of ash and charcoal. Or else they could seize a quicker and more merciful alternative and jump, as men had jumped from flame before them; a moment of terror, of exaltation, a splatter of brains across the rocks beneath, and they would lie broken, a long feast for crows and vultures.

He stooped and sought a finger-hold on the edge of the trap-door, idly rather than with any real intention. Escape down the interior of the tower was just as impossible as scaling its outer surface. Below them roared a furnace, and the only obstacles that delayed its grip upon them were the intervening wooden floors and the roof they stood on. Any descent below the roof would be an offer of instant sacrifice; a man might force his way down one storey, or even two, before choking at the end of a stairway whose treads themselves were being turned to embers at his feet.

In any case, the trap was bolted fast. Aware that Rigo was watching him closely, he rose and glanced across at Scudo, and the fetters jangled at his wrists. The roof was getting unpleasantly warm, and the smoke was thickening.

Leonardo crossed to the unconscious gunner, and slapped his face. Rigo joined him.

'Why bring him round?' he asked. 'Let him die in peace.'

'We are not going to die,' said Leonardo. 'And I need him awake.'

'You will never waken him with those love pats, then,' the Captain-Gunner said. 'Here.' He reached down and grasped a handful of Scudo's hair, wound the fingers of his left hand in it, and pulled, using the base of his palm for leverage against the giant's temple. The skin of Scudo's forehead bulged and puckered. 'He needs water,' Rigo said, continuing his task.

'Then pray for rain,' replied Leonardo.

Scudo's eyes opened, and his chained hands began to thrash aimlessly. He shook his head, and suddenly flailed at Rigo, throwing him half way across the roof in a reflex protest at the reviving pain. He hawked and spat.

'Where in hell am I?'

'A hundred feet in the air, and about to be roasted,' said Leonardo. 'Stir yourself. And you, too, Tesoro,' he added.

The young gunner had raised his head from his knees to watch Rigo's attempt to revive Scudo, but he now let it fall back listlessly.

'Move,' said Leonardo, 'or I will boot you to hell and back. It is close enough.' He aimed a kick at Tesoro, who scrambled reluctantly to his feet.

'What's happening?' demanded Scudo, hoarsely plaintive.

'I have work for you,' Leonardo told him. 'Are you listening?'

'What do you want me to do?'

'I want you to go and pull open that trap door yonder. You are the only one of us strong enough to do it.'

Scudo lumbered upright. Leonardo pointed him in the right direction, and he staggered across the smoking floor, shaking his head as he did so.

'This?' asked Scudo.

Leonardo nodded, and the huge gunner reached down and forced the tips of his fingers beneath the side of the trap.

'Have you lost your wits?' demanded Rigo. 'If he raises that, we are at the top of an open chimney! The draft will double the force of the fire.'

'Just so,' replied Leonardo. 'I'm not going to stay here forever while I fry. Follow me, and do as I do. Scudo.'

'Eh! It's *hot* under here,' said Scudo, still faintly puzzled by his circumstances.

'I know,' said Leonardo. 'Pull it open.'

Scudo wriggled the fingers of his other hand beneath the planks of the trap and heaved. The bolt that secured it gave way with a splintering crack, and the trap door opened, at once releasing a fiery spout of smoke and flying ashes.

'*Mother of God!*' shouted Scudo. 'Will somebody tell me what is happening?' He reeled back, singed, from the gaping rectangle. Leonardo at once made for the eastern side of the battlements. The others stared at him in astonishment as he swung himself into the notched opening. He raised his hands, reached over the stone pillar at his left, and draped the chain that fettered his wrists around it; then, stepping swiftly backwards into space beyond the castellations, he allowed himself to fall until he was hanging from his iron wristbands with his entire weight supported by the chain joining them.

Scudo's head appeared in the embrasure above him.

'Do as I have done, Scudo,' said Leonardo. 'Let yourself hang, like this. You see? Rigo? Tesoro? At my right and left. Come!'

A few seconds later his three companions had joined him. Ninety feet and more above the rocks of the Adriatic shore, they dangled like marionettes whose turn on stage is finished, with their faces pressed against the hot stone wall that now separated them from the inferno within the watchtower.

'And now,' said Leonardo to Scudo, 'Captain Leone will explain where you are and what you are doing here; and then I will tell you how we are going to escape our fate.'

After twenty minutes, Tesoro di Veluti began to complain bitterly; which at least, thought Leonardo, showed that he was recovering some of his spirits.

'My wrists are all but cut through,' Tesoro said.

'Then reach up with your fingers and grasp a link or two of your chain,' advised Leonardo. 'You can take a little of your weight that way. Rigo, how's your right arm?'

'Comfortable, I thank you,' Rigo said, 'though my left is somewhat strained. And as for my face and belly, I feel like a morsel of pork on a griddle.'

'But a live morsel of pork,' said Leonardo. 'This wall is an arm-span thick or more. It cannot keep us from discomfort, but it can keep us from death. Besides, the worst is over.' He laid his ear against the overheated masonry. The wall had cracked in places, but still stood firm. Behind it the roar of the flames grew in volume and fury, then steadied into a thunder like that of a foundry chimney. It was now diminishing. Overhead, tongues of orange licked at the sky, hurling smoke and chips of burning timber almost twice the height of the tower itself. We survive, he thought. A hot and dirty business, but we survive.

Beside him, Scudo voiced his own complaint.

'This is thirsty work,' he said. 'Did none of you think to bring a wineskin?'

It was an hour before Leonardo felt he should risk the ascent into the tower. He climbed with caution, setting the soles of his feet against the outer surface of the wall and pulling himself up until he could crawl between two of the pillars above him. He did not think they could be seen from the castle, half a mile distant, but he wanted to take no chances.

Inside the battlements the remaining waves of heat were almost more than he could stand. He looked down into the blackened hollow of the tower. Dusk had long since deepened into night, and yet the air shimmered visibly, distorting the small and glowing images of scattered embers a hundred feet below him so that they seemed like rubies glimpsed through dark and rippling water.

Little remained in the cylindrical gulf above which he was poised. He felt as though he were gazing down the barrel of an enormous cannon recently fired. Combustion appeared to have been almost complete; the conditions for it were after all wellnigh perfect. As his vision sharpened, however, he saw that here and there the charred skeleton of a heavy timber had remained intact. It takes a long time to burn away a fifteen-inch oaken rafter, and the fire had run out of fuel rapidly, as he had intended it should.

He called over his shoulder, and one by one the others joined him. They sat in neighbouring embrasures, Rigo beside Leonardo and Scudo with Tesoro di Veluti.

Rigo peered downward between his knees. 'And how do we get down? he inquired. 'It is a long way indeed without a rope—or with one, for that matter.'

'We have a rope, of sorts,' Leonardo pointed out. 'Though to make it available for our use will take many patient hours.' He held out his arms, indicating the four-foot loop of chain that hung between them. 'Your hook, I think, Rigo,' he said. 'Go to work.'

By midnight, they had some fifteen feet of chain in one continuous length, though several of its links were weakened by filing and hammering. It would do, thought Leonardo. Ten changes of anchorage would see them to the bottom. Since he had been the first to have his hands free, he had assumed the task of extracting and collecting a bundle of iron spikes; it required some nerve, as the spikes were imbedded in the under surface of a beam that still spanned the chasm beneath them. Not only were the spikes still hot, but the centre of the beam was smouldering as well, and threatened to collapse under his weight.

Nevertheless, he had his pitons for the descent, and

without further ado swung himself down the topmost niche that had formerly held the end of a stair tread. His fingers found a narrow crack in the stonework, the first of many such cracks, as he was gratefully to discover; he dislodged a piece of masonry, and hammered home a spike. Tesoro handed him one end of the chain, and he slipped a link over the head of the nail. He tested its firmness, and began his descent.

Eleven feet farther down the tower he stopped to drive in another spike. His companions now had a handrail of sorts, and began their own descent. When they had achieved handholds close above him, Leonardo jerked loose the top end of the chain and repeated the procedure he had just gone through, using his second piton as his upper anchorage. They rested in an embrasure before beginning the third relay of their descent; they rested again on the stub of a rafter before their fourth.

Within another hour, they were at the base of the tower where they kicked a standing place amongst the ashes. Heat and exertion had sweated them dry, and their thirst was appalling. They were safe enough in a sense, but still trapped. Rigo began to pick at the crevices beside the doorway, but the builders of the watchtower had set their masonry without mortar and their craftsmanship was excellent.

'We must break down the door,' Rigo said. 'The Count's handiwork behind it may have been more hasty.'

They were, unfortunately, working in near darkness, save for the faint glow of expiring embers about their feet. By feel, therefore, Leonardo examined the door itself. This, infuriatingly, was almost undamaged, except that its inner face had been badly scorched; the fire down here had been less fierce than higher up the tower, because of the lack of air. And—as he found after Scudo had heaved mightily at the handle and failed to budge it even a fraction of an inch—the door was bound in iron, which had expanded under heat, and was now immovable in its frame.

'I expect,' said Rigo, 'that you need to borrow my arm again, for use as a block and tackle.'

'It wouldn't be strong enough,' said Leonardo. 'I would need several pulleys to give me enough force to shift this barrier. Three would give us power of twelve men, but in any case the one above your elbow would be too weak.'

'Then what?' asked Rigo. 'Have we survived all this in order to starve like rats in a dungeon?'

'Let me think,' Leonardo said. He leaned against the door, and pushed away hastily, having forgotten how hot it was. He paced to and fro in the gloom, scattering ashes with his boots. 'We shall use a Spanish windlass,' he announced finally. Where is that chain of ours?'

Tesoro dragged it forward, and Leonardo drove one end of it through the massive iron handle of the door.

'Tesoro, he commanded, 'go one way around the wall. Scudo the other way. Feel along it as you go, and try to find me a place to fix this. A ring bolt, perhaps, or a hook.'

A minute later, Scudo called across the darkness.

'There are three hooks here. No, five. A rack for pikes, I dare say.'

'Stay where you are,' said Leonardo. Moving carefully, he carried the end of the chain across the room. As Scudo had said, there was a row of metal clamps, hook-shaped, set into the stonework of the wall. Leonardo stretched the chain as far as he could, and slipped a link of it over one of these. 'And now a crowbar,' he said. 'Search at your feet for a bolt from one of the traps, or any stout piece of metal.'

In the end, and after getting their fingers burned once or twice apiece, the best tool they could come up with for Leonardo's purpose was a twisted length of iron strapping from the inner surface of the door itself. Leonardo walked to the middle of the stretched chain, thrust one end of the metal strap into a central link, and began to twist the chain with the lever he had thus made for himself. He called Scudo to help him, since the chain shortened as it twisted and it needed the strength of more than one man to continue turning the metal bar. Leonardo prayed, fervently but silently, that the chain would not give way under the tremendous tension applied to it in this fashion; if that happened one of them might well be decapitated by the backlash. A moment later, however, the door squealed protestingly and gave way, exposing the recent brickwork of Girolamo Riario's masons.

'The twists and turns of life . . .' said Leonardo thoughtfully. 'Does it not amuse you to think that it is the twists and turns of the Count's own fetters which have saved our lives?'

'We are not out of this damned place yet,' growled Rigo. 'Keep your damned philosophy to yourself until we are.'

'Well. Riario's wall,' Leonardo said. 'Scudo?'

'Yes?'

'Kick it down.'

'Right,' said Scudo, and he did so.

Cool night air flooded in through the gap he had battered with one or two thundering heel punches. Tesoro would have shouted for joy, but was instantly silenced by Rigo. Leonardo pulled aside several more blocks of masonry, and crawled through to starlight and freedom.

'And now,' said Rigo, joining him, 'water. I am no lover of water as a rule, since it softens the brain, but for this once I will make an exception.'

When they had found a stream some distance north of Castello del Mar, and had drunk their fill and bathed, Tesoro announced that he was hungry.

'I am glad to hear it, infant,' said Rigo. 'For a while I was beginning to fear you had gone into a decline.'

'And so I did,' said Tesoro promptly and with a certain innocence. 'I despaired too easily. However, I propose to redeem myself somewhat now.' He buttoned his tunic.

'Oh?' said Rigo with interest. 'How?'

'I am off to steal one of Riario's chickens,' Tesoro said. 'Or possibly two.'

Scudo's stomach rumbled.

'You had better make it three,' said Leonardo. 'Two for Scudo, and one for the rest of us. And oblige me by not getting caught, Tesoro.'

'I was born in Pitigliano,' said Tesoro loftily, 'and in Pitigliano we learn to steal chickens before we can walk.'

Nine

THEY HAD FINISHED their dinner—or, perhaps, their breakfast—with the ravenous appetite achieved only by those who have recently escaped death, and were sitting on the sand a few paces from the gently surging waters of the Adriatic Sea. Scudo was still hungry, since he had in the end been forced to make do with a mere chicken and a half, and Rigo lamented the absence of ale; but otherwise they were contented.

'And now?' asked Tesoro.

Leonardo had already given the matter some thought.

'Since you are so expert a chicken thief,' he said, 'return to our encampment and take my stallion. Be careful, for Riario may have posted a man or two there, though I think it unlikely. And then ride for Florence.'

'Why?' Tesoro demanded. 'Is there nothing to be done here?'

'There is much. But someone must inform Lorenzo of what we know, namely that Riario is having fifty cannon built in Rome that fit *Turkish* shot and not our own! He and da Narni plot for nothing less than betrayal. This information must reach Lorenzo—and Cardinal Domenico della Palla—or the risks we have taken are for nothing.'

'Why me?' persisted Tesoro.

'Because,' replied Leonardo, 'when you came with us to Otranto you did so on the understanding that you would obey orders without question.'

'But—'

'Without question,' repeated Leonardo firmly. 'This is not some pleasant outing in the country, Tesoro, but a matter of all our lives and the welfare of Italy. Your mission is a vital one.' He reached into the pouch at his belt. 'Here are fifteen florins, which is all the money I have with me. There is more buried at our camp, but it will take you too long to search for it. You must be on your way north before the day breaks. Well?'

Tesoro opened his mouth to protest further, and then paused. 'Very well,' he said at last. He rose in the waning light of their campfire, and shuffled his feet uncertainly. 'I had best be gone,' he added, as though hoping for some warmer farewell.

'Watch out for wolves,' said Rigo, and grinned up at him.

Tesoro raised a hand in salute, and walked off into the darkness with an air of resigned dejection.

'Thank God I'm not his age,' Rigo said, 'when everything is either high comedy or black tragedy, as it is with him.'

'He will be a man,' said Scudo gruffly. 'What of us, Leonardo?'

Leonardo got to his feet and brushed the sand from his breeches. 'The lady Bianca is on her way to Constantinople,' he said. 'And therefore we are going for a short walk.'

'In what direction?' demanded Rigo.

'South.' He kicked sand over the remains of their fire, and led the way along the beach. They were in no hurry, and it was thus a little before dawn when they spotted the outposts of the Turkish army, or at least that portion of it which was quartered in the shore beneath Otranto's eastern wall. They continued on their way, still unhurriedly, making no attempt at concealment, until they found themselves challenged and surrounded by a party of Moors with lances, scimitars, and drawn bows. Leonardo raised his hands peaceably, and waited until the man who held a lance at his breast had stopped shouting in his incomprehensible Turkish.

'Take us to Sultan Mohammed, the Child of Allah,' he said.

His request meant nothing to their captors, of course, but upon hearing the names of their God and their Prophet, the soldier with the lance lowered it fractionally and relaxed. With two men guarding each of them, the gunners were marched down the beach amidst a growing crowd of the curious, and were thrust inside a tent. Here Leonardo at once lay down upon his back and closed his eyes.

'I hope you know what you are doing,' said Rigo. His only reply, however, was a gentle snore.

Some two hours later the flap of the tent opened. Two Janissaries entered, escorting a third man who stared at the Florentines as Leonardo opened his eyes and sat up.

'Sirs, sirs,' he said. 'It is you!' It was Stefano Morelli, the Milanese whom they had rescued from the tender ministrations of Girolamo Riario.

'Well, Stefano,' said Leonardo, 'I see that you have returned to the bosom of the All-Merciful. That was risky, surely, for a deserter?'

'There was no risk,' replied Stefano, and spat. 'After I had discovered that the mercy of Christendom was less than that of Islam, I simply came back here and told my Turkish masters that I had been taken by a Roman patrol and cruelly beaten. Since I had the lashes on my back to prove it, I was made welcome. I am now what I was before—second steward to my lord the Sultan. But what brings you here, sirs? You are in grave peril.'

Leonardo told him some of what had passed. 'So you see,' he finished, 'we are as little in love with the Count as yourself, and have come hither seeking passage for Constantinople. Can you smooth our road to the Sultan, your master, Stefano?'

'Alas,' Stefano Morelli replied, 'he has returned to Constantinople already, and his second in command Shan Khara with him. They left many days ago, in fact. Rome will not attempt to retake Otranto this winter, and there is nothing to keep the Sultan here. But let me see what I can do for you.'

He turned and spoke to the Janissaries in Turkish, evidently giving them some account of who their captives were. When he had finished, he turned back to Leonardo.

'I have not told them the truth,' he said, 'but what I have said will satisfy them for the present. You wish to rejoin your lady in Constantinople? That is all?'

'That is all,' replied Leonardo.

'And you do not, therefore, care how you travel there?'
'No.'

'Then, sirs, I may yet be of help to you. I owe you much—my life perhaps—and I am a man who does not forget his debts. Will you trust in my judgement?'

'By all means,' Leonardo told him. Stefano Morelli turned back to the Janissaries, made them another short speech of which the gunners could understand nothing, and then all three men left the tent.

'Cast your bread upon the waters,' Leonardo said to Rigo when Morelli had gone, 'and you shall find it after many days. Not so many, in this case. Who will say now that there is no reward in virtue?'

'Let's wait to see what Stefano achieves for us before we become pious,' replied Rigo sourly.

Their captors remained neutral towards them for the rest of the day, and food and water were brought to their tent at noon. In the evening Stefano Morelli returned, accompanied as before by two Janissaries.

'Sirs, I do not know whether you will be pleased by what I have done,' he said, 'but I have obtained passage to Constantinople for you. I have told the authorites that you are three famous mercenaries, and that you have quarrelled with the Count of Imola—which is true enough, after all.'

'And how did you account for our having walked directly into their lines?' asked Leonardo.

'Sirs,' said Stefano Morelli simply, 'I told them you were drunk.'

'Bravo!' said Leonardo.

'By Christ, I wish it had been true!' snorted Rigo.

'And how are we to travel to Constantinople, friend Stefano?' Leonardo went on.

Morelli hesitated before making his reply. Then: 'You are captives, sirs, and will go as galley slaves. I—'

'Be damned to that,' said Scudo. 'I am no slave.'

'Hold, now,' Leonardo put in. 'I cannot speak for you two, but I will gladly take oar and row if it brings me closer to the lady Bianca by one mile or one minute. Did you suppose they would transport us in luxury and by our own private vessel? We are, as Stefano says, prisoners. We can expect no better treatment.'

'Believe me,' Stefano said, 'I am sorry that I could do no better for you. Had you a ransom to offer them here and now, then perhaps . . . but no. If you could ransom yourselves, they would merely take your money and set you free—which would not get you across the Mediterranean.'

'It was well done, Stefano,' Leonardo said. 'I thank you.'

Rigo, who had so far made no comment, now spoke up with an air of triumph.

'A one-armed man cannot row,' he pointed out, and held up his hook for Stefano to see. Stefano at once turned and spoke with the Janissaries, whose faces remained stern.

'They say that you must pull your oar with your left hand,' Stefano said, looking miserable. 'If not, you will drown.'

'So be it,' said Rigo, shrugging. 'I row with my left hand.'

On the afternoon of the following day Leonardo shifted uncomfortably on the thin padding of his seat and took stock of his surroundings.

He was, at least, in the open air rather than confined in a noisome hold below decks. The galley which he and his two companions—along with one hundred and seventy seven other chained slaves—was long and sleek, an open bireme built for speed of passage and little else. Cabins stood fore and aft, and the rowers sat in deep wells at either side of a central platform running the length of the ship—a platform along which, he reminded himself, would stride overseers armed with whips to spur their charges into further effort if they should flag. A thousand miles to the Bosphorus, Leonardo thought. We will work.

The galley was anchored off Otranto, and rode slowly to the ocean's swell. Leonardo was at the inner end of his oar, which slanted downwards from his seat towards a port in the ship's side. A little below him and to his right Scudo sat, and beyond Scudo was Rigo Leone, nearest of the three to the timbers of the hull. All of them were chained by their ankles to bolts beneath their seats, and their hands were shackled to the oar handle, six inches thick and shining with the polish imparted by long years of sweated toil; the toil of men very like themselves, captured in one battle or another and sentenced to live out the remainder of their

92

days in these seats, in this ship, until sickness, starvation or brutality overcame them. How many men, Leonardo wondered, had died where he now sat? He suppressed the thought, and looked about him.

In front of him and behind were the sweeps of the lower rank of oarsmen, whose heads were on a level with his feet. To this extent the gunners had been fortunate, since the upper rowing stations were the more desirable. His own head was a little higher than the level of the central platform itself, and he could feel the sea breeze on his face. By his count, thirty Janissaries were travelling as passengers, and perhaps some thirty more of the common men-at-arms; their quarters were at prow and stern, open in the main to the stars and weather. A fighting ship, then, though Leonardo devoutly hoped they would not have to fight. All men had heard tales of the fate of galley slaves in a sinking ship; chained at their stations, they simply drowned like rats, since of all human beings the galley slave was the most readily expendable. Indeed, he was barely human at all. He took the place of canvas, spars, and rigging; that was all his purpose, until the grave took him, or the sea. Who cared whether galley slaves lived or died, or how they did so?

As though in ironic answer to his musings, a voice spoke from above his head.

'You are fortunate, sirs,' said Stefano Morelli, and squatted by the gunners' oar.

Leonardo held up his shackled hands and smiled grimly.

'Though you may find it hard to believe,' said Stefano, 'your conditions here are a rower's paradise compared to those in some of the galleys I have seen. This is a ship of the Sultan's own squadron, and must skim the waves like a dolphin. Therefore his rowers are carefully chosen, well fed and adequately rested, so that they may give him of their best.'

'I am glad to hear you say so. Though we are but animals chained to our burden, for all that. How long to Constantinople?'

'Twenty days, if the captain takes you across the portage by Corinth,' said Stefano Morelli. 'And he will, since it saves him nearly three days of sea journey.'

'And what is his hurry, then?'

93

Morelli stood up, and pointed along the central platform to a group of Janissaries carrying a wooden chest. 'Look yonder,' he said, 'Do you know what that casket contains? The Sword of Islam, sir, and a piece of the very robe once worn by Mahomet, the Prophet of the One God. It is a treasure beyond price. Ten days ago, by Allah's will, the Sultan's major-domo died of a fever; and his successor, through ignorance, neglected to send the chest you see there along with the Sultan's other baggage. Without it my lord will be like a lion driven mad by rage. Of all his possessions, that chest is the most precious to him, and therefore each day that passes before it reaches him in Constantinople is of vital account. I thank God that I am not responsible for its delay. Sirs, I said that you were fortunate, and it is the truth; but I am bound also to tell you that the Captain will make this ship fly through the water!'

'And thereby reach Constantinople the sooner,' said Leonardo, 'in which I rejoice.'

'Here, sir,' said Stefano, looking quickly from side to side before stretching down his hand. He gave Leonardo a small pile of coins. 'It is all I have to offer you; ten florins. A man with some money in his pouch wears a shield, if only a small one.' He straightened up. 'The captain speaks our mother tongue,' he added, 'and so does Hamoun, the overseer, though poorly. Guard what you say therefore. And now farewell, and may good fortune go with you.'

Stefano walked towards the prow, where the Janissaries were taking their precious burden within the fore cabin. Rigo craned his head to look at Leonardo from his station by the hull.

'And what was all that about?' he asked.

'The final settlement of a debt. Our Stefano is an honest man, and returned good measure for our kindness to him.'

'Oh? What did he give you?'

'A little money, and a great deal of information,' said Leonardo. He rubbed his palms along the tops of his thighs. Scudo grimaced.

'You would row this damned ship to Turkey all by yourself,' he said. 'Eh?'

'I might try,' replied Leonardo, and laughed. 'Be happy, Scudo. It is healthy exercise, and a means of seeing the world, though I wouldn't care to do it until the end of my days.'

Within five days, after passing inshore to Kerkira, Levkas, and the other islands of the Ionian coast, they left the Peloponnesian city of Patras to starboard and entered the Gulf of Corinth. Much of what Stefano Morelli had prophesied was true. If their conditons were not those of paradise, they were not hellish. True, all three of them had felt the whip of Hamoun, the overseer, more than once, but it had not been wielded with any real venom. They had eaten meat twice, albeit tough and stringy, and had been given a draught or two of thin wine, though this was forbidden to followers of Islam. Twice a day they were allowed to go aft, still fettered, in order to relieve themselves and bathe hastily in salt water. They, and those Italian captives around them with whom they managed to strike a meagre acquaintance, remained healthy men; and such was far from being the case, Leonardo knew, with the less fortunate among galley slaves.

In return for these marks of the Sultan's favour, the rowing pace they maintained was truly terrifying. While they rowed, their bodies became machines and their senses recognised only the insistent beat of the timekeeper's drum, a slow and merciless tattoo that hypnotised the mind and battered the soul. When they slept, it was in an exhaustion so profound that Leonardo, who normally dreamed often and vividly, was aware of nothing between the closing of his eyes and the hoarse bellow of Hamoun calling upon his charges to bestir themselves. Even Scudo, that bronze titan, was heard to complain every so often that his muscles ached, though his protests brought nothing but jeers from Rigo Leone. The Captain-Gunner, having voiced his own complaints loudly and with sarcasm before the start of their journey, considered it a waste of time and breath to continue doing so once they were under way. He therefore advised Scudo to keep his mouth shut, and pull.

On the evening of the sixth day out of Otranto, they reached the head of the Gulf of Corinth, and drove the prow of the galley up a gently sloping beach.

'It's to be a portage,' said Giorgio di Savona, a scarred Genoese whose station was immediately behind and below Leonardo's. 'You know what a portage is, Florentines? Tonight they give us a *good* meal. Tomorrow we drag the ship seven miles and more across the land to the Gulf of Salamis. After that it's the Aegean. I have made this land crossing twice, and have not grown to like it, though it is a change from pulling this oar, I admit.'

'Do they use rollers?' asked Leonardo.

'Yes.'

'Winches?'

'Why winches?' said Giorgio di Savona. 'They have our backs at their disposal, and they are quite prepared to break them. Hey, Scudo?'

'Yes?' replied Scudo, turning to look down at him.

'Is he always like this, your friend?' Giorgio jerked a thumb in Leonardo's direction. 'If you tell him something, does he always ask you questions like a damned scholar?'

'Always,' said Scudo.

'You must forgive him,' added Rigo, also turning. 'He is . . . you know . . . a little crazed in the head.'

'Oh,' said Giorgio di Savona, and looked up at Leonardo thoughtfully. 'Is he dangerous?'

'Not really,' Rigo replied. 'Or at least, only to his close friends.'

At this point they were shouted into silence by Hamoun, and food and drink were distributed in a disciplined silence. Undisturbed, Leonardo ate and drank gratefully, and fell once more into slumber like his fellows.

The next morning's ascent of the western slope of the Corinthian isthmus was accomplished by enormous effort and no incident of note. Shortly after dawn the galley slaves were freed from the shackles that held them to their oars, and some twenty of them were sent into the surrounding countryside, under guard, to fell timber for use as rollers. Of the remainder, half were organised into teams of ten men and given the ends of heavy cables to haul. The rest were chained to bolt heads set into the outer surface of the hull at either side of the galley, there to act likewise as draft animals.

When the woodcutters returned with their logs, the

beaching of the ship began. The crude rollers were set in sequence beneath the front of the keel, and the galley heaved onto them. The track they were to follow was a broad one, and well worn. It ran from the beach in a straight line to the top of the ridge, and the galley had surmounted this by noon. As each roller emerged from below the rudder post, it was lifted by a gang of Turkish soldiers and carried to the front once more; the captive oarsmen were confined to haulage, and were beaten mercilessly when ever the vessel's momentum slackened.

At the top of the ridge they rested, and were given water. Before them, under a burnished October sky, lay the narrow strip of land that joined Peloponnesus to the mainland of Greece. A trivial distance on map or chart perhaps, but daunting to those who now beheld it as a desert to be crossed, a torn and sandy roadway that ploughed its way to the horizon and beyond, along which they must drag a vast burden that would grow vaster and more stubborn with each hour that passed.

All the towing cables save two were now cast off, and every oarsman was chained to the hull itself. The open land to north and south presented too clear a temptation to any man, as the Turks were well aware. They toiled, therefore, like ants at a blade of grass, urged on by shouts and blows, each seeing only the ground at his feet, the wooden hull at his side, and the straining body of the slave before him. Those who stumbled were prevented from falling by their shackles. They were cursed, lashed, and set into forward motion again by their captors; and came, finally and unwilling, to a kind of a pride in their task, in the juggernaut-like progress of the ship and the squealing of the rollers beneath its keel.

It was at dusk that the first arrows rained among them, instantly killing six men on the port side of the ship and wounding as many more.

They were barely a mile from their destination, and their carved track ran along the bottom of a valley whose sides drew closer together and steepened in front of them. At the bottom of a wide notch, held at either side by bluffs, the track appeared to vanish, plunging downwards towards the dark blue sea beyond. Their attackers, whoever they might be, had chosen the perfect place and time for their assault; but no attackers were as yet visible.

Leonardo and his companions on the starboard side of the ship, hearing the cries and groans, could only guess at what had occurred. Their assailants were beyond a ridge to the north of the portage track, and had left their cover barely long enough to discharge their bows before sinking behind it and out of sight once more.

The ship came to a halt, while confused shouts rose from the Janissaries on deck above their heads. Both the Pelopponesus and Greece itself were under Ottoman rule, and the ambush was therefore unexpected. Leonardo glanced to his right, and shouted to Rigo and Scudo; he had seen ten or a dozen more archers to the south, their weapons raised. Arrows hissed towards them, and struck home with dull percussions into hull and human flesh alike. A white-robed Janissary toppled from the gunwale, to sprawl on the bare earth at Rigo's feet. Blood pulsed through the muslin which wrapped his side, and then was stilled by death.

'God's bones,' Rigo said, 'but here is poor sport! Are we expected to stand here like tethered pigeons at a fair?'

'Be still,' replied Leonardo. 'Now that they've seen their target plainly, they'll aim high. We're of little concern until the Turks are slain.'

His conclusion proved correct. The next volley from the north produced a whirring flight of shafts that cleared the galley and soared above the gunners' heads to bury themselves in the earth a hundred paces to their right. How many more arrows had struck home on deck they could not tell from their position at ground level, and nor could they gauge the effect of the subsequent curving hail from their own side, the south. The Turks, however, were clearly in no mood to wait until their unseen foes grew tired of this target practice from behind their ridges. Janissaries leaped to the earth, formed into a skirmishing line at either side of the vessel, and quickly up the valley slopes. Many fell to the arrows that rained among them, but most reached the summit and disappeared from the gunners' view.

Minutes later they returned. It was clear that they had found few opponents to engage in combat, and they regrouped around the galley talking angrily among themselves. Night was falling, and it appeared that, for the present at least, both Turks and captives were to be given a respite.

Half an hour later, Leonardo attracted the attention of Hamoun, the overseer. He came over to where the three Florentines were chained, coiling his whip as he did so. Leonardo beckoned him closer, and held out his hand.

'Here are five florins,' the artist said. 'I wish to speak with your captain.'

'For what purpose, dung of a goat?' inquired the overseer.

'For the purpose of ensuring you another five florins,' Leonardo replied. 'Not to mention the saving of your most worthy life.'

Hamoun tapped his jaw lightly with the stock of his whip before making up his mind. 'Very well,' he said. He unshackled Leonardo, and led him to the stern of the galley, where a plank had been set to give access to the after-deck. Leonardo followed awkwardly and was ushered into the Turkish captain's quarters.

'And who are you?' asked that officer brusquely. The sight of one of his galley slaves displeased him, since he had problems enough of his own to consider without—as he supposed—being faced with one of the nameless, faceless animals who drove his ship.

'I am Leonardo da Vinci,' the artist said. 'Some men call me the Taker of Cities.' Nobody, in fact, had offered him this title, but he judged the decoration appropriate to the moment and, as it happened, tolerably well deserved.

'Well?' said the captain, apparently unimpressed. 'And what cities have you taken?'

'Oh,' replied Leonardo softly, 'Castelmonte, and Venice, to mention only two. Sir, unless you make a decision which is difficult indeed, you are lost, and we are lost with you. I have come to offer you a way out of your difficulties, if you will accept it.'

'Say it since you are here,' said the captain grimly. 'But I will strip the skin from your body if you waste my time, Taker of Cities.'

'Sir, you have among your oarsmen many notable

99

warriors. They are captives, it is true, as I am, yet this is but the turn of fortune's wheel. Chained to your ship, we shall die tomorrow, before you or after you, it makes little difference. Dead men cannot move your ship. Living men can. Free men can also fight for you, it being in their interest to fight.'

The captain stared at him.

'What are you suggesting?' he asked.

'That you offer all your galley slaves their freedom, in return for their support in tomorrow's battle. It is as simple as that.'

'Oh?' replied the captain. 'And I dare say you will next propose that I arm them—and you? Well?'

'You might,' said Leonardo. 'But I expect that is too much to ask. We can do without arms, if need be.'

'They will surrender to the enemy,' the captain said. 'Do you take me for a fool?'

'They will do no such thing. I have a friend who is also a Taker of Cities,' Leonardo said. 'His name is Rigo Leone, and he is Master-Gunner to Florence. I assure you that he can put the fear of Allah into any man. Besides, where is their advantage? Leave their feet chained, then. But free their hands, sir, and they will fight.'

'No,' said the captain. 'It is out of the question.'

'Then you are prepared to lose the Sword of Islam, I take it. Not to mention the robe of the One Prophet?'

The Turk's eyes widened in shock.

'What do you know of such matters?' he whispered.

'Enough,' Leonardo said. 'And more than enough to imagine your fate were you to reach Constantinople alive—without Sword or robe.' He studied the captain's face for a moment or two. 'Come now,' he said. 'Accept my suggestion, and you have a chance, however slim, of completing your mission successfully. Ignore me, and these brigands will cut us all down, man by man. Let us fight, sir. Let us fight!'

A mile away, the leader of a band of dissident Greek militia spiked a morsel of cheese with his dagger and bit into it. The cheese represented the last of his supplies.

'We are two hundred,' he said to his lieutenant. 'Next month we shall be five hundred, and the month after that, a thousand. Meantime, let us take this Turkish ship.'

'And bring a Turkish army down about our heads,' said his lieutenant.

'I care nothing for any army of Turks. I care for my belly, and for the bellies of my men. How many are they? Twenty? Twenty-five? We will have them at dawn.'

'And what of the galley slaves?'

'Kill them. Who needs more mouths to feed?'

Advancing at daybreak to the top of the northern ridge, the Greek leader found that nine tenths of his opposition had mysteriously vanished. The Turks had deserted their vessel under cover of the night's darkness, it seemed, leaving only their unwilling oarsmen still chained pathetically to the sides of the galley, looking about them with nervous eyes.

'So much for the Turks,' said the Greek leader. 'So much for their famous Janissaries.' He hawked and spat. 'Well. Let us finish this business, and we will have a ship of our own as well as her supplies and cargo—whatever that may be.'

He waved his men onward, shouting wildly, and they poured down the hillside. The ill-fated galley slaves shifted their feet in apparent and fearful anticipation of doom; some of the advancing Greeks even sympathised with them.

Such feeling, where it existed, ceased a few short seconds later, when the chained men detached themselves—swiftly and magically—from the bolts to which they were supposedly fettered, and began to wield the chains at their wrists with deadly effect. The Greek commander, his archers left encamped, was outnumbered by at least two score. He himself was unlucky enough to end his unhappy life three feet away from Scudo, who kicked his head in like a rotten pumpkin. Few of his soldiers survived him for long; those who were not strangled or flailed to death were taken in the rear by the Turks, who had been hiding below the twin bluffs that guarded the exit to the valley. One or two, more fleet of foot than the rest, escaped. The rest were massacred, and their bones served for many months as a reminder to others who might have considered challenging the Ottoman Empire.

When it was all over, the Turkish captain took a count of his own casualties; thirty-three dead and twelve wounded. Barely half of these were Janissaries, a fact which piqued him somewhat. But the galley-slave's plan had worked and he had a promise to fulfil. He summoned the artist to his cabin.

'I owe you my thanks, sir,' he said. 'I will order your leg irons removed at once.'

'And those of all the rest of us,' said Leonardo.

'The thought distresses me greatly,' said the captain. 'You cannot expect me to make them free men here and now. I have my ship to think of.'

'And the Sword of Islam,' Leonardo reminded him. 'And the robe of the Prophet. Keep your word, else you are no man at all.'

'And how will I get to Constantinople?'

'We shall row you to Constantinople. But we shall row as free men row, with neither whip nor chains. Some of your own men must help us.'

'But . . . haste is essential, sir. You must see that. I cannot be at the whim of . . . of—'

'Free men?' said Leonardo. 'Why not? We will get you to Constantinople faster than your wildest hopes, since a man who is his own master always works better than a serf. Moreover, if you will take my advice, you will allow us to set up our own shifts at the oars. We can give you three quarters of your maximum speed, but steadily, day and night. The racing beat gives you a spurt, but the fatigue that follows loses all you have gained. Let Captain Leone seek out your most experienced oarsman, and give him the pace drum. And keep Hamoun out of our way, for there are one or two amongst us who might take it into their heads to toss him overboard. I myself will assist your navigator, for I was taught by one of your own countrymen, Ibn Hazim.'

The captain surrendered, with as good a grace as he could muster.

'Sir,' he said, 'you have deserved honour at our hands, and you shall receive it. And so shall all those who have served us under your command. As for my promise to set

102

them free, they shall be unchained now—though I know not what my promise may be worth when we reach Constantinople.'

'Have no fear,' replied Leonardo. 'All you need do is ensure that the Sword and the robe reach the Sultan at the same time that I do. I'll see to it that your debt is discharged with honour.'

He returned to Rigo and Scudo, around whom a milling crowd of former galley slaves had gathered.

'Well?' said Rigo.

'*No chains!*' shouted Leonardo. For a minute he could make himself heard no further above the cheering. 'Now we have a ship to move, to launch, and to drive for Constantinople! Captain Leone here is your commander. If you dispute it, do so with my friend Scudo, who will be delighted to offer you any small persuasion you may need. Is it agreed?'

A hundred and fifty voices roared their assurance and twenty minutes later, the galley was moving again.

Hamoun, who was discovered later to have both eyes blacked, spent the rest of the voyage in the forecabin. In this he was wise; but he was annoyed to find that the journey from the Gulf of Salamis to the Bosphorus took exactly three days less than the best time his whip had ever achieved.

Ten

'*Is it really possible?*' asked Lorenzo de' Medici. 'Can Rome's own Captain-General, the blood relative of the Supreme Pontiff himself, do such foul treachery? God knows he is a brutal and self-seeking man. Yet to steal the secret of my guns, the most dangerous weapons in all Italy, not for Rome but for Rome's *foes*—for Italy's foes! It almost passes belief, even for Girolamo Riario!'

It was a chill morning in late October. With the Cardinal Domenico della Palla at his side, the two men paced their daily path through the meadow that ran behind the Medici Palace. Now, in his agitation, Lorenzo paused, his hand on the churchman's arm. Between the two men, Roman and Florentine, Cardinal and temporal ruler, there had blossomed a friendship that was a surprise to them both; a friendship, perhaps, of men who are opposed in many things and yet find themselves to have similar minds, a fundamental understanding of the nature of power.

Cardinal della Palla had no business to hold him in Florence. He should have returned, long since, to his Chancery and the network of information from which he derived his strength. Instead, he had tarried through autumn in almost continuous discourse with Florence's ruler, that free-thinking republican who was, on the surface, Rome's sworn enemy. Their daily walks through this meadow had become something to which they both looked forward with much anticipation, though neither could fully understand why this should be so.

'No,' Lorenzo continued. 'No, by God! I am growing old, it seems. All treachery is possible, even this. And Leonardo da Vinci, may plague and the devil take him, is seldom wrong. If he has sent me young Tesoro di Veluti with this news, I had best force myself to believe that he knows whereof he speaks. Damn him.'

'My lord,' murmured the Cardinal gently, 'it seems to me that you curse this man overmuch. I will remind you that he has won you this information at considerable risk.'

'Risk?' said Lorenzo. 'Do not speak to me of risk! What of my ward, the lady Bianca? I need Milan's friendship. How can I keep it when I must account for her welfare to Lodovico Sforza, Milan's ruler and her cousin? I turn my back, and she is gone to Leonardo da Vinci in defiance of both scandal and her safety. Now she is half across the world, and a captive of the Turks. Whose fault is that if not Leonardo's?'

'Hers,' replied the Cardinal. 'My lord, if she is wilful, consider that it may be her destiny and God's purpose that she is so. Perhaps you had better stop brooding over her like a mother hen, and allow her wings to carry her where they may.'

'Even to death?'

'I doubt that she is dead,' said Cardinal della Palla.

'She is a slave in the *seraglio* of a heathen if she is not,' replied Lorenzo.

'Perhaps. Will you forgive me, my lord Lorenzo, if I point out another curious fact to you? Whenever you complain of her behaviour, which I admit is scandalous, you always add that it is not her welfare that concerns you so much as your relationship with her powerful cousin Sforza, or Florence's relationship with Milan, or some other specious argument. I find this odd; the more odd since I was present when your gunner brought you the news of her capture, and I saw the pallor of your face when you heard him speak.'

'I am fond of the child,' mumbled Lorenzo. 'Her conversation pleases me.'

The Cardinal laughed outright, and took Lorenzo's arm. 'And she has a mind of her own. I know. And when you speak of Leonardo, you swear like a soldier. Shall I tell you, my lord, what your behaviour puts me in mind of? You are like a man who has lost a woman of whom he is very fond to a friend of whom he is equally fond—or a brother, perhaps? Loving both of them, you are enraged when they

105

conspire against you. Let us be honest. You feel towards Bianca as though she were part way between a daughter and something more than a daughter. And as for Leonardo, will you swear that he does not, in however small a measure, put you in mind of your brother Giuliano? Giuliano is dead, and you have admitted to me that you seek to bind Leonardo da Vinci to Florence. Is it to Florence, my lord, or to yourself?'

'Your imagination is running away with you,' snorted Lorenzo. 'There is not a word of truth in your suggestions.'

'No? I am not so sure,' Cardinal della Palla said, mildly. 'It is you who are walking with your eyes closed. Well, let me try to offer you some direct comfort. Wherever the Lady Bianca Visconti may be at this moment, I will wager you that she is in command of her situation.'

El Fatih, The Conqueror and The Right Hand of Allah, Sultan Mohammed II, was indeed entranced with his newest and most beautiful possession. Her fair hair and delicate northern features had captivated him from the moment of their first meeting. But it was not until Bianca had complained acidly—and with no little wit—at being confined to his *seraglio* along with—as she put it—a hundred empty headed and chattering females that he had been intrigued by her mind.

Her complaints might well have brought her a whipping, or worse. Instead, they earned her a cushion at the Sultan's left hand when he held court, together with his amused indulgence. After an hour or two spent in discussion of commodity exchange rates and the relative stabilities to be found among the currencies of the city-states of Italy (for Bianca had been an excellent listener at the knee of her guardian Lorenzo de' Medici, that shrewd banker) his indulgence had turned to surprise and then to delight.

'Little one, you have a head that would sit well upon the shoulders of my wisest Vizier,' he had told her. 'In fact, I think I shall here and now appoint you my guide in matters of trade and finance.'

'It pays well, my lord?'

'The preservation, from sunrise to sunrise, of your life,' Sultan Mohammed had replied. 'You would not, surely, advise me to pay more for your counsel than I need.' He had smiled thinly at this small joke, and so taught Bianca her first lesson in Constantinople. She walked a tight-rope. She proceeded thereafter to do so, and with skill.

She had other feats of balance to perform. For one thing, she shared the Sultan's bed chamber, but not yet his bed; he had fondled her and caressed her, but no more. She wondered why, since he was not yet fify and seemed at the height of his vigour. On the whole, she regarded her calculated flirtation with a man who could force her to submit at any time as something of a game, pleasurably exciting but little more.

She had already told herself, firmly, that Leonardo was dead. She did so not because she believed it, but in order to provide herself with some kind of shield against the day when she might receive word that Girolamo Riario had indeed killed him. In a sense, then, she neither hoped nor despaired; at best, she was in Constantinople and he at Otranto, half the world away. Her heart insisted that he was indestructible, while her mind argued that all men were mortal and that Leonardo could be no exception.

Meanwhile, she charmed Sultan Mohammed, and tried not to think that a night was approaching when she would be forced to accept or repulse him in earnest. He toyed with her, and fed her a succession of sweetmeats; they were not to her taste, but she was careful not to say so. When he asked about her childhood, she told him tales of Milan and Abbiategrasso. His courtesy, though faintly mocking, was unfailing; he did not ask her whether or not she had a lover. At times she thought he might be impotent, yet he had several sons, all of whom were tedious and quarrelsome. One evening he dismissed her from his chamber and spent the night in solitude. He gave no explanation for this, but welcomed her as readily the next day as always.

Shan Khara, his handsome commander, was more importunate. Meeting Bianca in the corridors of the palace one morning, he touched his forehead and breast in a faintly ironic salute while flashing her a brilliant smile.

'My lady,' he said, 'a suspicious man might wonder whence you had obtained your magic; but the sight of you disarms all suspicion and answers all questions, since it is clear that your beauty is all the magic you will ever need.'

'Thank you, sir,' answered Bianca gravely.

'Truth requires no thanks.'

'Then may I compliment you upon your command of my language? There are many here who speak it well enough, but such graceful compliments as yours would put the courts of Florence and Milan to shame.'

Finding himself thus encouraged, Shan Khara grew bolder.

'My lady, I would that I might spend all my days at this court and in your company; but I am a soldier, and cannot do so. I have no wife, and had delayed all plans to marry. But now I see that my days have been spent in the folly of childhood, and that Allah may never again cast my way such a treasure as yourself. It is in my mind to ask my lord the Sultan for you. Are you willing that I should do so?'

'Your lord and mine, Sultan Mohammed, may be unwilling to lose his adviser in matters of high finance,' said Bianca. 'Have you considered that?'

'He will relinquish you to me,' Shan Khara replied, 'though he might refuse another man. You are my lord's favourite; but so, for different reasons, am I. For such a prize as yourself, my lady, I am happy to risk his displeasure. How say you?'

Bianca, who had foreseen none of this, was thrown into some confusion. It was possible, for all she knew, that if she raised no objection Shan Khara might simply ask the Sultan for her at once, and that she might find herself married and bedded by nightfall. Even in Italy, women were chattels to be disposed of at a word. It was only the bargaining for their disposal that took time, and Shan Khara had the air of a man whose bargain was all but made.

'But I would need to renounce my faith,' she said to him.

'That is true,' replied the Turk. 'And the knowledge that I had been the means of your salvation would add to my happiness.'

'You must give me time. One's faith is not something to be cast aside like a worn slipper,' Bianca said. 'I cannot believe that Allah himself would have it so.'

Shan Khara smiled again at this, and took her hand.

'You do not, then, reject my suit out of hand?'

'Sir, you are a man of courage, courtesy, and most pleasing appearance. I do not imagine that many women have resisted your attentions, or would want to.'

Shan Khara was, perhaps, not entirely satisfied with this answer, but chose to interpret it as the beginning of consent. He bowed to her, and took his leave. Bianca went to her apartment, two small private rooms overlooking the garden of the *seraglio*, and threw herself down on a divan. For the first time since she had been taken by Girolamo Riario, she wept.

Cipriano di Lucca found her some minutes later, and tried to comfort her. Most men were barred from the women's quarters on pain of instant death, of course, but Cipriano had found his own peculiar solution to the problems of watching over his charge.

'What is it, my lady?' he whispered.

She raised a tear-streaked face to him.

'I wish Leonardo were here. Cipriano, tell me he isn't dead. Tell me, even if you know it is a lie.'

'Of course he is alive,' said Cipriano softly. 'I do not say that he'll find us at once; we cannot expect him to sprout wings and fly across the Mediterranean. We have a game to play here, and it will be a long one. But do not give up hope, madonna. You play your part with exquisite skill.'

Bianca surveyed him, smiling ruefully as she dried her tears.

'And so do you, Cipriano,' she said. 'Or your head would have been forfeit long before this.'

At this precise moment, Leonardo da Vinci, with his two companions Rigo and Scudo, stood side by side, facing the Sultan. At one side of the tiled room in which the Turkish ruler held his daily levee stood the casket they had brought with them, under escort, from the galley.

'My lord,' Leonardo said, 'as for ourselves, you may do with us as you see fit. But I gave your oarsmen my promise that they should be freed, to honour that promise as though it were your own, though my right to ask this boon of you is only that of a man who seeks the preservation of his own honour.'

The sultan fingered his chin, and beckoned to the captain of the galley, who was still prostrated at his feet.

'They fought well?' he asked.

'Lord, they were like lions,' replied the captain, 'and, though I ordered their fetters to be struck off, they drove your ship here more swiftly than I could have believed possible.'

'You are an honest man,' the Sultan said. 'For having endangered that most precious burden entrusted to you, I shall have you flogged. Your sentence is twelve lashes. For having taken the correct decision to save that same burden, my Chamberlain will give you a hundred pieces of gold. Return to your vessel. *Insh'Allah.*'

'May His Mercy preserve you always, lord,' said the captain, as he backed his way out of the chamber.

'Now, as for those to whom you made your promise,' continued Sultan Mohammed, addressing Leonardo, 'has not the Prophet instructed us that, being bidden to walk one mile, we should praise the Name and walk two? Your word, and more than your word, shall be mine also. To any man who may wish it, I will grant rank in my own armies, making only the condition that he become a true believer. To the rest I will give passage home, a reward in gold, and their freedom. Will that preserve your honour?'

'My lord, I thank you,' replied Leonardo simply. 'I am deeply in your debt.'

A suspicion of a smile touched the corners of the Sultan's mouth.

'Very true,' he said. '*How* deeply remains to be decided. I am told that all three of you are famous mercenaries in your own land. In which arts of war are you most skilled?'

'We are gunners, my lord.'

'Are you? My own gunners are known throughout the world. Well, I shall in due course decide what your ransoms shall be. Meanwhile, you may have the freedom of my court and my palace, excepting always the quarters used by my women. If you wish to bear swords, you may do so. My servants will find you what you need. That is all.'

The gunners bowed deeply, and retired.

'Why,' said Rigo in the passageway outside, 'he is a good fellow, for a heathen. I am surprised.'

'Keep your comments to yourself,' Leonardo advised him. 'He put half Otranto to the sword, this good fellow.

110

Do not be deceived. We walk on eggs here.'

They came into a courtyard whose walls were decorated with pierced and gilded metalwork. Brightly coloured birds flitted about pausing now and again to take seed from a marble table.

From a corner of this pleasant square they were suddenly greeted by a gorgeous apparition dressed all in pink and with painted cheeks and fingernails.

'*Carissimi!*' this figure called to them, and proceeded to undulate in their direction. 'How wonderful to see you!'

'Dear God,' muttered Rigo. 'Can it be—it *cannot* be Cipriano! Is it? By Christ, and it *is!*'

Cipriano di Lucca bore down upon them like a ship in full sail. His pantaloons, gauze over rose-coloured silk, billowed with his passage, his short jacket—which on closer examination proved to be embroidered with crimson and orange butterflies—swayed with the motion of his hips.

'Darlings, I could *eat* you,' he trilled. 'I thought you were all a *million* miles away!'

'What in the devil's name do you think you're doing?' asked Scudo. 'God's bones, I always knew you were a pox-ridden pretty boy, but—'

Cipriano took his arm affectionately. 'Don't be so *cross* with me, Scudo,' he implored. 'Aren't you pleased to see me, you great thing? Give us a kiss.' He puckered his lips.

'What!' roared the giant, shaking himself free as though from the embrace of some loathsome creeper. 'What! Have you gone out of your mind, blast you?'

Rigo, now speechless, stood dumbfounded. As for Leonardo, he was so racked by helpless laughter that he was forced to stagger away, bent almost double, to collapse upon the stone rim of a fountain. He plunged his head into its waters, then shook his dripping head, fighting for control over his ribs.

'All right, Cipriano,' he gasped, when he was able to speak. 'All right. Steady, now. Tell us what all this is about.'

Cipriano minced across and plumped himself down beside the artist, intertwining his fingers with Leonardo's.

'It is very simple,' he whispered. 'I am attempting to

111

preserve the lady Bianca's virtue, and at the same time certain valuable parts of my own anatomy. It came about like this. We arrived here some ten days ago, and I perceived several things almost at once; the first being that I had fallen among peasants, whose appreciation of fashion was rudimentary. I was, as always, dressed soberly but with a certain flair . . .'

'Ah,' Leonardo nodded. 'I begin to see.'

' . . . Whereupon,' continued Cipriano, 'certain lewd fellows made advances towards me, and I realised that they thought—for what reason I cannot imagine—that I was of a kind with themselves. After that, when they sought to shut the lady Bianca away in their damned mare stable, I protested that I must stay with her, but to no avail. So I looked around, and discovered that a few men *were* allowed among the Sultan's women folk. They were either eunuchs or else known to prefer the attentions of their own sex. So that's the way, I said to myself. Well. The notion of becoming a eunuch did not exactly entrance me. Therefore, I thought, since I must remain at the side of your mistress, Leonardo, and since the wind sits in *that* quarter, my dears, I would take advantage of it. So I made eyes at this boy and that; and by and by along came a learned doctor of some sort, asking me whether I had ever felt any carnal desire towards the lady Bianca, having been her constant companion for many weeks.'

'So,' Cipriano continued, 'I answered him as best I might, telling him that I had seen her both with her clothes and without them. and that I felt towards her as one might towards a sister. At which . . . all this being the very essence and perfection of truth, as you know—'

'Of course,' said Leonardo with difficulty. 'Go on, brother.'

'At which, then, the doctor laughed, and I poked my tongue out at him, and begged him to get me that sweet, *sweet* boy called Abou Nouass, who is a well known harlot. Thank God he did not grant my request. But I must have persuaded him, and have thereafter spent the rest of my time here guarding the lady Bianca's person and my own. And so far as I am concerned,' he added, returning to the precious falsetto he had for the moment abandoned. 'I've had a positive *onslaught* of invitations from the most *terrible* people.'

And the lady Bianca is well-guarded, I hope?' inquired Leonardo.

'So far, yes,' replied Cipriano. 'The Sultan treats her like some sort of *kitten*, and has barely laid a hand on her. But there is a son of a whore called Shan Khara who has fallen head over heels in love with her, and seeks her as a gift from the Sultan, *so*—'

'And how can I see her?'

'You cannot,' said Cipriano bluntly. 'Unless of course you are prepared to put on a performance like my own. She has her own rooms in the *seraglio*. Any man who goes within two hundred paces of them will lose either his head or other more important parts of himself within the hour. I would strongly advise you to stay away.'

To the surprise of neither Rigo nor Scudo, though to their considerable fury, Leonardo at once proceeded to disregard this sage advice. No sooner had the moon risen over the Golden Horn than he was searching the outer wall of the palace for a path from their own quarters to the Sultan Mohammed's harem. He found one without difficulty, since the ornate decorations that topped nearly every window, door, and partition were a heaven-sent gift to any climber of moderate ability; if Otranto had presented him with little problem, the *seraglio* gave him none at all.

He crossed the palace from end to end by means of the roof, avoiding its guards wherever he found them. Natural instinct, sharpened by practice, made his soundless passage like that of a wraith, and he reached the garden outside Bianca's window within ten minutes of bidding farewell to his friends. No light showed within her rooms, however, and he therefore settled down on the beaten copper dome of a summer house to wait for her.

Below him, like a shining plain, lay the Sea of Marmora and the Strait of the Bosphorus, the corridor that led to the vast northern reaches of the Black Sea. Constantinople was on the same latitude as Naples, and the air was still warm even this late in the year. At his back were six of the hills that formed the city, the seventh being occupied by the sculptured building on top of which he sat. Mosques and minarets dotted the peaks and slopes at either hand; the breeze carried scents of spice, camphor and wood smoke. It was an alien perfume, which reminded him that for many of the Mediterranean peoples the city he now overlooked was the end of the world. Turkey itself was a mystery; Persia a land of travellers' tales; beyond them were to be found deserts, dragons, and the legendary territories of the Indies and Cathay.

How long he stayed in reverie at his comfortable post he did not know. The moon reached its zenith, and a soft voice called to him from the garden beneath.

'Leonardo?'

'I'm here, Madonna,' he called in reply, and slid from the cupola to the ground. Bianca was already running towards him; her embrace enfolded him and she began, happily, to cry.

'Cipriano told me,' she breathed. 'Oh, Leonardo! I tried not to believe that you were dead, but it was too hard for me. I thought I should never see you again. I should have known better, shouldn't I?'

Leonardo drew her into the summer house and held her tightly. 'Bianca,' he whispered. 'My own Bianca. I love you. Don't cry, little one.' He kissed her, and smiled down at her. 'After all, I've travelled a very long way just to tell you so. When we're old and our hair is grey, remember that I once rowed half the length of the Mediterranean to be with you.'

Bianca dried her eyes, and began to smile too. 'I'll remember,' she said. 'But now you'll have to go again, and quickly.'

'Go?' asked Leonardo innocently. 'I've only just arrived.'

'And I would have sent you a message, had I been able to leave the Sultan's side, to tell you that it was enough for me to know you were here,' Bianca replied. 'We have seen and touched each other now. What will happen if you are found here?'

'You are beginning to sound just like Rigo and Scudo,' said Leonardo. 'Why is everyone raising objections to my simple wish to see the woman I love? I cannot understand it.'

Torn between laughter and vexation, Bianca stamped her foot. 'You sound like a boy stealing apples from an orchard!' she declared. 'I knew of course, that you'd come here, and that nothing could stop you. When I saw you from my window a minute ago I felt no surprise whatever.'

'And what did you feel, Madonna?'

'Joy. Relief. Love. What else, Leonardo? But I also knew that I would see you tomorrow, and *safely.*' A sudden thought struck her. 'Unless you intend to carry me over yonder wall this instant?'

'Well, no,' Leonardo admitted. 'I toyed with the idea, but what then of Rigo, Cipriano, and Scudo? I'm afraid I am not enough of a romantic.'

Bianca nodded. 'Better. Much better. You cannot carry all four of us off on your shoulder. A fact is a fact; so you have taught me. Therefore, patience, my heart—and go now, *please!*'

'Your cruelty knows no bounds,' said Leonardo, and kissed her once again. 'But I acknowledge your good sense. Until tomorrow, then.'

He left her inside the gazebo and, taking a short run, pulled himself to the top of the garden wall. As he did so, the gateway to the courtyard opened, and he was at once seen by Shan Khara, who had four guards with him. The Turk hailed him furiously, and sent two of his men around to the far side of the wall.

'Infidel!' shouted Shan Khara. 'Dog!'

Leonardo stared down at him from the wall top. He had already observed that none of his opponents carried a bow.

'What are you doing here?' he asked. 'I was told that this place was strictly out of bounds to all men.'

'I have been seeking you,' replied Shan Khara grimly. 'Come down from there, and die.'

'Come down? I think not—with respect,' said Leonardo with composure.

Shan Khara frowned. 'I have seen you somewhere before,' he said.

'From a distance,' agreed Leonardo. 'It was in the city of Otranto. May I ask your name?'

The Turk told him. His rage at the thought of a stranger and a Christian invading the privacy of Sultan Moham-

115

med's harem had cooled, and he rested the tip of his scimitar against the tiles at his feet. The infidel, naturally, would still die, but Shan Khara found time to be curious about him.

'There is a small matter between us, sir,' Leonardo said. 'I must ask you to cease paying court to the lady Bianca Visconti. You will understand that I bear you no ill will, since you could not have known that she is mine, as I am hers. Now that you are aware of it, however ...'

Shan Khara grinned. 'Come down,' he purred, 'and let me cut you to pieces.'

'Tomorrow, perhaps,' Leonardo said. 'If Allah wills it.'

He ran along the top of the wall and jumped to a neighbouring roof. He was under no illusion; this Turk would do exactly as he had threatened, if given the opportunity. The escape Leonardo sought, therefore, was merely a temporary one, but he sought it nevertheless. He was surrounded several hundred yards away when he finally descended to the Sultan's courtyard, where the guards there took him easily and clapped him into a locked cell without delay.

He was joined there shortly after dawn by Rigo and Scudo.

'Admirable!' said Rigo bitterly. 'From oven to fire and back again, all within the space of a few days. This is becoming wearisome.'

'But why are *you* here?' Leonardo asked. 'The offence was solely mine.'

'We were foolish enough to plead for your worthless life,' Rigo answered. 'That is why. We explained to the Sultan that you were Italy's genius and *our* simpleton, and that you found it difficult to undertand that laws which apply to all men apply to you also. He did not accept our pleas, and threw us into prison along with you.'

'He looked very angry, this Sultan,' rumbled Scudo. 'I think we're in trouble.'

116

Eleven

SULTAN MOHAMMED WAS less enraged than might have been supposed. Around the middle of the morning he summoned Cipriano di Lucca, whom he found entertaining.

'His friends have told me that Leonardo da Vinci is mad,' the Sultan said. 'Is that true?'

'My lord,' replied Cipriano, 'it is not exactly that he is mad. His mind works in a fashion rather different from yours and mine, that is all.'

'Does he not recognise authority?'

'He recognises it, my lord, but he regards authority as something with which he can hold a conversation.'

'Is he reckless?'

'My lord, he appears to be, and yet he is not,' Cipriano said.

'That is something with which I am familiar,' said Sultan Mohammed. 'I am not, for instance, entirely convinced that you are altogether what you appear to be. But go on.'

'When he is faced with a difficult situation, my lord, he performs certain calculations in his head,' Cipriano went on. 'I dare say that all of us do likewise, balancing risk against gain. But the results of his computations and those of other men in similar circumstances seldom agree.'

At this the Sultan smiled. 'And what lies between him and the woman Bianca Visconti?' he asked.

'My lord,' said Cipriano, 'they have been lovers these past two years and more.'

'And are they true to one another?'

'Yes, my lord. Nothing can come between them.'

'Do you regard him as a friend?'

'The best a man could have,' Cipriano answered.

'Your disguise is slipping, Cipriano di Lucca,' said Sultan Mohammed, and summoned two Janissaries. 'Take this Florentine to the same prison room as his companions,' he ordered, 'and see that you guard all of them carefully.'

He rose from his dais, and went to find Bianca, who was locked in her rooms in the *seraglio*. She rose at his entrance, and saluted him, laying her fingers against her forehead and bosom.

'My child,' the Sultan said to her, 'your life is forfeit. 'You know this?'

'I have been threatened with death before now, my lord, and I have seen that since death is but a gateway through which all must pass, its threat is not so great as many suppose. It is the most that can be inflicted upon any man or woman. Beyond it we are out of reach and safe from further harm. And besides, are we not all in the hand of the One God, no matter by what name we choose to call Him?'

'You speak truly,' said Sultan Mohammed. 'You are not, then, disposed to plead with me?'

'Why should I waste your time, lord, or my own? You will do as you wish. Are you a man easily swayed by tears or cries for mercy? I know you are not. The city of Otranto knows you are not. And will Leonardo plead with you? I doubt it. If the penalty for setting foot in your women's quarters is indeed death,' said Bianca forthrightly, 'then I think it is a very cruel and unnecessary one. But it is not my opinion which counts here.'

On the next day a distinguished visitor arrived in Constantinople, and was received in state.

'You are welcome,' the Sultan told him. 'What gifts do you bring me this time?'

'I have but two, my lord,' replied Antonio da Narni. 'Yet they are gifts of some consequence, rather than mere playthings for your entertainment.'

'Oh? And what are they?'

'The cities of Venice and Rome,' said Narni. 'Twin jewels for the crown of the Ottoman Empire.' He sat back and took an almond from a golden dish beside him.

Sultan Mohammed rubbed his chin.

118

'Precious gifts indeed, and as you say, of some consequence. Are you certain that you can deliver them?'

'I offer them to you for the taking, my lord. Or perhaps I should say, rather, that I offer you Venice, and the Count Girolamo Riario will give you Rome. I am, as before, joined with him in this enterprise. Rome? Rome is an overripe fig already, and the Count can pluck it, since he is the commander of Rome's armies. As for Venice, I am able to inform you that six months from now I shall have effective control of her fighting fleet, and can therefore pluck her too.'

Sultan Mohammed stared at the Venetian with a carefully veiled contempt. Well had he earned his nick-name, the Sultan thought; Gattamelata, the honeyed cat. The Prince of the Ottoman Empire had lived too long to appreciate treachery, be it at home or among his enemies.

'And your price?' he demanded. 'For, though you speak of giving, I assume that you are not offering me your gifts unencumbered.'

'Our requests, my lord, would be to rule your new lands in northern and southern Italy, when you have taken them,' said Antonio da Narni. The south for Count Girolamo, the north for myself. A fair bargain, I think.'

'I will consider it. And meantime?'

'You have Otranto, my lord. There are a thousand square miles and more of open plains around that city. It is an area large enough for the assembly of the mightiest army the world has ever known. *Your* army, my lord, served by your own supply routes.'

'Protected, no doubt, by the Count and yourself,' said the Sultan.

'Precisely.' Antonio da Narni's voice grew more confidential. 'Rome's forces oppose you there in theory, but not in practice. Girolamo Riario will pretend that he is trying desperately to prevent your expansion, but that he finds it impossible to do so. By next summer you can march where you will, my lord, and who will hold against you? Not Riario. Who will cut your supply routes by sea? Not myself. Naples is spread too thin; Florence, Milan and Genoa are too far away; Siena, Mantua, Ferrara and Mont-ferrat are too weak. On the eastern shore of Italy, Imola belongs to the Count, and Forli to myself; thus you may have unhindered passage to the northern marches. You can swallow Italy whole before the year is out. Such is our grand design.'

'It is well conceived,' said Sultan Mohammed. He smiled blandly. 'But of course I must confer with some advisers of my own.' He clapped his hands and addressed his guards. 'Bring the prisoners hither,' he commanded, 'and also the girl Bianca Visconti.'

'With all respect, my lord,' said Narni apprehensively. 'I have no wish to meet with the lady Bianca. I gave her to you, and she is your concern, my lord. And who are these prisoners?'

Sultan Mohammed waved an indolent hand. 'They are condemned to death for having displeased me,' he replied. 'My pleasure and displeasure are somewhat capricious, Venetian, but here they rule supreme. Do you find your quarters comfortable, by the way?'

'They are admirable,' said Narni, fidgeting. The Sultan gave no sign of having heard him. He was looking towards the side entrance of the chamber with a gleam of anticipation in his eye.

'Ah,' he said. 'My little Vizier approaches.'

Bianca prostrated herself before the dais and then rose, her face pale with fury.

'You know the most excellent Antonio da Narni, of course?' said the Sultan to her. 'He gave you to me, as a token of goodwill from himself and Count Girolamo Riario, did he not?'

'That, and more besides,' said Bianca. She was trembling. 'He is a viper, my lord! A vile traitor, a murderer. He would have killed—'

But the Sultan held his finger to his lips, and she fell silent. Something was in the air, or so she felt; and a moment later she perceived that her instinct had been correct. From the far side of the room Leonardo came across the floor, along with Rigo, Scudo, and Cipriano di Lucca. They were under escort. Leonardo bowed deeply to the Sultan, and then turned towards Antonio da Narni, who had started from his seat with an ashen countenance at the sight of the Florentines.

'Why! Messer da Narni,' Leonardo said to him. 'You seem surprised. As though, perhaps, we had risen from the grave. Does something trouble you?'

The Venetian's mouth worked, but no words came. Amused, Sultan Mohammed addressed Leonardo.

'I guessed that you might know each other,' he said suavely. 'And I see that it is so. Leonardo da Vinci, I require your advice. I am about to enter into a contract with this man by way of trade, and I would like to know your opinion of his character.'

'Why, my lord,' replied Leonardo, 'that is easily given. He is a friend and associate of the Count Girolamo Riario, who would betray his own father and his own country. As for da Narni here— he is an assassin, which matters little to your purpose. He is also a pimp, a dealer in human flesh, a liar, a breaker of his word, a traitor himself, a fool too devious to recognise his own folly, and very probably a coward.'

'All of that? You do not think you are prejudiced against him?' asked Sultan Mohammed with interest.

'It is true that he tried to burn us alive,' replied Leonardo, 'but I have not allowed that to influence me.'

The Sultan beckoned him forward. 'He proposes to sell me Italy. What would your advice be?'

'Payment . . . *after* delivery, my lord,' said Leonardo.

'My lord Sultan,' said Antonio da Narni, finding his voice at last. 'This is a grave breach of confidence. This man is our common enemy. Do you play some game with him—or with me?'

'Did I not warn you that my will was capricious?' replied Sultan Mohammed. 'I like to know the temper of the men I deal with. Nor have I said that I believe Leonardo da Vinci. And if I choose to play games, be sure that they have a purpose apart from my own amusement.'

'No man plays games with an empire, nor with the prospect of one,' Narni said, allowing anger to get the better of his judgement.

Sultan Mohammed was silent for a long while. He gazed at Narni as a man may look at some insect of curious form before crushing it, and the Venetian quailed. Then: 'The Will of Allah shall guide us here,' he said, softly, 'for I propose another game. You will fight each other, to the death. How does that strike you?'

'Folly,' said Narni.

'Now?' Leonardo said. 'With pleasure, my lord.'

'You hear?' the Sultan said to Narni. 'Whatever offence you have committed against Leonardo da Vinci, he is ready to kill you for it. You, on your part, must perforce kill him, since if you do not and I allow you to return to Italy, your own life will be worth very little. I advise you to draw your sword, and defend your honour—such as it may be.' He clapped his hands. 'Bring the Florentine a weapon,' he ordered.

Leonardo bowed to him and removed his doublet. Accompanied by Rigo, Scudo, and Cipriano, he crossed the room and accepted a rapier from one of the Sultan's attendants. His own sword being still at the Castello del Mar in Italy, he examined his present weapon carefully, testing its balance in either hand and running his thumb along its edge.

'Be careful of Narni,' advised Cipriano. 'He may be a better swordsman than he looks.'

'I'm sure he's skilled,' replied Leonardo,' but I think he has done too much of his killing at second hand. Well, we shall see.' He worked his shoulders, took the hilt of the rapier in his left hand, and advanced to the middle of the floor. Narni came from the dais to meet him, sweeping his own weapon to and fro in a businesslike fashion.

'Proceed,' said Sultan Mohammed.

Narni walked unconcernedly to within a few feet of his opponent, the tip of his blade now lowered and motionless. Then, without warning by eye or hand, he slashed upward, striking like a snake for Leonardo's groin. Had his edge bitten home, the duel would have ended then and there, with the artist's entrails spilling across the tiles. But Leonardo dropped his own blade, parrying the blow and allowing Narni's sword to sweep past his left thigh and his arm until the point of it was shoulder high. In the same movement he stepped a pace forward and punched the Venetian, right handed, squarely upon the nose.

His arm had the force of a pile driver, and Narni was totally unprepared for such an assault. The sound of

snapping bone and cartilage broke through the silence of
the chamber like the crack of a whip; Narni reeled back
with outflung arms and fell on the base of his spine,
skidding a few feet before he came to rest.

Scudo laughed.

'A true gunner, by Christ!' he said. 'For a moment I was
afraid he might prance about as noblemen do.' He cupped
his hands about his mouth. Bang him again, Gunner!' he
yelled.

Narni struggled to his feet. Blood was pouring down his
face, and dripped from his beard onto the front of his tunic.
He was blinded with pain and fury; but he had, so he
thought, learned his lesson. He extended his blade in front
of him and advanced upon Leonardo once more, using the
formal duellist's stance which, had he been wiser and less
cunning, he would have adopted from the very beginning of
his bout. It was too late now, though Narni could not know
this. Leonardo stood his ground, poised on the balls of his
feet, awaiting Narni's move. He presented an open and
inviting target. Narni essayed a feint, reaching for his
enemy's stomach, then lifting his point in the last fraction
of a second to lunge instead for the throat.

Leonardo ducked aside and hit him again, with the same
force and precision as before and in exactly the same place.

This time the Venetian did not fall. He gave a screech of
pure animal fury, threw caution and skill to the winds, and
flung himself at Leonardo, hacking wildly with the edge of
his blade. He felt the side of his wrist connect with
Leonardo's shoulder as the latter moved inside his guard
for the third time, and heard the clatter of his lost weapon.
But he never felt the thrust that killed him, sliding between
his third and fourth ribs at the left and severing the main
arteries that fed his lungs.

Leonardo stepped back, releasing his sword hilt. Blood
gushed from Antonio da Narni's mouth, choking off the
curse he was about to utter, and he pitched face
downwards, threshed once, and was still.

Leonardo walked towards the Sultan's dais, rubbing his
bruised knuckles.

'My lord, I thank you,' he said. 'He was a foul man and
deserved to die.'

123

'Just so,' responded the Sultan. 'It was as Allah willed it. And you, I perceive, are a dangerous man; I have yet to decide what I shall do with you. For the present your lives and the life of my small and beautiful Vizier,' he inclined his head at Bianca, 'are spared. Stay in the quarters assigned to you, for I shall give you no second chance. I am told that you have difficulty in understanding what orders mean; I request you, therefore, not to put me to the trouble of beheading you. That is all.'

Leonardo da Vinci's next meeting with Sultan Mohammed, which took place two days later, was devoted to business.

'A hundred thousand florin ransom for each of you?' the Sultan said. 'It is a small sum. Such mercenaries as yourselves must have amassed it long since.'

'We are not mercenaries, my lord. That tale was not started by us, but by another—though we did not deny it at the time. We *wanted* your commander at Otranto to send us to your court. But I have now to confess that we are only citizens and soldiers of Florence, and that while Lorenzo de' Medici may place some value on our services, it will not be a hundred thousand florins each.'

'Then he is foolish,' said the Sultan. 'You, at least, should carry such a price. You are a dangerous fighter, as I have said; and what drew my attention was not that you killed that dog of a Venetian, but the manner in which you did so. It was done in the fashion that gave you the least possible trouble. You enraged him and ran him through. You could have defeated him more straightforwardly, since you were the better swordsman; but you did not choose that road. You chose efficiency, and that is what makes you a danger. Well, no matter. Tell me, truthfully, why you sought to come hither?'

'To obtain the release of the lady Bianca,' said Leonardo.

'And that was all?'

'Yes, my lord.'

'And how did you hope to obtain her freedom?'

'I do not know,' replied Leonardo. 'Nor did I know at the time. I knew only that I must join her as speedily as possible.'

'And now that you are here,' the Sultan said, 'is there nothing else you seek of me?'

'My lord, I know indeed that it is in the mind of my patron, Lorenzo the Magnificent, to extend his banking interests throughout your empire, if you are willing. Also, he made me some discourse upon trade in alum with you. I would be happy to represent him in such things, but they were not my reasons for coming.'

Sultan Mohammed considered this for a while. 'Well, Leonardo da Vinci,' he said, 'all these matters can be discussed when you have made me an offer for your freedom and that of your companions, and not before. I like you, but I have not grown soft of heart.'

'Your courtesy, my lord Sultan, has always been in evidence,'. said Leonardo with a smile, 'but I have seen none of your kindheartedness.'

'Bargain with me, then. I am a trader.'

'And I know not what I can offer you. My own fortune amounts to some twenty thousand florins, since I have little use for wealth.'

'Foolish,' said the Sultan. 'You have a use for it now.'

'That is a lesson, my lord, which you have taught me, and I am grateful for it.'

'Then you are not wasting your time here. What of your companions?'

'They are but poor gunners,' replied Leonardo. 'Or rather . . . wait! Yes, my lord, we have something to offer you, after all.'

'Speak, then,' said the Sultan. 'My trader's ear is cocked.'

'A means of improving your gunnery,' Leonardo said. 'Invented by myself, and proved by them. The greatest advance in the art of war for a hundred years. What of that?'

'My gunners are the best in the world,' said Sultan Mohammed.

'With respect, I will wager that they are not,' replied Leonardo. 'We can outshoot them easily. Come, now. You are a notable player of games, my lord. The proof—and the secret of our accuracy—for our freedom. How can you refuse?'

'I don't like it,' Rigo said. 'You have offered him the secret of the Medici Guns? And he is Italy's foe? No, by God!'

'You are talking without taking thought, as usual,' said Leonardo unkindly. 'Use your head. If we do not get back to Italy, he'll have the secret of the Medici Guns before long in any case. Have you forgotten that Riario is giving him fifty of the damned things? We have nothing to lose here.'

'He's right, you know,' observed Cipriano.

'I don't like it either,' said Scudo. 'But if Leonardo says—'

'Oh, go to Hades,' said Rigo.

'This is my field commander,' said Sultan Mohammed, 'and my finest gunner. His name is Shan Khara—though I know you have already met. You have considered the conditions of your contest?'

Leonardo looked at the young Turk who stood easily by the Sultan's side. Shan Khara's expression was neutral; he seemed to harbour no resentment at having been made to look something of a fool in the *seraglio* garden. A professional, thought Leonardo, approvingly.

'We have,' Leonardo replied. 'First, we need a gun from you, and two days in which to make ourselves familiar with it. Is that fair?' Shan Khara nodded, the condition being reasonable. 'Its size and bore are your choice,' Leonardo continued, 'so long as it is the same weapon you will use yourself. The range at which we fire is your choice as well. Each gun team will fire three shots, all shots to count in the reckoning.'

'Including the sighting-in shot?' asked Shan Khara.

'Yes. Three shots, including the first,' Leonardo answered. 'We are gunners, not amateurs.'

'Agreed,' said Shan Khara. 'What else, Florentine?'

'A pair of scales.'

'What for?' asked Shan Khara.

'In order to weigh our shot, of course,' replied Leonardo, grinning at him. 'Only a fool would use three balls of unequal weight in a contest of accuracy. And we would like to make our own choice of powder from whatever supplies

126

you have in your arsenal. I shall also need the services of a gunsmith and a shipwright. Other than these, I can think of nothing.'

'It's a fair weapon,' conceded Rigo Leone early the following morning. They were on a practice range overlooking the Sea of Marmora, its landward side screened by a dense belt of trees. Cipriano and Scudo circled the cannon they had been lent, examining the ornate decoration along the barrel, poking their fingers into the touch-hole, and feeling the interior of the muzzle for smoothness. Rigo crouched beside Leonardo at the breech. 'I see they still use a wedge for adjustment of range, which is clumsy; but the bore is excellent.'

Leonardo peered at the bronze wedge that supported the breech-block. It was, indeed, an old-fashioned method of raising and lowering the barrel, the triangular piece of metal being hammered forward to depress the muzzle and allowed to slide backward if one wished to increase the trajectory length. The mechanism was crude and gave only a limited amount of range variation, but it was undeniably strong.

'Tell me what accuracy you hope for,' Leonardo said.

'Three feet above or below my point of aim at four hundred paces,' said Rigo. 'We used guns like this at Forli.'

'That isn't good enough. I'll make a longer wedge with a finer taper,' said Leonardo. 'In any case we must mark it with graduations, as this has none. Will the gun itself hold to within a foot either way?'

'At four hundred paces? Yes.'

Leonardo levered out the wedge with a crowbar and looked at it critically. 'Then I'll make the wedge to the same accuracy. It will need to be about twice as long as this one; I'd prefer a screw, but I cannot cut one in two days. You'll have to do the best you can.'

'And your rangefinder?' asked Cipriano, coming to stoop beside them.

'I'll build that tonight,' Leonardo told him. 'Meanwhile, let us accustom ourselves to the habits of this thing.'

They fired forty-five rounds during the course of the

day. The Turkish weapon proved reliable, with a constant throw to the right of some two and a half feet in a quarter of a mile. The gun itself had a barrel seven feet long, with a five-inch bore and a shot that weighed about seventeen and a half pounds. It was thus a good deal larger and heavier than their own Medici Guns, but still handled relatively easily.

Leonardo stayed up all night making his rangefinder, the foundation upon which the fabulous accuracy of the Medici Guns was built.

Other men might be forced to sight in their cannon by firing several trial shots at their target in order to find its distance from them, though a good gunner could make a fairly close guess at his range by eye if conditions were right. Leonardo da Vinci, with a simple apparatus of wood and brass, could determine how far away his target lay before firing a round; and he had taken a city in the pitchblackness of night by way of proving his case.

It was for this reason, of course, that he had stipulated that all shots should count in his contest with Shan Khara. So he built his contrivance and calibrated it, and stood over a metalsmith while the latter forged him a ranging wedge with three times the accuracy of the one it was to replace; and on the second night he went without sleep again while he assembled his computations.

By the morning of the third day, he was ready.

Shan Khara, holding his mouth loosely open as did all gunners who sought to preserve their eardrums, stood away from his cannon and looked down range through the clearing smoke of its discharge. The eyes of the gun crew, ten men strong, followed his glance. The echoes of the shot died away through the trees and spread across the open sea to left and right of the range; beneath the trees stood the packed ranks of spectators, the palanquin which held Sultan Mohammed II himself, and the whinnying chargers of the mounted Imperial Guard. Twenty paces away at his right was the four-man Florentine crew. Shan Khara was surprised to see that Leonardo da Vinci was lying prone on the brown grass. Before him was an instrument consisting of a transverse plank of mahogany. The artist appeared to be taking sights through apertures at either end of this contrivance. Then he rose and spoke to Rigo Leone.

A runner came pelting back from the far end of the range.

'Two arms' lengths high and to the left, sir,' the man reported. Shan Khara frowned slightly. He had chosen the maximum range he could achieve, given the length of the field selected for their contest; it was not too bad for a ranging shot, though he had hoped for better.

'Five hundred and twenty paces,' Leonardo said to his colleagues. 'You'll need to lay off another hand span to the left to take care of the lateral drift. Scudo?'

Rigo knelt behind the breech of their weapon, and sighted along the barrel while Scudo set his back against the carriage tree and heaved.

'Done,' Rigo announced.

Leonardo set his calibrated ranging wedge a fraction behind the five hundred pace mark, and checked the seating of the range block with obsessive care.

'Ready,' he called.

Cipriano di Lucca crossed himself, and set his slow-match to the powder train. Smoke drifted above the cannon's breech. The fuse hissed, and then grew suddenly silent as it burned down within the belly of the gun, bringing their hearts to their mouths in that fear of a misfire which bedevils every artilleryman, no matter how firmly he assures himself that no misfire will occur.

The cannon roared, bucking slightly before its wheels rolled back in recoil.

'A good one,' Rigo said.

'How do you know that?' asked Leonardo, his head singing from the crash of the gun's detonation.

'She told me,' Rigo replied. 'You do not understand her language yet.'

All of them looked towards the distant target, a rectangle of canvas thirty feet square, supported by a wooden framework. The ball, of course, would pass through it like a knife through paper, and they could not see the mark of their impact. Scudo turned back and began to sponge out the barrel; he was a meticulous craftsman, and had grown fond of his temporary charge.

129

'A good one,' Rigo repeated. 'A florin that we are within five spans of the centre.'

The runner approached them, gesticulating. He did not speak Italian, and Rigo drew a representation of the target on the ground, indicating that the messenger should point out where their ball had struck. He did so, afterwards spreading his fingers to show by how much they had missed the centre.

Shan Khara walked across from his weapon.

'You did well, infidels,' he said. 'Less than one arm's length to the right of aim. I thought I had not performed too badly, but your shot was magnificent. What *is* that device of yours?'

'It gives me my range,' Leonardo replied. 'Which is why, although we are probably on a level with yourself as gunners, we shall win. Lay your cannon.'

'No,' said Shan Khara. 'I concede the match. We are, as you say, all gunners; and if you have found your range at the first attempt, I do not suppose that Allah will strike you with sudden madness for your second, or your third. My lord will give you your freedom. I will settle for your range-finding technique.'

'Sir,' said Leonardo, 'it seems that we find courtesy wherever we turn. I am sorry that I annoyed you when we first met, but you caught me at something of a disadvantage.'

The young Turk laughed. 'So I did,' he said. 'So I did.' Still laughing, he looked around at Scudo, Rigo and Cipriano. 'Well, infidels,' he said, 'let us be friends—for the time being, at least.'

He walked with them across the field to Sultan Mohammed's seat.

'My lord,' said Shan Khara, 'whatever price you have agreed with these Florentines, pay it gladly. You have the best of the bargain, for I am a defeated man.'

Leonardo turned towards the target. He was nearer to it now, and could see the marks of both shots. 'My lord Sultan,' he said, 'your captain does himself an injustice. He has come within five feet of his aim— at five hundred and twenty paces—with his ranging shot. Were we to meet in battle, he is a gunner all of us would respect.'

'And it may happen so, if Allah wills it,' replied the Sultan. 'Since you will give us the secret of your aiming machine, you are free to return to Italy when you wish, according to our bargain. I do not suppose that you will refrain from opposing me there.' He patted Bianca's cheek. 'As for your lady,' he went on, 'I return her to you freely, though it means the loss of my favourite adviser. Guard her well, Leonardo da Vinci, and remember that a few minutes in her company almost cost you your life.'

'He who faces life gladly must also face death willingly,' Leonardo said. 'I thank you, my lord, as do we all.'

Six days later the Florentines were on their way home in the same galley that had brought them. This time, however, they travelled in state, and Hamoun, the overseer, gave Leonardo his whip.

'I have little need of it, sir, since you and your companions showed me how free men can row,' he said. 'Three quarters of my oarsmen are wage earners now, and the rest are working for their liberty.'

And the captain, who owed them his life, treated them as honoured guests. They were laden with the riches of Asia, with silks, jewels, wolf furs from Tartary, and a large package wrapped in oilskin, the contents of which Leonardo would not disclose. He had spent many hours in the company of Arab physicians at the Sultan's court, however, and his friends assumed that it contained medicines.

In a way, they were correct.

By Christmas, they were in Tuscany, and beyond Christmas lay a spring that was to prove eventful.

Twelve

LORENZO DE' MEDICI, unlike lesser men, was not a lover
of spring. Others might revel in its promise, might give
thanks in church and field for its arrival; but for Lorenzo it
was but a reminder of the death of his brother Giuliano at
the hands of the Pazzi family, by the connivance of Rome.
Moreover, for one who ruled the Republic and City of
Florence, it was an awakening not of hope or desire, but of
the political and military problems that lay like dangerous
bears, dormant throughout the harsh yet peaceful winter.

None the less, on the fourteenth of March—for spring
had come early to Florence in the year 1481—Lorenzo de'
Medici felt a certain anticipation stir him. He was about to
interview Leonardo da Vinci and even he himself found his
own mood difficult to understand. Argument with his
errant gunner, artist and engineer was ever frustrating.
Leonardo had a relentless habit of slicing through to the
bone of an argument before his opponent realised it.
Perhaps, thought Lorenzo, it was simply that the artist never
admitted defeat; no man could possible be in the right so
frequently, and so annoyingly, as Leonardo da Vinci.

The truth of the matter was that once Cardinal Domenico
della Palla had returned to his Chancery in Rome, Lorenzo
de' Medici found few about him who were worth the
trouble of arguing with. At all events, when the door to his
private library opened and Leonardo entered, the Ruler of
Florence was unaccountably pleased to see him.

He opened his conversation exactly where he had closed
it on the previous evening.

'Volterra,' he said. 'I will give you Volterra. Castelmonte

is yours by right, but I will add another fief to it. Count of Castelmonte and Volterra?'

'I have no wish to be Count of anything, Magnifico. I am sorry if I did not make that clear.'

'What of the Dukedom of Arezzo, then? That is my highest offer.'

'Sir,' said Leonardo, laughing, 'you are by instinct and experience a republican, and you cannot scatter duchies about like favours at a feast. It is improper. And I do not see myself as a duke.'

'Let me restate the case,' said Lorenzo. 'I cannot chain the lady Bianca Visconti to the wall of her room as though she were a bitch in heat, and if I do not then she will follow you into any lunacy you have a fancy to indulge in. Well, I surrender. It is my wish now that she should marry you. The Regent of Milan will not permit her to wed a commoner, of whatever brilliance. Therefore, you need position.'

'I need nothing,' said Leonardo. 'At least not Castelmonte or Volterra, or even Arezzo. Have you asked the lady Bianca whether or not she wishes to marry me?'

'She will marry you if I tell her to do so.'

'Ah,' murmured Leonardo. 'Sometimes I wish that she would do as I tell her, too, but I am bound to point out to you, sir, that she does not.'

'Your behaviour together is becoming a scandal.'

'In Florence? A scandal in Florence?' said Leonardo incredulously. 'There is no such thing.'

'Be reasonable,' pleaded Lorenzo. 'I am ready to give way to you in this. Do you not want to marry her?'

'I think not,' said Leonardo. 'Sir, may I offer you some advice?'

'I have never known you to refrain from doing so,' said Lorenzo.

'Then stop troubling yourself over the lady Bianca and myself. It is your mistaken belief that if I were to marry her I should become a good citizen of Florence, settle down, and so be available to you whenever you wished. In this, Magnifico, you are wrong. We should go where we pleased. No diplomatic manoeuvres can keep us in the service of Florence; we serve her, and you, because we love

133

her—and, amazing though it may seem, we love you also. Now,' said Leonardo, 'how can I help you?'

Lorenzo eyed him keenly. For a moment he seemed about to make some reply to Leonardo's declaration. Instead he asked, quietly, 'Are you returning to Otranto?'

'Yes.'

'When?'

'Very soon,' Leonardo answered. 'If it is spring here, the season will be the more advanced down there.'

'Do you propose to take the lady Bianca with you?'

'If she wishes to come, yes.'

'Disregarding the fact, of course, that we are at war with the Turks,' said Lorenzo, knowing, as he spoke, that his sarcasm would be fruitless.

'Italy was at war with the Turks before Christmas,' Leonardo rejoined, 'at which time the lady Bianca and myself—and three of your gunners—were in Constantinople, the enemy's capital city. How are your negotiations over the alum trade progressing, by the way? Satisfactorily, I hope.'

'Well enough,' grunted Lorenzo. 'And your point is taken. Yet if harm should befall her—'

'The responsibility will be mine.'

'Or hers, I dare say.'

'Or hers.'

'In any case,' Lorenzo went on, 'what I want to know is your purpose in going to Otranto. You've convinced me that Rome's siege there is a farce. Sweet Jesus! And Rome has the impertinence to demand that I humble myself before her!'

'It's a habit in Rome,' Leonardo pointed out.

'Quite. What enrages me is that the same cry goes up wherever I turn. Rome's Captain-General is plotting to betray Italy, and all I hear from every side are voices beseeching *me* to repent and kiss Rome's foot!'

'That doesn't surprise me either.'

'I didn't say it surprised me,' said Lorenzo. 'I said it enraged me.' He raised his fingers and ticked them off one by one. 'Bologna, Mantua, Capua, Pavia, Verona. Ferrara, Rimini, Senegallia, Padua. Milan would like to agree with them, but when I asked Lodovico Sforza if he would

134

submit in my place, he had the grace to say that he, personally, would invite the Holy Father to do something entirely different with his foot. But for the rest of them, what do they cry? "Oh, Lorenzo! Oh, Magnifico! We know you have been grievously wronged by Rome, we know Rome has sought your death and achieved your brother's. We know you have suffered grievously, but submit! Italy must unite against the Turk." That is their wail, Leonardo. They are like children in a nursery.'

'Well, be damned to them,' said Leonardo. 'I have a better plan.'

'God knows I am ready for one!'

'Let the Medici Gunners retake Otranto. All Italy will ring with the news, and Florence will be seen to have done Rome's work for her. Sixtus will be a laughing stock, and if he seeks your submission thereafter *none* will support him, it seems to me.'

'Now, by all that is holy,' said Lorenzo, 'here is a notion unsurpassed in excellence! But—fifty gunners against Otranto? Can it be done?'

'Sir,' said Leonardo, 'can you doubt it?'

Lorenzo de' Medici laughed. 'And yet,' he said, 'Florence has but ten of your cannon, even now.'

'And Rome has another fifty,' said Leonardo, 'since Riario had had them cast there, in order to give them to Sultan Mohammed.'

'And what of Riario and his farce at Otranto?'

Leonardo shrugged negligently and smiled.

'Well,' Lorenzo said. 'God knows I will not forbid you to try, no matter how impossible I may think your enterprise. Succeed, and you will have Arezzo no matter whether you choose to marry my ward or not. But I was forgetting; you do not want to be a duke.' He sighed. 'You make it hard for any man to offer you a reward, Leonardo da Vinci.'

'Sir,' replied Leonardo, 'I ask you to recall the philosopher Diogenes, who was the wisest man in Greece and who lived in a barrel. It is recounted that the tyrant of Athens went to him, and found the famous sage sunning himself outside his simple home. "What can I give you?" the tyrant asked; and Diogenes thanked him, but would take no gift. "And is there nothing, then, that I can do for you?"

135

said the tyrant. "Yes," replied Diogenes; "you could stand aside a little, out of my sun." The tale impressed me, I remember, when I first heard it told.'

'Very apt,' said Lorenzo with heavy sarcasm. 'But I doubt that it made your philosopher a popular man. What happened to him in the end?'

'I believe he may have been beheaded,' said Leonardo, grinning widely. 'Or perhaps I am confusing him with someone else. Still, he was only a philosopher.'

'Your accusations are monstrous. Do you think I believe them for a moment? Monstrous!' said Pope Sixtus IV, in his gilded library. He shook his head, his jowls flapping in outrage.

'Your Holiness,' Leonardo da Vinci replied, 'if they are monstrous, it is because the Count of Imola is a monster. When will you open your eyes to the fact? He tried to burn us alive while we were under safe conduct issued by your own hand. Is not that proof enough of his cruelty and deceit?'

'I do not believe that either,' the Supreme Pontiff said. 'God knows,' he added piously, 'that we rejoice in your safety, but we were informed that you had perished in an attack by the Turks upon the Count's headquarters at Castello del Mar. Later we heard that this was not so, and that you had been taken prisoner by Sultan Mohammed, and our hearts became lighter. But this tale of yours . . . no. No, it is *not* possible.'

'Your Holiness, then, considers me a liar?'

'Do not be presumptuous. You are a Florentine, Master da Vinci. That does not necessarily make you an evil man, but of a certainty it makes you an enemy of Rome and of your Mother the Church. Whispers of heresy have been heard concerning you. When did you last confess your sins before Almighty God, my son?'

'My sins are not at issue here, and in any case, Your Holiness will forgive me if I am unable to remember for the moment whether I am under excommunication or not. When one dwells in Florence—'

The Pope swelled. 'Those who live in Florence are dwellers in the cities of the plain,' he intoned. 'Sodom and

Gomorrah! Sodom and Gomorrah! Florence is worse than either, since she has been shown redemption and refuses it.'

'Perhaps. But Florence can pull your chestnuts from the fire at Otranto,' said Leonardo.

'Your impertinence knows no bounds,' said Pope Sixtus IV. 'You have our leave to go. *Now.*'

Cardinal Rodrigo Borgia, in private conference with His Holiness later the same day, refrained from committing himself strongly to one point of view or another. This was a natural skill improved by years of practice, and one which was eventually to bring him the Papacy itself.

'It is unlikely,' he said. 'But I do not insist that what Leonardo da Vinci says is impossible. Count Girolamo Riario is your nephew, and yet I recall Your Holiness once expressed to me the opinion that he was a dangerous tool, in the hands of the Church or elsewhere. If Your Holiness were to press me, I would suggest replacing him as Captain-General of your armies; but beyond that I would not care to go.'

Though he did not say so, Cardinal Borgia was in no doubt concerning the issues presented. He would believe anything of any man, particularly in the spheres of treachery, political manoeuvre and double dealing. As for Girolamo Riario, the Cardinal would sooner have taken to his bosom a poisonous toad than have any dealings with Rome's military leader.

'I thank your Eminence,' the Supreme Pontiff said. 'May I take it, then, that you would not accede to this request from Lorenzo de' Medici and give him the cannon he asks for?'

'Accede to it?' said Cardinal Borgia. 'No, I don't think I would, were I in your place. Lorenzo's aim is clear. He seeks to diminish Rome and exalt his own republic in the eyes of Italy, and that is something which Your Holiness cannot afford.'

'And what is your advice?'

Cardinal Rodrigo Borgia affected a world-weary drawl. 'My counsel would be to withdraw entirely from Otranto, and the sooner the better. Whether or not there is any particle of truth in the Florentine allegation concerning

137

Girolamo Riario—and I do not, of course, admit that there is—it is quite plain that Otranto cannot be retaken this year. Every day that your armies sit outside the city's walls twiddling their thumbs makes Italy more certain of Rome's impotence. It was not, frankly, a good idea to have gone there in the first place, as I believe I told Your Holiness from the outset.'

'It will be worse if we withdraw,' said Sixtus.

'On the contrary,' said Borgia. 'It will be bad if we withdraw, but far worse if we do not. As for the fifty cannon, it is my belief that they will make very little difference one way or the other.'

Pope Sixtus summoned Leonardo da Vinci to the Papal palace the following afternoon. The Pontiff—much irritated—suffered from a sense of impending catastrophe, and made no attempt to prolong his interview more than necessary.

'Your request is denied,' he announced coldly. 'My cannon left Rome four hours ago with a detachment of my own Swiss Guards. You are no longer welcome in Rome.'

'Can your Switzers fire cannon?' inquired Leonardo.

'You have outstayed your welcome, Master Leonardo,' said the Pope. 'The matter is closed.'

'I ask because giving artillery to an infantryman is like offering a razor to an infant,' Leonardo said.

'Persist further,' Sixtus interrupted, 'and I will have you *thrown* out of Rome, neck and crop.'

'For a Florentine to be ejected from Rome is a proclamation of virtue,' said Leonardo, and withdrew, calculating the depth of his farewell bow to a hairsbreadth. In the hall outside he found Cardinal della Palla, who greeted him softly.

'You have annoyed His Holiness,' said the Chancellor.

'And how does Your Eminence know that?' asked Leonardo. 'You have not seen him yet.'

'I do not need to see him. I need only look at *you*,' replied Cardinal della Palla, and proceeded on his way.

Thirteen

LEONARDO RODE FROM Rome to Aquila, high in the Apennines near the headwaters of the Pescara river. Here he had arranged to meet Rigo Leone and the Medici Gunners, and he blessed his own foresight in choosing a route which avoided the journey all the way back to Florence. Events were moving faster than he wished, and even his own light artillery would prove a hindrance in the mountains. He consoled himself with the thought that the Swiss would be delayed still more by their fifty guns; his own party carried only five.

He found Rigo with a complaint. It was not a very serious one, but he found some difficulty in expressing it.

'It is a question of the lady Bianca,' Rigo said uncertainly. 'She is here with your consent, I know. But my gunners are a foulmouthed and gutter-bred crew, for which I make no apology, and they find her presence among them . . .'

'Disturbing?' said Leonardo, kindly helping him out.

'No,' said Rigo. 'Well, that too, I dare say, since they are men like any others, but that isn't exactly what I meant.'

'Inhibiting, then? You mean that they find it hard to restrain themselves from passing wind when they please and invoking the pox with every second word? Rest easy, Rigo. She may even civilise them somewhat, and if they enlarge her store of words she is so much the better educated for it. She is not a trembling novice at a convent, Rigo, for all her tender years.'

Rigo laughed. 'True, by God,' he said. 'I presume she is with us for some good reason?'

'She is,' said Leonardo.

'Some reason, that is, apart from your own comfort.'

'Be assured,' Leonardo said, 'that her purpose is vital to our enterprise, and not merely my consolation. Besides, the fact that she is accompanying us will annoy Lorenzo de' Medici, which is excellent for his health and constitution. Where is my wagon?'

'In our rear. And that is another thing. What does it contain? It's a blasted nuisance.'

'But, like the lady Bianca, essential,' Leonardo replied, 'and in any case it is hardly a four-horse dray.'

'It's still a damned nuisance. And now tell me about the Pope's cannon.'

Leonardo told him, at which the Captain-Gunner's grumbling increased. 'What are we to do, then?' he asked. 'Kill these Swiss, and take their cannon from them?'

'No. They have done nothing except follow their orders, poor fellows, though I doubt if there is one man among them who knows muzzle from breech. But treachery can be made into a two-edged weapon, and I think I've designed a plan to make these guns fight upon our side after all. Have you a map?'

Rigo shouted for Cipriano di Lucca, who brought over a rolled chart. He also brought with him Bianca Visconti, who was clad in a riding-dress of green.

'Madonna,' asked Leonardo, 'do your friends use foul language in your presence?'

'Often,' said Bianca. 'Though sometimes they splutter and turn red.'

'And do their oaths distress you?'

'Not in the least.'

'There you are, you see,' said Leonardo to Rigo. He spread the map out on the grass, between two patches of snow. 'The Swiss are marching by way of Isernia and Campobasso, as we did on our first journey to Otranto, and we must therefore cross from where we are now, to Pescara, and turn south east in order to meet with them inland from Foggia.'

'And when we meet them?' inquired Rigo.

'We shall put them to sleep.'

'Ah,' said Rigo, having at last come across something he could readily grasp. He swung his hooked right arm, miming a downward blow. 'You mean—'

140

'No,' said Leonardo. 'I do not mean that, particularly since Scudo, for one, might hit their heads with such enthusiasm that some of them would never wake up again. We shall be more subtle, but they will sleep soundly none the less.'

At about the same time, in a pavilion of blue and silver silk pitched on the beach beneath Otranto's seaward wall, Girolamo Riario was in conversation with Shan Khara. The Count was far from happy, because he believed that his high position entitled him to deal with principals rather than underlings, and he regarded Shan Khara as an underling.

'I regret, sir,' said Shan Khara, 'that my lord the Sultan will see nobody, not even yourself. He remains upon his ship, which you can see in the bay yonder if you turn your head. But no person other than myself is likely to be allowed to board it. What exactly is your difficulty?'

He did not add, as he might have, that Sultan Mohammed II held Count Girolamo Riario in contempt, making in his heart a clear distinction between treacherous allies and honourable foes. Nor had Shan Khara himself any liking whatever for Rome's Captain-General, a feeling which he took little trouble to conceal.

'Gold,' Riario said. 'I have bought Forli, which was easy. I needed only a majority of their city's elders in my pocket, and obtained them mainly through the use of promises. But if I am to deliver you safe passage through Ravenna, it will cost nearly a hundred and fifty thousand florins, which must come from the purse of your master.'

'A trivial matter,' said Shan Khara. 'The money will be in your hands tomorrow—or whenever you feel able to slip away from the leadership of your armies to visit us. Where are the cannon you promised?'

'They are on their way here. The Holy Father, I gather, has sent them under escort, but I foresee no difficulty. You can arrange some sort of attack, I dare say?'

'They had better prove to be worth the trouble, if we do.'

'They will,' Riario said. 'They are the finest weapons in the world, and their bore is identical with that of your own

141

small guns. As you know, I arranged for this special design.'

He rose, and walked to the entrance of the tent. Out at sea, a supply convoy of Turkish galleys had appeared on the horizon, making its way towards them. The city of Otranto itself, Riario knew, was already stuffed almost to bursting with food and arms, clothing and transport vehicles, against the day when the main body of the Ottoman army would arrive and take possession of the peninsula. He had investigated certain of Otranto's warehouses, and the sheer volume of material they contained had impressed even him.

'You must be ready by the end of May at the latest,' he said to Shan Khara. He ran a finger around the inside of his collar, beneath the edge of the fluted steel breastplate he wore always—even, some said, while he slept. 'May,' he repeated. 'You cannot take the republics and duchies of the western plains this year, but you must be in winter quarters and ready to march upon them by October. Well?'

'Everything is arranged,' replied Shan Khara smoothly. 'Do not trouble yourself. You will not oppose us when we move, after all. Will you?'

The Count tugged at his neck again, as though his doublet chafed him. 'Not I,' he said.

'And your Germans?'

'They have not been paid to fight. But it will be a cold day in hell before I discuss my affairs with a rabble of *Landsknechts*. I expect six thousand more from Maximilian of Austria, but not until the middle of June, and by then . . .'

'If Allah wills,' said Shan Khara. 'And now forgive me, for I have work to do.'

Guard-Lieutenant Johannes Wendt and his Swiss, of whom there were a hundred and ten, came trudging down from the foothills of the Appenines towards the plain around Foggia. They were extremely weary and thirsty beyond belief, for their last river crossing had been at Fortore some twenty-five miles behind. Their descent from the high mountain passes had been a cruel one—their wagons proving both stubborn and difficult to manage—and they had lost three of their fifty guns in a ravine.

The worst of their journey was, however, now behind them, and they joked among themselves in the gathering dusk. When they saw, toiling up the track a quarter of a mile ahead of them, two men struggling with a cart drawn by a highly cantankerous mule, their amusement was that of men who perceive others heading for misfortunes which they themselves have overcome. They were, accordingly, ready to be diverted even before they realised that one of the approaching pair was almost incapably drunk.

Lieutenant Johannes Wendt called his column to a halt as the mule cart reached them. He leaned down from his saddle and addressed the more sober of the two, a taller man whose rough clothing was heavily stained with mud.

'Where are you bound for, fellow?' he asked.

The man bowed as he removed his hat, which was of a kind worn by the hill peasants of the region.

'Sir,' he said politely, 'we are for Naples. How is it up there?' He pointed up the trail.

'Bearable, but only just,' replied Lieutenant Wendt. 'Naples is a goodly journey—for any man,' he added, staring distastefully at the drunkard, now reeling against the side of his vehicle.

'Tell him to kiss his horse's arse,' said that individual belligerently. 'Tell him . . . tell him . . .'

'Hold your mouth,' said the first carter. He was, the lieutenant saw, a well-built man with a pleasantly deferential manner.

'All right then,' said his companion. 'In that case, ask him what the hell his company of pox-ridden, fart-arse foreigners are doing in *our* path! Eh?' He staggered and grasping the bridle of the lieutenant's mount, peering up at him and laying a finger wisely alongside his broken nose. 'Foreigners!' he said. 'I can tell. It is impossible . . .' here he belched loudly in punctuation of his discourse, '. . . abs'lutely impossible to fool me. I know, you see. I know a God damned, pox-ridden foreigner when I see one, by Christ, I do. They speak *foreign*, that's how!'

Lieutenant Wendt slashed at him with his whip, but missed. The man had already begun to lumber in the direction of his fellow, whose cloak he now held while he retched hollowly. He stuck a finger into his mouth, and at

143

once spewed forth a stream of vomit all over his friend's boots. Those at the front of the Swiss column broke into hearty laughter.

'Where in the name of everything holy did you pick him up?' asked the lieutenant, aghast. 'He is barely fit to walk a dozen paces, let alone cross a mountain range.'

'Sir,' replied the tall man earnestly, 'he is my father's cousin and is employed in our family's vineyard, and is a sore trial to me.'

'Vineyard?' said Lieutenant Wendt, with interest. 'What have you in the cart?'

'Wine, good sir. We sell it to the court of King Ferrante himself, for he will drink no other. It is a profitable trade, but I have begged my father again and again not to send this lout with me. It is worse than putting a sailor in charge of a whorehouse.' He slapped his companion's face, and the latter straightened up again, his stomach now apparently empty.

'Where are we?' he mumbled.

'Exactly where we were five minutes ago, Cipriano,' said the first carter angrily. 'Where do you suppose?'

'Wine?' said Lieutenant Johannes Wendt. 'Wine?'

'Give them some wine,' said the man called Cipriano. 'Eh? They're only poor foreign arses, but they can't help it.' He weaved toward the lieutenant, who backed his horse away nervously. '*Nectar,*' he shouted. '*Wonderful!* The best in Italy, this stuff is! It's called . . .' he spun on his heels, keeping his balance only by a miracle. 'What's it called? I cannot remember.'

'Get back to the cart, fool!' gritted Leonardo da Vinci. He had brought Cipriano on this mission with some foreboding, and was beginning to think his qualms justified. Playing a role was one thing, histrionics another, but he had little choice except to follow Cipriano's lead.

'We will buy your wine, fellow,' said the Swiss Lieutenant, who had paths of his own to pursue. 'Why take it all the way to Naples?'

'Sir,' replied Leonardo uncertainly. 'Sir, my father . . .'

'*Lacrimae Christi!*' bellowed Cipriano. 'That is what it's called! *The Tears of Christ!* The most marvellous, perfect, wonderful wine in all the land! Eh, you foreign arses?' He leaned against the cart with his head in his arms a moment. When he stood upright again, he was apparently, to Leonardo's astonishment, weeping tears of his own. '*Give* it to them,' he sobbed. 'They are so far from home. So far. Besides, they'll only have foreign money.'

'*In vino, veritas*,' said Lieutenant Wendt, smiling. 'But we'll pay you, just the same. What do you say?'

'Sir, who are you?' asked Leonardo timidly.

'We are a detachment of the Pope's own guard in Rome. I am indeed, as your friend observes, a Swiss, and so are all my men. Does not Rome rank above Naples, and the Pope above kings? Sell, my friend.'

Leonardo thought for a moment.

'Twenty florins,' he said. We have ten barrels; two florins a barrel.'

'*Robbery!*' screamed Cipriano. 'Offer him twelve,' he urged the lieutenant. 'Go on, go on. Twelve!' At this, one of the officers collapsed across his horse's neck, too weak with mirth to sit in the saddle.

'Ten florins,' suggested Lieutenant Wendt.

'Fifteen,' Leonardo said.

'Eleven. Whatever your drunken friend says, it is not *Lacrimae Christi*,' said Lieutenant Wendt, 'which as all men know is grown only on the slopes of Mount Vesuvius.'

'I admit that he could not tell *Lacrimae Christi* from vinegar,' replied Leonardo, 'but it is good wine for all that. Thirteen florins.'

Cipriano began to advance on the lieutenant, his gaze fixed and glassy. 'Are you calling me a liar?' he said. 'Eh, foreigner? Are you?'

'Control him,' said Wendt. 'Keep him away from me. Twelve florins.'

'Done,' said Leonardo.

'Pah!' Cipriano said. 'Twelve florins is half its value. A quarter. A tenth. It is beyond price.'

'Unload the cart,' Leonardo ordered him, and hit him a clout that made his ears sing. Whether or not his command was meant seriously, there was no need for Cipriano to obey it; the Swiss company, almost to a man, descended upon their wagon like locusts and bore off its contents in an uproar of delight.

An hour later, all of them were unconscious, many snoring happily. The wine was indeed excellent, since Leonardo da Vinci was no skinflint. But the large quantities of opium tincture, carefully extracted with brandy from the package of poppy resin Leonardo had brought back with him from Constantinople, were an addition which the Swiss, in their greedy thirst, had not quite perceived.

Twenty of the Medici Gunners—the remainder were two miles away, in hiding with their own weapons—moved silently among the sleeping men, heading for the huge six-wheeled wagons that carried Rome's cannon.

'That poison of yours . . .' Rigo said, looking around.

'It is not poison,' said Leonardo. 'Only a soporific. I wish I had known about it when we played the surgeon with your arm; it's far more effective than wine.'

'How long will they sleep?'

'I am not sure. I tested it upon myself, by the way, but I think it will depend upon how much each man here has drunk. Long enough for our purposes, anyway. They will wake, and sleep again.'

'Again?' said Rigo. 'Why?'

'Because I have put a *second* dose of it in their drinking water,' laughed Leonardo, 'and from the dreams of the poppy one awakens with a raging thirst, as I found out from my own experience.'

They reached the wagons, and watered the horses which were harnessed to them. Rigo, Scudo and Cipriano went from one to the next, checking their burdens.

'Forty-seven guns,' Cipriano announced, 'and four cart loads of powder charges. There are no shot.'

'They need no shot,' said Leonardo. 'The Turks have enough of their own.'

Rigo walked to the nearest gun and ran the fingers of his left hand over the bronze of its barrel.

'Not bad,' he said. 'What next, Leonardo? Spike them?'

'That would be of no use. What we do must not be evident. Otherwise we might just as well steal them, and have done with it.'

'What, then?' Rigo asked. 'We could score the insides of the barrels, which would thwart their accuracy. But that might be found out as well.'

146

'And it is not enough,' said Leonardo. 'No. There is a simpler way to achieve what I want. Where is the wagon I loaded in Florence?'

Rigo pointed to a ridge behind them. 'Beyond, and out of sight,' he said. 'If you need to bring it hither, it will take an hour or more.'

'Its contents will do. Or at least some of them.' He told the gathered artillerymen what he had in mind, and they laughed.

'You have an evil mind,' said Rigo.

'I know,' Leonardo replied. 'It comes of long association with men such as yourself.'

Fourteen

FOLLOWING THEIR ENCOUNTER with Lieutenant Johannes
Wendt and his Switzers, the Medici Gunners marched
south and east for twelve days, following the same route by
which Leonardo, Rigo, Scudo and Tesoro had first reached
Otranto. This time, however, they made certain that
nobody, Turk or Italian, saw their arrival; they undertook
the last fifteen miles of their journey by night, and pitched
camp some six miles west of the city among the low hills of
the peninsula.

Leonardo da Vinci, during the following week, played
little part in the life of the encampment. The gunners,
under Agnolo Fulvio, Cipriano, Scudo and Giunta di
Lenzo, performed their daily ritual of stripping down and
reassembling their cannon, a task which they could now
perform in well under a minute. Leonardo and Bianca, in a
small gully within hailing distance of these exercises,
unpacked what was left in the small wagon he brought from
Florence, and busied themselves in what appeared to be
several days of carpentry and sailmaking. At least, so it
seemed to those gunners who were curious enough to climb
the ridge that separated Leonardo's working area from the
camp itself. All who did so returned to their fellows shaking
their heads in bafflement.

'He is building a new kind of boat,' said Balestraccio.

'I would not put anything past him,' replied Tomasello
Cennini, 'even though the nearest water is three miles from
here, and that is only a stream.' Tomasello, who rarely tried
to understand Leonardo's undertakings, had long ago
adopted an attitude of humorous cynicism towards them,
at least until he was called upon to take part in their results.

On the evening of the last day in April the gunners'

supper was interrupted by Marco di Carona, who was on
sentry duty. He marched into the pool of orange light cast
by the fire, holding by the arm an indignant young man
with fair hair.

'Who is this?' asked Rigo.

'I don't know,' said Marco. 'He's a German.'

'My name is Carl Otto von Thalen,' the young man said,
pulling free of Marco and drawing himself up to a posture
of rigid attention. 'I am lieutenant to my lord Manfred,
Landgrave of Konigshaven, and with the forces of the most
excellent Captain-General Riario, Count of Bosco and
Imola. And you, sirs?'

Rigo was about to reply to this, but Leonardo cut him
short.

'For the moment,' he said, 'you may assume we are
bandits.'

'That was my presumption,' the young German said
stiffly.

'Well?'

'Are you hungry?' Leonardo asked him.

Von Thalen relaxed slightly. 'Yes,' he admitted.

'Then eat with us while we decide what to do with you.
Come, man. Sit down. We have not harmed you yet.' Thus
invited, the lieutenant complied, and fell upon the piece of
meat offered him as though he had not eaten for days. 'And
meanwhile,' Leonardo went on, 'tell us what you are doing
in the wilds so far from your headquarters.'

'Walking,' said Carl Otto von Thalen. 'With me, it is an
exercise. I have been here for eight weeks doing nothing. I
do not allow myself to get out of condition.'

'You are hired to Rome, then?'

'Against the Turks. Yes. It is a question of retaking the
city of Otranto.' Still chewing greedily, the German looked
around, and saw the Medici Guns. 'If you are bandits, why
have you cannon?' he asked. 'It is unusual, I think.'

'Quite so,' said Leonardo. 'Well, sir, we are not outlaws,
since you have discovered the truth of it. We are a
detachment of artillery, recently arrived from the west. We
prefer to practise here rather than joining the main body of
the Italian forces. Gunners, sir, tend to be unsociable men,
I fear.'

The lieutenant's face cleared.

'I do not blame you,' he said. 'It is a swamp down there. So you are from Rome, are you? The rest of your weapons arrived this afternoon.'

'We are not—' began Tomasello, but never finished his remark, finding himself almost paralysed by a kick from Rigo Leone. Oblivious to this piece of by-play, the young German settled himself more comfortably and grew confidential.

'It is a farce, of course,' he said. 'I cannot answer for yourselves, but I do not believe we are here to fight. So my friends say. We are . . . what would you say? Decoration.'

'Oh?' said Leonardo.

'Of course. In any case, Otranto will not fall to those tiny guns of yours, nor to any others. It is my opinion that it cannot be taken at all. The main gate faces eastwards, to the sea, and the Turks hold the shoreline for a mile at either side. And the rear gate . . .'

'Yes?'

'I thank God *I* do not have to take it,' said Carl Otto von Thalen. 'Since you are only just here, you will not know how it is defended. Last year a small group of men with more courage than sense penetrated the city by crawling through a drain. They performed a reconnaissance, and do you know what they found?'

'No,' said Rigo, as though fascinated. 'What *did* these heroes find?'

'Let me show you.' The lieutenant picked up a stick and drew a rough plan of Otranto in the ashes at his feet. 'The Turks have knocked down half the buildings in the city. They have twelve large cannon inside, all trained on the back of the landward gate, and they have cleared a line of fire for each gun, like this . . . You see? To set foot inside the rear gate is instant death for any man, or for a thousand men if it comes to that. Even to bring a ram against it is impossible, for all the Turks have to do is swing the gates open and fire their guns at the attacking party.'

'I see,' Leonardo said. 'What of the walls themselves?'

'Any wall can be scaled, of course,' said von Thalen. 'But these will require siege towers, and I hear no news of any such equipment coming. Even if we were to employ them . . . but, sirs, it is as I told you before. We are not here to recapture Otranto. Some say we are not even being paid to fight. The Count of Imola has some two thousand men of his own, and four cannon, which he has not used this year. We Germans are four thousand more, but we have brought with us tents for eight thousand—and they are pitched and empty. You see? Is it not plain? We are an army for show, and that is all. We appear to be twice as numerous as we are. And we are not here to take Otranto, but to discourage the Turks from breaking out. Not that we should be likely to succeed in that, either.'

'Why not?' Leonardo asked him.

'Because the Sultan has already brought in arms and provisions for an army of one hundred thousand,' said von Thalen. 'That is my own estimate, at least. I take exercise, as I have said, and I use my eyes. One hundred thousand men, and he brings in more supplies daily.'

'But no troops, as yet?'

'No. What has he already? Ten thousand, perhaps. I tell you, sirs, an army the like of which has never been seen before in Europe is on its way, and when it arrives . . . But also, there is something else afoot. Something I do not like, though I do not know what. I am young, but I am no fool—except,' he smiled, 'that I may talk too much.'

'You have no enemies here,' Leonardo said.

'And I thank you for my evening meal,' said Lieutenant von Thalen. He looked at the rising moon. 'I shall have to leave you shortly, if I may. From midnight I am supposed to stand guard over the rest of your cannon at Castello del Mar. I will keep them safely for you, though they will do you no good.'

'Finish your meal,' Leonardo told him, and rose, tapping Rigo on the shoulder. Together they walked a little distance up the canyon, until they saw in front of them the shadowy form of Bianca Visconti. She was sitting on a rock.

'I thought it best he should not see me,' she said as they came up to her.

'Your beauty, madonna, is equalled only by your good sense,' Leonardo said, and kissed her.

'We shall have to kill him, none the less,' said Rigo.

'Why?' demanded Bianca, shocked.

'Because he will certainly let slip—in innocent conversation at the Castello del Mar, Riario's headquarters —that he has seen us here,' Rigo replied. 'We can hardly keep him prisoner. Nor can we ask him to refrain from mentioning us.'

'We cannot harm him,' Leonardo said. 'He is a sensible lad, and an innocent one. It's the misfortune of war that he stumbled upon us, just as our success with the Swiss was our good fortune. We are not assassins, and must therefore adapt our plans to fit life's accidents. But I have the feeling that he will not live long in any case, poor fellow.'

'What do you mean?' Bianca asked.

'I mean that he has a quick brain, and is drifting too close to the truth for Riario's comfort. He does not know all of it yet, but he may discover that treachery is afoot. He believes that he and his compatriots are here for show, and so they are. He believes that this show is for the benefit of the Sultan, but in that he is wrong. He scents *something* in the air, and yet, he's not quite sure. Well, when the Turks are ready to move out of Otranto, Riario will allow them to slaughter the Germans like sheep. If he should smell that out, he is lost.'

'Can you not warn him?'

'No, my heart,' said Leonardo. 'That we dare not do. And although I may not take a knife to his throat, neither will I sacrifice our chances in Otranto, simply to protect him. He is in the hands of Providence, as are we all.'

At the Castello del Mar, Girolamo Riario supervised the stowage of the last cannon in the cellars. He rubbed his hands together, with much satisfaction.

'Return to Rome at once,' he ordered Lieutenant Johannes Wendt.

'My lord,' said the Swiss, 'my men need rest.'

'They can take it where they find it, then, but not here. You will leave within the hour, and be in Lecce by dawn.'

Lieutenant Wendt would have protested more strongly, but one glance into Riario's eyes changed his mind and he said nothing. He strode out of the castle, gathered his men, and rode northwards in a foul temper, cursing the lack of consideration common to all of high rank. In obeying the

Count he saved his life and the lives of all his subordinates, but this he was not to know.

When the young German, Carl Otto von Thalen, presented himself for guard duty a little after midnight, the Count reviled him.

'You are late,' he said.

'Sir, I apologise,' said von Thalen. 'I was delayed by a small—'

'I do not care to hear what small thing happened to you. Your orders were to report to me at midnight. It is now morning, and by how many minutes you have failed in your orders does not concern me either.'

'Yes, my lord,' said von Thalen, his back like a ramrod.

'Go to your post. How many men have you?'

'Twenty-four, my lord.'

'Your turn of duty, and theirs, is extended until noon,' said Riario, and left him, his mouth twisted oddly as though in hidden amusement.

Lieutenant Carl Otto von Thalen descended to the cellars of the castle for his last night on earth. He fingered the rows of gleaming barrels, the wheels of oak, and the iron-bound gun carriages. He knew nothing of gunnery, but he understood discipline, and none of his men moved so much as an eyebrow when he informed them that their watch duty had been extended from eight hours to twelve.

Nor was he surprised that the Count had shown no inclination to listen to his explanation about the small company of artillerymen he had found in the hills. Superior officers seldom listened to excuses, and Lieutenant von Thalen accepted this without question. He would discuss it with the Count tomorrow, if opportunity arose; though Girolamo Riario, he thought, had of late developed a curious gleam in his eye, a gleam almost of madness, so some of von Thalen's fellow officers said. Since his own master, the Landgrave Manfred von Konigshaven, had been three parts mad for years, the notion did not disturb Carl Otto von Thalen very much.

'Well,' said Rigo Leone, 'it is something to know that the Sultan has not moved his guns. It is no comfort, but useful.'

'Their guns do not matter,' Leonardo.

'What of the sewer?' put in Cipriano. 'Doubtless there is a heavy guard upon it.'

'The sewer matters a little,' rejoined Leonardo, 'but not very much.'

Recognising in Leonardo a tone that foretold trouble, Rigo grew annoyed.

'And what does that matter?' he asked.

'The supplies.'

'You mean the food and equipment for a hundred thousand men, the mightiest army the world has ever seen, and so on? Very impressive, except that we knew that already,' Rigo said. 'In any case, I don't see how they affect us. Girolamo Riario, perhaps, but not us. *We* are not going to fight a hundred thousand men, I take it?' He said this a shade uncertainly, as though he were afraid that Leonardo might announce cheerfully that this was exactly what he proposed they should do.

'No,' replied Leonardo with a smile. 'Not even with five cannon.'

'Then what about the supplies?' demanded Rigo. 'You want to steal them? Is that it?'

'Not exactly. They might prove a bit burdensome. Let us leave robbery to the Turks for the present. They, after all, are about to steal some fifty of Rome's guns; and whenever they choose to do it, we will wish them good luck.'

Shan Khara, leading one hundred and fifty mounted Janissaries, swept northward along the beach as dawn's first glow began to touch the Adriatic horizon. Behind him rolled seven carts, drawn by oxen.

He did not need a hundred and fifty men for this enterprise, he knew. Thirty would have sufficed, together with the ox wagons; but he had agreed that some show of force should be used, and he was a man of his word. Besides, his appetite was sharp.

When he had first learned through a network of agents in Rome, Naples, Sicily, Malta and Crete that the guns offered him had been built to an original design by the very man who had so honourably defeated him in Constantinople, Shan Khara rejoiced. It was true, of course that the secrets of Leonardo da Vinci's rangefinding accuracy were already his, having been exchanged for the Florentine's freedom and that of his comrades. None the less, the building of guns in Turkey to Leonardo's specifications would take until the end of summer. The thought of immediately obtaining such weapons gratified him beyond measure. With fifty of these cannon, he thought, he could master the Mediterranean for Islam; with three hundred, the whole of Europe. But Europe could wait.

He turned inland, as arranged, by the blackened shell of the watchtower that guarded the seaward approach to Castello del Mar. Reining in briefly, he surveyed the cracked wall and thought again of the Florentine engineer who had harnessed to the craft of gunnery the power of mathematics. He wondered if this extraordinary man might be anywhere nearby. Shan Khara believed he was; he felt the prickling anticipation of yet another contest between himself and Leonardo, not under tournament conditions but those of war. A glove of challenge had been cast down in Constantinople, and retrieved. All that remained to be decided were time and place.

He spurred his horse, and headed for the distant castle.

Lieutenant Carl Otto von Thalen saw the Turkish vanguard against the morning sky, and went into action with a precision learned almost by rote. He at once sent his *caposquadra* and three men-at-arms to check the security of all the possible means of entry to his stronghold. Another man was sent off to alert his commander, the Count of Imola. He had eight crossbowmen and two arquebusiers, and these he ranged at strategic points around the battlements. The remainder of his force he gathered in a large bedchamber on the first floor; they would be sent wherever they might be needed later.

When his messenger returned with the news that Girolamo Riario was nowhere to be found, Lieutenant von Thalen was momentarily puzzled, but concluded that the Count had returned to the main encampment near Otranto without telling him. It was his privilege to do so, though von Thalen thought it careless. He went in search of the Count's valet or any other of his servants, and found the civilian household staff huddled in the ground floor hall, terrified by the clatter of feet and shouted commands that echoed about them. He reassured them, and ascertained from the valet that none of them knew the Count's whereabouts either. Then he climbed up to the battlements, at the foot of which a howling company of heathens in flowing robes were dismounting from their horses.

Shan Khara, on seeing von Thalen's face overheat in the growing light, hailed him and invited him to surrender. There was something odd in his manner, the young lieutenant thought, as though he were requesting a formality he assumed would at once be complied with.

'Take your dervishes and go home,' advised von Thalen. 'There is nothing for you here, Turk.'

Shan Khara repeated his invitation, without heat.

'No,' said Lieutenant von Thalen, and signalled to his arquebusiers. They discharged two shots from neighbouring embrasures, and a Janissary fell to the ground.

'Fool,' said Shan Khara, and retired a distance of several yards. A suspicion entered his mind which he would have dismissed at once were it not that he was dealing, ultimately, with Girolamo Riario. He cupped his hands. 'We have come for the guns!' he shouted. 'Open, and let us in.'

Lieutenant von Thalen seized a crossbow from the man nearest to him. 'You have come for a bolt through the head,' he called, as he fired it. He missed Shan Khara, whose suspicions were now confirmed. The Count of Imola had not told his own subordinates what was to happen, and they would have to be killed. The fact did not distress Shan Khara unduly, but it was something else about Girolamo Riario to be stored in his memory.

He signalled to his Janissaries, and began to seek the best means of entrance to Castello del Mar.

As for Lieutenant von Thalen, he remained unworried. 'After all,' he told his *caposquadra*, 'how long have we to hold out? It is already morning, and relief will come from our south within the hour.'

'Two hours,' said the *caposquadra*, who was a middle aged man of some experience.

'Very well. Two hours. If we cannot hold them off that

long, we are not worth our hire,' said Lieutenant von Thalen.

Four miles away, outside Otranto, two of von Thalen's German colleagues emerged into the mist that lay about their encampment and listened to the faint and distant sounds of battle.

'Carl Otto is in trouble, I think,' said Werner von Landau, a stocky youth whose uncle was a *landsknecht* in Bavaria. 'Come.'

His comrade agreed and they went in search of their immediate superiors, who looked in turn for Rome's Captain-General. Informed by Riario's page that his master was at the Castello del Mar, they bothered their heads no further; whatever was going on up there, it was no concern of mere mercenaries.

Now, a dozen Janissaries battered at the main doors to Castello del Mar with a heavy log. They were surrounded by thirty more of their fellows who waved scimitars. Lieutenant von Thalen, however, had taken pains to assure himself of the doors' thickness and the strength of their bolts, and—apart from picking off several of the men below him with arbalest fire from the towers that overlooked them at either side—he remained confident. A rough count of the enemy told him that he was outnumbered by six to one, but that did not worry him either. He had a cool head for his age. The bars over one or two ground floor embrasures might be sawn through, given time, but otherwise he was perfectly certain of his safety until reinforcements should arrive.

He walked back through the rooms on the first floor, and had no sooner reached the top of the main stairway when his confidence fell in ruins about him. A shrill scream, choked off in mid-utterance, told him that the castle's defences had been breached—how, he did not know—and that he was doomed.

He shouted for his halberdiers, and prepared to hold the stairhead. Turkish troops poured into the passages and hallway below, their weapons red with blood of the hapless servants they had slaughtered. They looked upward and began to climb the stairs.

'To the roof, sir,' said his *caposquadra* urgently, 'Make a signal! Fire, smoke, *anything!* It is our last hope!'

Lieutenant von Thalen thought it a slender hope, but took his subordinate's advice. The *caposquadra* and eight pikemen levelled their halberds and descended the staircase, which was soon a mass of yelling Janissaries, each of whom pressed upward over the bodies of his dead fellows. Death in battle, for the follower of the Prophet, was the gateway to paradise, and against such fervour the defenders could do nothing.

Finding a ladder to the roof, the lieutenant climbed quickly, dragging with him a tangle of curtains with which to build his fire. In the half light before sunrise, he crossed to the seaward parapet, and saw beneath him the first cannon being carried out of the castle's rear doorway. The ox wagons were drawn up in a neat column, the flanks of the animals steaming; every now and again, one of them would shake its head, rattling the chains that yoked it to the cross-tree. He realized now that his fire was a hopeless gesture, he would not be granted time in which to build it before death in one shape or another overtook him. But what he felt most of all was curiosity, coupled with mild annoyance that he would never know how the castle had fallen or why. He had lived his life by discipline, good sense and attention to detail, and all had failed him in the end, leaving him only questions.

He climbed down the ladder, and a hand tapped him on the shoulder as he stepped off its lowest rung. He turned, and found the answers he sought.

'So, my lord,' von Thalen said. 'It was you.' Girolamo Riario plunged his stiletto into the side of Lieutenant Carl Otto von Thalen's throat and stepped back calmly, to watch him die.

'No survivors,' said Riario, either to himself or to the dying man at his feet. 'I cannot afford survivors.'

He went downstairs. None of the Janissaries molested him. Shan Khara was at one of the windows at the back of the great hall, watching the loading of the guns into the ox-wagons; he did not acknowledge Riario's presence in any way. If the Count noticed this discourtesy, he gave no indication. He crossed to a writing desk, took out parchment and inkhorn, and began his report on the unhappy events at Castello del Mar and the regrettable loss of forty-seven cannon to the Ottoman Empire. 'A surprise attack by night caught our German soldiers off-guard,' he wrote. . . . . . .

Fifteen

CURRENTS OF AIR, so Leonardo saw and felt with the eyes and fingers of his mind, were ebbing all about them. Air trickled down neighbouring gullies and ravines, spilled over the edges of low cliffs in cascades, and drifted towards the far-off sea, whence it would return in flood at eventide. Sailors called this daily rise and fall the sea breeze and the land breeze, being affected by its flow only in so far as it filled their sails and bore them towards the shore or away from it. Yet sailors, of all men, Leonardo thought, should recognise a tide for what it was, whether they could see its surge or no.

To Rigo Leone, standing beside him on the crest of a bluff two miles from their encampment and gazing over the plain that lay between Otranto and themselves, the wind was just a hill wind, and a cold one. It was at his back, and chilled the nape of his neck so that he hunched himself inside his leather jerkin.

Seated on a tussock next to Leonardo, Bianca shivered and drew close to him, concerned with human warmth rather than with wind and weather. Sunrise was approaching, and from afar all of them could hear the sounds of battle, not from the city, but from an invisible point several miles to its north. The sounds were faint, and fought to reach them against the prevailing breeze, rising imperceptibly, only to die away again while they strained their senses to hear.

'They are taking the guns,' Rigo said. 'Did the German not say they were at Castello del Mar? It must be.'

'In that case we're short of time,' said Leonardo. 'We must move tonight, or tomorrow at the latest. I had hoped for a few days at least, but if we are not to be granted them, so be it.'

'Move,' said Rigo. 'move! You keep saying "move," but you never tell us how. Can we mine the walls of Otranto? No, we cannot. Can we scale them? No. Neither can we get underneath them by way of that sewer, which must by now have a full platoon of guards at its inner end. The rear gate is covered by six cannon, and the front is held by the entire Turkish army. Move, you say! How, man, *how?*'

'We take wings, and fly.'

'Or grow shovels for hands, and dig like moles. Come, Leonardo. It is clear that you have a plan. What is it?'

'I have just told you, Leonardo said. 'We shall fly.'

'He means it, Rigo,' said Bianca soberly. 'I promise you he does.'

'Not I,' said Cipriano di Lucca flatly, surveying the monstrous sail-like contrivance of black silk, whipcord, bronze wire and timber that lay spread out before them on the pebble-strewn floor of the dell. 'Not for a million florins.'

'Nor me,' Scudo said.

'It looks to me like an invention of the Devil,' said Giunta di Lenzo. He had, indeed, crossed himself as soon as Leonardo led the gunners from their morning campfire to the open air workshop. Several of Giunta's fellows had done the same. Nobody, as yet, had come right out with the opinion that Leonardo had this time taken leave of his reason, but the feeling was abroad even if unexpressed.

They stood in an uncertain semicircle around the expanse of cloth and rigging, while Leonardo adjusted a lashing at its centre. Crouched in the early light, he gave the impression of being a winged man even while earthbound. At either side of his body the curving triangles of dark and shimmering cloth, each five paces from base to tip, stretched across the grass and rippled in the breeze as though impatient to leave the ground. Near the forward edge of each wing Leonardo had painted—from pure lightness of heart, perhaps—a circle in various hues of red, orange and yellow; so that, seen from above as they saw it, the glider had the appearance of a gigantic skate or sting-ray, with a pair of malevolent eyes at its forward end and a drawn-out tail, or rather a prolongation of each wing,

161

extending some eighteen feet behind the point where his feet now rested.

He looked up from his task.

'It is nothing but a kite,' he said. 'A child's toy, grown to the stature of a man. It reminds you of the Devil only because it is black; and the reason it is black is because it must fly at night, unseen. There is nothing to be afraid of.'

'No kite will carry a man,' replied Giunta di Lenzo with an air of finality.

Tesoro di Veluti, who had not spoken yet, looked around the dell. Some ten paces from Leonardo's proposed flying machine stood a row of four winches, the drum of each wound with layer upon layer of fine cord. Farther up the small valley, several large bundles of silk and spars appeared obviously to represent other flying machines like this one, not at present assembled and braced.

Tesoro was still too young to have reached that closing of the mind to all things new which afflicts men sooner or later — for the most part, sooner — and while he did not exactly believe flight possible, neither did he hold it to be impossible. After all, who had thought of the first wheel, he asked himself? A man, in all probability, much like the man who now knelt in front of him, making secure a knot in a leather harness. Another man, of like mind, must have been the first to set himself astride a horse and thereby outdistance his more timorous friends: although, Tesoro reflected, he had most likely been thrown for his pains and broken his skull. There was that to be considered, too. Tesoro smiled to himself, and kept silent.

Leonardo got to his feet, and inspected the wings of his device. Four hundred and twenty square feet of silk had gone into the building of each machine, and he had four of them. The backbone of each consisted essentially of three long spars of planed and varnished spruce, while another transverse spar, light and whippy, supported the leading edge of each wing. The pilot would hang below them, his feet in stirrups, his body leaning forward and supported by leather straps, his hands grasping handles let into the under surfaces of the tensioned poles that formed the roof struts of the wings. He thought of the weeks of calculation and experiment that had gone into the planning and design of this machine, this challenge to the angels themselves; of the models he had built, tested and discarded as failures. And all the while his mind held firm to the vision of two hawks, floating and soaring above him, telling him by their graceful motion that wings which flapped or whirled were unnecessary to flight, that the power to sustain a man above the earth was to be found not in the muscles of his own body but in the wind itself, if that wind could be tamed. He wished suddenly that Cardinal Domenico della Palla could be here with him, so that he could explain to the Chancellor how the wheeling hawks had swept away a barrier in his mind and enabled him to see the principles of gliding flight, the answers to the problems of turning, balance, and control, clearly and as though he had walked out of a mist into a sunlit plain. Cardinal della Palla, no doubt, would point out gently that it had been God who had swept away the barrier, using the birds as His instruments; and Leonardo would not dispute it.

Meanwhile he had other barriers to surmount, not in his own mind but in the minds of others.

'Well, we are ready,' he announced briskly. He saw little by way of enthusiasm or encouragement in the faces around him.

'You are going to *fly* in that thing?' said Tomasello Cennini, voicing the thoughts of all.

'Me?' said Leonardo. 'I would not be so impolite. The lady Bianca Visconti has chosen to fly it, she being light of heart.'

Bianca left Rigo's side and came down the short slope of the dell to meet him. She was wearing a short tunic and breeches, in russet.

'Giunta and Marco, lift the tail,' commanded Leonardo. 'Cipriano, Scudo, Balestraccio, Tomasello, the front of the wings. Come.'

The six men he had selected gathered around him, while he showed them how to perform their tasks. It was not, he explained to them, a question of lifting the machine's weight—one man alone could have done that, with ease—but of preventing the wind from catching it before they were ready to launch it.

'We're going to the top of that ridge,' he said, pointing to

163

the southern rim of the dell. 'Up there, the breeze is strong and steady, and you will need to hold the wings down and the tail high. Do you understand?'

They nodded and muttered doubtfully. Leonardo checked the attachment of the mooring line both to the winch nearest the machine and to the glider-kite itself, and they carried it up the slanting side of the valley. Its nose was facing inland, to the west, since that was the direction from which the morning wind was blowing. Once at the summit of the ridge, the six gunners held the black wing head high while Bianca took her place beneath it and Leonardo fastened the light straps of the harness around her shoulders and waist.

'Don't rest your feet in the stirrups until you have left the ground,' he told her, and hang from your hands as much as you can. You have no need to control it yet.' They smiled at each other, conspiratorially and a little nervously, for this was a scene they had rehearsed many times.

The idea that she should make the first flight had been Bianca's. Weeks ago, Leonardo had foreseen the nature of the problem that confronted him. Put in its simplest terms, this was one of persuading a group of brave but sceptical men to accept a course of action which appeared to be merely a somewhat imaginative form of suicide. Any one of the Medici Gunners would storm a breach with an even chance of dying or less, and do it without a second thought. That was not the difficulty. It was the unknown, the crossing of a new frontier, that would paralyse their will to try.

'But you'll show them that it is not impossible,' Bianca had said, in the garden of their villa outside Florence. 'You'll give them proof.'

'I don't think that will be enough, somehow,' Leonardo had replied. 'They know me as a friend, it is true. But they also regard me as being part way between a genius and a dreamer. Cipriano, for instance, is quite capable of watching me fly above him for hours, and then of telling me calmly that what I have done is all very well for me, but that he will have none of it. And he'll carry the others with him. Oh, if I had a week or two in which to soar and swoop over them, then sooner or later one of them would become intrigued enough to try it. But I may not have a week.'

'Then the answer is simple,' said Bianca. 'Let me fly. For once they have seen me do it, there is not a man among them who would dare refuse to do likewise, even if he thought he were facing instant death. I am but a poor, frail woman; and men have peculiar notions about their honour.'

So now, as Leonardo tightened the harness about her and the great expanse of silk above her bucked and fluttered in the airstream, they smiled at each other with the complicity of actors. Their performance, after all, was an historic one. To left and right Cipriano, Scudo, Balestraccio and Tomasello Cennini cast sidelong glances towards them as they fought to prevent the wings from breaking free of their grasp.

Leonardo checked the tethering line once more, confirming that the entire length of its run down the side of the ridge to the valley floor was free from obstruction.

'Are you ready, Bianca?' he asked her.

'Ready,' Bianca said, and he stood away, watching the airflow pluck alternately at the upper and lower surfaces of the wings. Then he walked beneath them, making a last examination of the lashings, until he reached the tail.

'When I raise my hand,' he told Giunta di Lenzo and Marco di Carona, 'lower the spars you are holding until you feel the wind catch the silk and begin to lift. Then let go at once and kneel, so that the machine does not strike you as it rises.' They nodded, and he ran quickly down the side of the ridge to the winch, around which the other gunners were gathered. He felt for the iron pawls that locked the drum. It was about eighty feet from winch to kite, and he did not intend to let out any more cord than already lay between the two. Bianca would be swept sideways when her feet left the ground as the kite ascended to float directly in line with the winch, but he had decided that it would be safer for her to land in the bowl of the valley than to try to do so up on the ridge.

He climbed back and stood in front of Bianca and the four gunners who held the leading edge of the wing.

'When I raise my hand,' he said 'do nothing. That is a signal to the men holding the tail. The moment I lower it again, let go. Understood?'

'Yes,' Cipriano said.

'Very well,' said Leonardo, and took several paces backwards until he could see the whole of the kite and the ground at either side of it. He watched the bending of the grass on the ridge, felt the air blow cold on one of his cheeks and then the other; he waited, poising himself to choose the right moment, the right wind force, the right direction.

Bianca took a firmer grip on the handholds above her head, feeling the kite sway powerfully, and listening to the flap of the silk and the occasional creak of the spar-lashings. She closed her eyes momentarily, then decided this was a sign of fright and opened them again; whatever happened to her, it would not be made any better or worse by whether she could see or not, she told herself firmly.

Leonardo raised his hand. Giunta and Marco, holding the tail, depressed it until it was level with their waists.

At once the wind surged under the leading edges of the wings, throwing the silk into a smooth upward curve. To the four men who held the wing spars, it seemed as though a huge and invisible force gripped the machine suddenly, seeking to wrench it from them and hurl it towards the sky.

'Hold firm!' Leonardo shouted. He waited for as long as he dared, while the lift under each wing equalised, then swept his arm down again.

The four gunners let go, and the wings tilted sharply for an instant. Bianca felt the soles of her feet leave the ground and then settle. Marco and Giunta released the tail, and immediately, magically, the great horizontal sail rose swiftly into the air, drifting backwards and sideways under the pull of the mooring line, soaring over those in the little valley who watched its ascent with awestruck eyes. Leonardo ran down to join them, he checked the winch once more and then, like his companions, looked up.

Sixty feet overhead, Bianca hung beneath the aircraft, her feet resting securely in the stirrups, her waist and shoulders supported by the leather straps of the harness, her fingers lightly gripping the shaped handles at the front of the two uppermost longitudinal spars. The great kite yawed slightly from side to side as though searching for freedom, but was always returned to equilibrium by the weight of her body. From the end of the third spar between

166

her knees, the tethering cord dropped away in a smooth arc to the winch drum below.

Tesoro di Veluti, shading his eyes, watched her with an excitement that threatened to overwhelm him. He imagined himself up there in her place, sensing without having to be told how it must be possible to control that vast sweep of silk by leaning this way or that, by taking more weight on hands or feet. He wondered what would happen if the line that held her to the earth were cast adrift, and even as he pondered this heard Leonardo's voice at his ear.

'Remember never to lift the front edge of the wing too high,' the artist murmured, as though reading his thoughts. 'Once you are free, you must always skim forward, or you will fall. That is the hardest thing to keep in mind. But I will show you, later, For now, help me to bring her down in safety.'

'By God, *yes*,' Tesoro said. 'A *triumph*, Leonardo! For you, and for her! I believed it, and yet I could not fully believe it until I saw it.'

He stooped to the winch handle and, with Leonardo, began to turn the drum. The kite descended slowly. Once below the rim of the valley, it began to tilt and swing erratically with the eddying wind. But little harm could come to Bianca, for even had she plummeted straight downwards there were more than fifty willing arms to catch her. Her landing, in fact, was far from perfect, since the machine slewed violently when it was still a dozen feet from the ground and one wing tip caught against a boulder. Leonardo freed her from the harness, and found her undamaged by her experience save for a bruised knee.

'How did it feel?' Tesoro di Veluti asked her, eagerly.

'Well,' replied Bianca diplomatically, 'I am ready to do it again, but not until somebody gives me some wine.'

At this the pent-up tension among the gunners gave way to relief, and they began to laugh and cheer. Four of them brought wineskins, at the sight of which she protested until it became clear that not all of it was intended for her.

After drinking her health, the gunners spent the rest of the day assembling three more aircraft, under Leonardo's careful supervision. When they broke for the noon meal, Rigo and Cipriano buttonholed the artist and led him aside.

'It is a miracle,' said Rigo, 'but . . .'

Leonardo grinned. 'No, it isn't a miracle,' he said, 'except in the sense that the flight of birds and butterflies is also a miracle. But go on.'

'How does it get us over the wall?' asked Rigo. 'If one rises and falls to the same place, then I do not see . . .' he scratched his head.

'Call Tesoro here,' said Leonardo, 'since it is the four of us who will make the attempt.'

Rigo beckoned, and the young gunner joined them.

'Tell us how you think we can use these machines to cross a wall, Tesoro,' Leonardo said to him.

'Why . . . I presume that if you cut free of the line that ties you to the winch, you will swoop forwards and downwards until you reach the ground again some distance away,' Tesoro said. 'Isn't that so?'

'You see?' said Leonardo. 'He is born to fly. That is exactly what happens.

'Indeed,' Cipriano said. 'Well, whatever may be the case for our infant here, I assure you that I was not born to fly.'

'Nor were you born to swim,' pointed out Leonardo, 'yet I have known you do so, after a fashion and under duress. If you want to take Otranto, you must fly. Make your choice.'

'I will fly,' sighed Cipriano. 'I surrender to this latest madness of yours, Leonardo. I trust you will allow me a little practice? Even young birds are permitted that.'

'This evening, and tomorrow,' said Leonardo. 'Have no fear, Cipriano. You will take to it as a duck takes to water—although now that I think of it, perhaps in your case I might have chosen my words better.'

In the last rays of sunset, Leonardo looked down at the eight or nine men surrounding the winch beneath him and felt for the knife at his side, observing as he did so that this was a risky manoeuvre which caused the machine to tilt as his body shifted. The breastband of the harness chafed a little, and he made a mental note to substitute a wider strap in its place. Also, it was proving harder than he had expected to transfer his weight from the handgrips above him to the stirrups at his feet, this being his means of altering his rate of descent or climb in the wind. In any case this was all to the good, since the most disastrous of errors in control was the one he had pointed out to Tesoro di Veluti—that of lifting the forward edge of the wing too steeply, and plunging earthward. Centuries in the future, men were to give a name to this hazard, whether intended or accidental; they would christen it *stalling* and, as Leonardo had done, would warn novice flyers against allowing it to happen. So far as he was concerned, it was something he had observed while gliding models across fields; he understood in a general way why it should occur, and even what action to take if it did. It was almost the only dangerous flight characteristic he had been unable to correct in his machines and the best he could do was to impress upon Rigo, Tesoro and Cipriano that they should on no account shift too far back on their heels.

Earlier in the evening, all three of his pupils had made tethered ascents, as Bianca Visconti had done, in order to accustom themselves to the dizzying sensation of floating in the void unsupported by anything except the black silken canopies above their heads. All three had survived the test, landing with varying degrees of pallor on their faces.

It remained, now, for Leonardo himself to sever the cord that still tied him to Mother Earth, and undertake man's first free flight.

The wind was flooding back from the sea, rising and filling the gullies from which it had ebbed that morning. He was soaring about a hundred and fifty feet above the winch, and would land another four hundred feet lower, on the plain at the escarpment's foot. Aside from the winchmen, all the gunners were gathered down there; he could see them as brown dots on the grass, about a third of a mile distant, beyond the edge of the cliff directly in front of him.

He took a deep breath, dropped his right hand to the level of his knees, felt for the cord, and slashed through it. He released the knife at once, so that it no longer hindered him, returning his hand to the spar it must hold, to preserve his balance and that of the glider.

The sensation of plunging downward and forward gripped his stomach, and he fought against the temptation to swing his weight in the opposite direction. He imposed upon his mind, by conscious effort, the notion that he was merely sliding rapidly downhill, like a child playing a game on a haymow or a bank of snow, and his fear turned to exhilaration.

He became a bird, as men have become birds in dreams ever since the beginnings of time.

The edge of the cliff rushed towards him, and he swooped over it into the open sky above the plain. The dark wings overhead seemed to fuse with his hands, his arms, to attach themselves directly to his mind and muscles, so that he no longer flew his machine as a thing apart but clove the air as the hawk or the heron must cleave it, making no decisions, no calculations of lift or equilibrium, but simply flying. He leaned, and his wings leaned with him against the wind; the ground tilted, levelled, and rose toward him. The men who watched his progress with upturned faces scattered in the path of his descent upon them, and then he became a man again even as they were—a creature of the earth who dared to seize hold of the sky for an instant and now relinquished it again, stumbling and with a certain relief.

Leonardo disentangled himself from the harness and rigging of the machine and pointed at Tesoro di Veluti.

'Now you,' he said. 'And keep your weight forward.'

'At once,' Tesoro said. 'Leonardo, what is it like? Without the line and the winch, I mean?'

'Like nothing you have ever known,' Leonardo said. 'But remember to keep your weight forward.'

By the time of their morning meal the next day each of the four aviators—Rigo, Cipriano, Tesoro, and Leonardo himself—had made two free flights. Their third, as Leonardo now explained to all the gunners, would be made in battle.

'For we must take the city tonight. We are as ready for it as we shall ever be; and we dare wait no longer, since Shan Khara already has Rome's forty-seven guns.'

'And we have five,' Scudo said, heavily.

'True,' agreed Leonardo, 'and of those I propose that we leave two behind. Three are all we need.'

'And are you going to fly them in, too?' Scudo asked.

'No. My air machines will lift a man and his personal gear,' laughed Leonardo, 'but not a cannon. Not even one

170

so light as ours. You and the rest will bring them in, Scudo.'

'How?'

'Through the same sewer by which Rigo and myself entered the city. They will be guarding it, to be sure. But it will be our task to open the way for all of you when we have flown over their heads.'

'And then?' said Cipriano. 'The Sultan is not likely to surrender Otranto to us merely because we have a handful of the Medici gunners and three cannon inside his walls.'

'I am not necessarily seeking his surrender,' replied Leonardo. 'All I seek is to prevent his expansion across Italy.' He leaned back against a moss-covered rock. 'Consider, my friends,' he went on. 'He's gathering provisions for a hundred thousand men at least, perhaps more. Our young German friend told us so, only confirming what we already knew of Sultan Mohammed's plans. Now, he holds a vast store of supplies.'

'And so?' asked Cipriano.

'His supplies must include gunpowder,' said Leonardo mildly.

Rigo whistled.

'By God,' Cipriano said, 'you are right. Powder and shot! And therefore, a magazine.'

'Which we can fire,' said Leonardo.

'When we find it,' said Rigo, and began to perform computations in his head. 'It will be a great deal of powder, by my reckoning,' he said when he had finished. 'A great deal. Perhaps a thousand tons, if he has a year's supply. I trust we shall not stay too close while it goes up.'

'Close be damned,' said Cipriano, becoming enthusiastic. 'I care not how close we are, so long as we fire it! Do you know where it is, Leonardo?'

'No,' said Leonardo. 'But I foresee little difficulty in finding it once we are inside the city. It's almost certain to be in one of the warehouses on the seaward side, and I shall be amazed if the magazine is not the most heavily guarded building in Otranto.' He took the remains of a burned twig, and began to outline his plans in front of him, drawing—as Lieutenant Carl Otto von Thalen had done—in the ashes of the fire. 'Here are the Turkish guns,' he said. 'We must

171

land beyond them, of course, since, it will do us no good to risk our necks only to be shot down the moment our feet touch the ground. Our immediate task will be to surprise the guards at the inner end of the sewer, and let Scudo and the rest of you into the city. Then we will go along the back of the wall, thus . . . you remember, Rigo? And when we find the magazine, we'll lay powder-trains to it and blow it up. The resulting confusion—'

'Will be considerable,' put in Rigo. 'A *thousand tons* of powder? Confusion is not the word.'

'Quite so. I imagine that we shall find it possible to make our escape,' Leonardo said. 'We can take their own cannon in the rear, since we know that they cannot turn them from their fixed lines of fire towards the landward gate.'

He looked around the circle of gunners, all of whom were nodding approval.

'Very good,' Rigo said, 'Very good indeed.'

That things did not go quite according to this admirable plan was due to unforeseen circumstances; and these, of course, are liable to plague the most brilliant of strategists.

Sixteen

'THAT WAS WONDERFUL,' said Bianca, 'but now I am cold, Leonardo. Wrap your cloak around me, please.'

Leonardo complied, and they lay in silence for a while. It was after dark, and they had built their own small fire in a ravine half a mile from the gunners' camp. Low walls of sandstone enclosed them on all sides, save for a narrow entry where a stream tumbled over the edge of a natural weir some distance from their couch of soft grasses and myrtle.

'You are angry,' said Leonardo presently.

'How did you know that?'

'From holding you,' Leonardo said. 'What is it, Bianca?'

'Oh, I am not angry with you,' replied Bianca. 'Or perhaps that is not true. I keep remembering that in an hour or so from now you'll be with Rigo and Cipriano and Tesoro in Otranto, risking your own lives and taking the lives of others. The idea frightens me, because I may lose you. But it has given you the greater pleasure in making love. Men have always gone from love to war, I suppose, but it angers me.'

'And adds no sweetness to our loving?'

'Not for me. I am a woman.'

'You . . .' began Leonardo, and then fell silent.

'Go on,' Bianca said.

'I was about to say that you have the courage of a man, until I reflected that this was a kind of arrogance; as though men had courage but women none. Since that is plainly untrue, it is also discourteous. As for love and war, my heart, I cannot deny that you're right. But don't imagine that I am not frightened too.'

173

'Apprehensive, perhaps, not *not* frightened. You look forward to it.'

Since this also was true, Leonardo said nothing.

'And these beautiful flying machines of yours,' Bianca went on. 'Why is it that the first thing they must be used for is battle? Why always war, and never peace?'

'Because men give only of their best in war. I sometimes think that Providence has ordained it so. Our gunners yonder are but half alive when they have no battle to fight. If they have no enemy outside Florence, they fight Florentine infantrymen out of pure high spirits, and if there are no infantrymen about, they fight each other. You have seen it. What's the easiest way of obtaining money from a patron? For purposes of war. If I had gone to Lorenzo de' Medici three years ago and begged him for a thousand florins, or a hundred, to enable me to perform experiments in the science and the mathematics of ballistics, would I have got them? No. He gave me the money and the support I needed because he himself had a military need. He desperately wanted the city of Castelmonte recaptured from Rome, and I offered him a chance of taking it. Now he has his cannon, and I have my knowledge, and both of us are satisfied. But it was war, Bianca, that brought this happy state of affairs to pass. And if a ruler wishes me to make a statue for his glorification, does he ask me to portray him as a wise man with a book? He does not. He wants to be shown astride a war horse, wearing armour and holding a sword aloft. War is the mainspring of endeavour, and most men seem half asleep except when fighting.'

'Or making love?'

'Perhaps,' said Leonardo. 'It may be that love and war are more alike than I had thought.'

'And you?' asked Bianca, putting her arms around him.

'I cannot cast stones, even if I wished to,' answered Leonardo. 'How long have I considered the possibility of flying, casually and as an exercise of the mind? Many years now. How long have I known that flight was possible? A year, perhaps. I have a hundred pages filled with notes and sketches, diagrams of this type of wing and that, studies of the way in which birds soar, or flap, or glide. But it took

174

Sultan Mohammed and his invading armies to impel me into making human flight a reality. Do you see?'

'But that's terrible,' Bianca said.

'Is it? I wonder. There are things which I believe concerning Almighty God, and other things which I do not believe, but there is one thing I *know* of Him. He must be an engineer, even as I am. I have only to look around me to see at once that this is so; for what is a tree, a leaf, a river, a grasshopper, if not an exquisite piece of engineering? And if Almighty God is an engineer, perhaps He has an engineer's problems, as I do. I cannot build a flying machine without accepting the possibility that it may fall from the sky and be dashed to pieces, since this risk is a part of flight itself. Perhaps God could not have created man with desires and aspirations without accepting the likelihood that he would fight and kill for those desires and those aspirations. So perhaps war may be a necessity, to remain so until a larger enterprise be found to unite mankind.'

Bianca turned to lie on her back, still holding Leonardo's hand.

'I cannot imagine what such an enterprise might be,' she said. 'To fly around the world?'

'That is merely to fly farther than I have done, and is inevitable,' Leonardo replied. 'But to fly *higher* . . . what do you see above you, Bianca?'

'Stars.'

'To fly to the stars, then,' Leonardo said. '*There* is an enterprise which might absorb all man's energies, and leave him no time for war.'

'It might also be impossible.'

'No,' said Leonardo. 'Everything is possible. Have you not learned that yet, little madonna?' He leaned over her, and kissed her mouth gently. 'Is anything impossible? Tell me.'

'Nothing is impossible,' Bianca said. 'Nothing at all.'

From an upper floor window in the Turkish command headquarters, Girolamo Riario looked out over the city's main square and the gun emplacement immediately below him. He had been drinking steadily since midday, and the fingers of his left hand now played incessantly with the neckband of his doublet. He stared up into the darkness of the night, his mouth working soundlessly, repeating some secret litany over and over again. He drank deeply, the wine spilling over his lips and to his chin.

'*I have seen them,*' he whispered, hoarsely. 'Last night I saw them, and again this morning. A portent.'

'Of what?' said Shan Khara impatiently. He was seated at a table at the far side of the room, dealing with an interminable stream of dispatches and orders.

'Who knows?' Riario said, without turning. 'Of death, or destruction. But I have seen them. They are black winged, and they ride the night wind like angels—or devils.'

'Or dreams, Roman,' said Shan Khara, with faint contempt. 'Or dreams.'

'They are not dreams. I do not speak of dreams, but of what I have seen with my waking eyes. They were as shadows, true; but shadows are not cast by nightmares.'

'You are sick, my friend,' said the Turk. 'Sick in your mind, and growing worse daily. These fancies of yours, when did they begin? When I gave you the news that Leonardo da Vinci had escaped your claws and was still alive. Your eyes started from your head as though I had told you he was a genie. He is not. He is a man like you and me. Therefore kill him if you can; and if you cannot, then leave him to me. In either case, stop behaving as though he had bewitched you.'

Riario left the window, and pressed finger and thumb against his closed eyelids. 'My hand trembles,' he said. 'Of course you are right. All men can be killed, Shan Khara, can they not?'

'All men,' agreed the Turk. 'And now leave me in peace. I have no time for visions, or shadows, or angels of destruction. Return to your own castle, if you can face the ghosts of your own conscience there.'

'I will stay here in Otranto,' Riario said. 'With your permission.'

'Anywhere,' said Shan Khara indifferently, 'so long as it is not in this room.'

Rigo Leone settled the hook at the end of his right arm

176

into a notch he had carved for it in the handgrip above his head; he shifted his feet in the stirrups, and looked downwards along the line that still anchored him to the ground. He could barely see the winch men below him, since the moon was a mere sickle blade that drifted in and out of the clouds. Just as well, Rigo thought, otherwise any moon gazer in Otranto or the Roman army would be able to see him and his three companions plainly.

How high he was he did not know, though the men at the foot of his line could have told him from the markings on their drum that he was eight hundred feet above their heads and almost a thousand feet above sea level. The four flyers had left their camp shortly after eight that evening, and had marched circuitously, dragging with them the wagon that carried their gliders. Climbing the lower ridge, they had been smoothly launched from a point where they could not be seen by curious eyes.

The landward wall of Otranto lay about half a mile distant and thus well beyond the tents of Rome's army and those of her German mercenaries. It seemed a long way off, and Rigo hoped that Leonardo's calculations would prove correct. He was not an over-imaginative man, but he could envisage—with pitiless clarity—the results of failure to clear the top of the wall, or indeed of falling to earth beyond the Turkish cannon inside the city. He turned his head cautiously to the right, and was reassured to see Leonardo himself some fifty paces away—if the word *pace* held any meaning up here in the vault of night—and at the same height as himself. On his left, at an equal distance, Cipriano di Lucca hung beneath another curved quadrilateral of silk, and beyond him was Tesoro di Veluti.

All seemed well so far, thought Rigo, and strained to pick out the details of the terrain that lay before him and to the grey line of Otranto's wall. The river he could see plainly—a thread of silver across the almost featureless plain. Around it winked a thousand red pinpoints of glowing braziers. It is God's gift to the artilleryman, this incredible achievement, he said to himself. How often had he longed to be given one clear glance at the whole of whatever stronghold lay before the muzzles of his guns, to see its redoubts, its turrets, its ravelins, its strengths and weaknesses? If it were daylight, he could have that view now.

He looked towards Leonardo again, waiting for the signal and feeling his hooked right hand slide awkwardly in its notched grip. The black sail above him tilted, humming. How many men, he wondered with a sudden thrust of ironic happiness, could ever claim that they had exchanged a hand for a pair of wings?

He saw Leonardo's glider leap forward like a falcon loosed upon its prey, and reached for his knife. He cut himself free, allowing the wind and the earth to drive him towards the far city a thousand feet below.

Cipriano di Lucca fought to suppress the laughter that threatened to burst from his lungs and throat, just as it had done on each of his two previous flights. On both occasions his friends had been forced to unwind him from the leather straps and the cords of his machine and drag him bodily out from beneath the collapsed silk that covered him, while he did nothing but roll and gasp helplessly.

This was not a sign of sheer amusement, though everybody assumed this was the case. When the cord at his knees parted and he began his glide, he would in quick succession be overcome by absolute terror, insane delight, and then a disbelief in the reality of what was happening to him—that he could be taking part in it—and particularly that he might even survive it. The sweep of the knife that freed him was, to Cipriano, utter suicide, as surely as though he had plunged its blade directly into his heart. It was therefore ridiculous, it was dangerous beyond all fantasy, and yet it was happening. And so by the time he was half way to the ground, his mind found its own relief from terror and joy in huge gusts of laughter that ended only when he had crawled away, exhausted, to the refuge of some tuft of long grass.

On his second flight, Scudo had found this performance so disconcerting that he had booted the reluctant pilot to his feet and poured the contents of a water flask over his head.

'What's so funny?' the big gunner had demanded, shaking Cipriano until his teeth rattled. 'What in God's name is the joke, eh, pretty boy?'

But Cipriano could only shake his head.

Now, as the summit of Otranto's wall hurtled towards him, he took a firm grip on his emerging laughter. To swoop over the heads of Turkish gunners and sentries like an invisible and audibly cackling vampire bat might throw them into confusion, but it was not the way he must enter their city. He held his breath, and the battlements which were clearly about to break every bone in his body, slid away a hundred and fifty feet below him. Three seconds later he was equally convinced that he was going to land squarely on top of the sleeping crew of a cannon. Then they too fell away and he found himself rushing down a wide canyon, one of the channels blasted through the city's vitals by Sultan Mohammed as part of its defences.

Cipriano's landing was a poor one, though this was only partially his fault. Deprived of wind by the buildings around them, his wings began to droop, but he was too occupied searching for a clear space in which to set down to make the necessary gentle correction to their angle. While still ten feet and more from the ground, he suddenly caught sight of Rigo and Leonardo as dark and struggling shapes against the paler greys of the street's surface, and at once committed the sin he had been warned against. He instantly pulled himself backwards in a reflex attempt to stop. At once the leading edges of his wings flapped upwards, caught the air again, and collapsed. By good fortune he was already well past his two companions; otherwise he would undoubtedly have knocked them flat. As it was, he fell like a fledgling crow in a welter of spars and silk, with a wrenched shoulder and a doublet torn from neck to hem.

Leonardo and Rigo, in alarm, ran towards him. They found him cursing briskly and fighting free of the last of his harness. Then all three of them stood in a doorway and looked up at the sky.

Rigo sucked at a loose tooth, testing it. 'Well?; he said. 'Where is the infant?'

Tesoro di Veluti was in fact more than a minute from landing, on a mission which had taken—quite literally— an unexpected turn.

Whereas the others, sliding down the wind in front of him, had followed one another in almost a direct line,

179

Tesoro had indulged in one or two gentle turns and slide slips out of sheer high spirits. As a result of these experiments, he had crossed Otranto's outer wall several hundred feet to their right. This would have made little difference were it not for the fact that by some accident of topography and airflow, he crossed the wall at a point where there was a sharp up-current.'

Tesoro was surprised, and then momentarily alarmed. His glider, unaccountably, was now thrown skywards, interrupting its continuing downward glide. A man with less instinctive control of his machine—for Tesoro, as Leonardo had previously observed half jokingly, was a natural pilot—almost surely would have crashed. Tesoro did not, and his alarm turned to pleasure when he discovered that he now been granted an extra one hundred feet of altitude. He wheeled exultantly and, as the narrow moon appeared from behind a cloud, saw that he was immediately above the roof of the cathedral, and well past the point at which he was already supposed to have made a landing. Not a whit put out by this, and in fact convinced that God had offered him an excellent field of roof slates upon which to set down, Tesoro made a last triumphant turn into the wind and prepared to land.

'Did you see?' said Cipriano, pointing. 'A glimpse only. He must be coming to earth over there.'

'I saw him,' Leonardo replied. 'He knows where to meet us, and we dare not waste a moment trying to find him. Come.'

A quarter of a mile away, Girolamo Riario staggered back from the window with a soft moan, and went in search of another wine flagon. He, too, had seen Tesoro di Veluti; but he did not say so to those whom he found in his way, and who were impelled to call silently upon Allah when they saw the ghastly expression on the Count of Imola's face.

Beneath the city, Scudo took an impatient grip on the heavy iron grille that blocked his path, set his feet in the current of the sewer's flow, and began to pull. Shan Khara's masons had strengthened it and reset its crossbars in the stonework at either side of the sewer. They might as well have used fabric and thread for all the resistance it offered to Scudo. He banged it idly against the tunnel wall when he had torn it free, and washed his hands in the water that foamed around his calves.

'Give me the lantern,' he said to his men, and led the way forward. He was in a foul temper because, as Leonardo had predicted, he had been forced to submerge his three guns, and his entire assault crew some fifty paces from the point where the outflow left Otranto's wall. Wrapped carefully in oilskin, only their powder remained dry. They were forced to submerge not because of the water's depth but in order to avoid the possibility of being seen by a stray sentry from above. Scudo would rather have kept himself and his equipment dry, entering the stream nearer to the base of the wall, but he had timed the march of the sentries and had decided not to risk it.

He reached the domed chamber at the far end of the drain, gathered his twenty-four men about him, looked calmly up at the trickling mouths of the pipes that discharged all about them. He waited.

Leonardo, Rigo and Cipriano converged like wraiths upon the alley leading to the storm sewer's outlet. As they had expected, both ends of the alleyway were guarded by sentry teams, each of four men. Leonardo climbed to the roof of the terrace of empty houses lining one side of the alley, and returned ten minutes later to report that six more Turks were guarding the storm sewer exit.

'They will change their watch at midnight, unless we are exceedingly unlucky,' he said. 'We have plenty of time before then, and Scudo must be waiting by now.'

'Good,' said Rigo. 'Just so long as Tesoro does not come charging into the middle of us like a stuck boar.'

'He has more sense than that, I hope.'

'Then your hope is greater than mine. Personally I do not think the boy has any sense whatever. But let us do what we can, and pray.'

They took the nearest group of sentries without further ado. When they had dragged the men—three of them unconscious, and one dead—into a deserted carpenter's shop, Cipriano wondered aloud whether it might not be an

181

excellent idea to change into Turkish uniform.

'You have a mania for costume,' said Leonardo. 'No.'

They climbed to the roof tops, as he had done, and crossed to the far end overlooking the alley. Here they saw, conveniently, that the second group of guards had divided, two men having gone into a nearby house to rest or take refreshment. The three gunners descended the stairway in silence, and found one man at a table; Rigo laid him out with a single blow on the head, and Cipriano felled the other as he returned from his ablutions. Leonardo whistled softly at the entry way, and the second pair of watchmen walked toward the door, asking a question idly in Turkish. As they reached the doorway, the artist put an arm around each of their necks and rammed their skulls together with a thud he feared must be audible all over the city, then laid them tenderly side by side in the narrow passage.

With this end now secure the three companions then walked along the backs of the houses until they reached the angle in the alleyway. Here, Leonardo entered the nearest door, and found immediately inside it a stairway leading to a cellar. Feeling his way cautiously down, he discovered a candle on a ledge, which he lit. In the cellar itself he came upon several kegs of wine and a large jar of vinegar. This he brought upstairs, leaving the candle burning on the cellar floor. He satisfied himself that the door at the head of the stairs was a stout one, and beckoned to Rigo and Cipriano.

'After this, no subtlety,' he whispered. 'Are you ready?'

They nodded, and Leonardo tossed the pottery jar down the cellar steps. It broke with a crash, and the acid smell of vinegar at once filled the passageway.

Hiding themselves in a room opposite the cellar door, they waited to see how many victims their bait would ensnare. Three men entered the passage from the front of the house; one of them held a lantern. They whispered volubly, sniffing in puzzlement as they advanced. When they reached the head of the cellar stair, their leader caught sight of the candle's gleam below, drew his sword, and dashed heedlessly down the steps, followed at once by two of his supporters. It was not clear what they imagined they would find—a cat, perhaps, or a thief with a fondness for vinegar—but no sooner were they below stairs than

Leonardo stepped quickly out of hiding and closed the cellar door, bolting it securely.

Rigo and Cipriano at once charged into the alley at full tilt, taking the three remaining Turks completely by surprise. As soon as one had been disabled, Leonardo left Rigo and Cipriano to manage the other two and ran to the circular trap that opened the way from the sewer. He pulled it aside, and peered down into the watery darkness.

'You've been having yourself a late supper, have you?' Scudo inquired. 'We were just on the point of going home again.'

Leonardo stretched down an arm, which was something of a mistake, since Scudo's weight almost toppled him into the chamber. He braced himself, however, and the giant emerged, very damp and smelling powerfully of sewage water. He was disappointed to find that Rigo and Cipriano had already disposed of any possible foes, and that he had only to bring up his three guns and his twenty-four men from the drain-head below.

Twenty minutes later the Medici Gunners were ready to move forward into the city.

'Where's Tesoro?' asked Giunta di Lenzo. 'Has he broken a leg, or something?'

'Doubtless he will tell us when he finds us,' said Rigo. 'Move out.'

'It's a problem,' said Tesoro di Veluti to himself.

It had taken him some time to detach the harness from around his body. Not that the task itself was too difficult, but he had found it tricky to avoid falling a hundred feet or more from the gutter where his aircraft had come to rest on the cobbles of the cathedral square below him. His landing had been well executed, but the slates were so smooth that had it not been for a wing spar wedged between two gargoyles, he would by now have been dead.

He could not immediately find a way down, until it dawned on him that he must first climb to one of the roof ridges of the great building and make his way into the tower, one side of which had been torn away by gunfire.

He set himself to wriggle up the slates, trying—fruitlessly—to use the palms of his hands like the suckers of a

183

wall lizard. After a few minutes and one near-disastrous slide towards the gutter, he removed his boots, which at once made his ascent much the easier, though still somewhat nerve-racking. Thus it was that he reached the gable, and balanced his way along it like a tight rope walker until he grasped the base of the cathedral tower. Edging his way around the lead flashing where it overlapped the roof, he found an oriel window and pulled himself inside.

He peered down into the nave, far below. At first he could see little in the gloom, which was relieved only by faint moonlight entering from the east window. As the minutes passed, however, his vision sharpened, and he suddenly recognised why the darkness below him was so much blacker than it might otherwise have been.

'*Mother of God,*' said Tesoro quietly. 'Dear, sweet Madonna!'

Slowly and with great caution, he began to search for footholds by which he might descend into the cathedral.

Seventeen

FANNED BY TWO Nubian slaves, Sultan Mohammed II sat in the great after-cabin of his galley and listened to his young commander's midnight report. When they had dealt with such matters as the disposition of the sentries and the readiness of the Ottoman artillery, the Sultan posed another question.

'What of the Count of Imola?'

'Lord,' replied Shan Khara, 'Allah has seen fit to smite him, so that he wanders in his wits. He babbles of spirits riding the wind, of black-winged demons and the like. Also, he is drinking to excess.'

'Does he interfere with you in the performance of your duties? Should he be confined under lock and key?'

'Not yet, lord,' replied Shan Khara, 'though it may come to that before long. But what of his own command? That is what troubles me. Until now he has come to us in secret, unsuspected by his Romans and his German hirelings. Today he rode into our lines shortly after dawn as though chased by ten thousand devils, scattering our picket lines and overturning a tent or two in his frenzy. He has been in the city ever since; and, however poor a leader he may be, his field captains must have noticed his absence by now. If we confine him, we shall be forced to announce that we have captured him. If we do not, then we risk exposing his complicity with us.'

The Sultan thought for a moment. 'It is in God's hands for the present,' he said reluctantly. 'But what has brought him to such a pass?'

'Is it not plain enough, lord? He was but half a man to begin with, being a traitor and a coward. He has long been obsessed with his desire to kill Leonardo da Vinci. In this he has failed repeatedly and his mind now whispers to him that Leonardo da Vinci is immortal.'

'Ah,' said Sultan Mohammed. 'It comes back once again to Leonardo da Vinci, does it? Tell me, do you believe that he and his gunner friends are hereabouts?'

'I believe they are, lord,' Shan Khara said, 'or, at the least, that they will come to face us at Otranto before long. I would guess that neither he nor his companions are men who could resist a challenge.'

'That is what I believe also, and it does my heart good to know that we have *some* opponents who are worthy of our respect.' The suspicion of a smile touched his mouth. 'Look to your defences, Shan Khara, and look well. Leonardo da Vinci has been inside Otranto once, and I am not prepared to wager that he will never set foot here again.'

Otranto's warehouse quarter occupied most of its eastern and seaward edge, lying for the most part immediately behind the perimeter wall. The area spread out untidily at either side of the main thoroughfare from the harbour gates to the central square. It was one of the few parts of Otranto left intact by Sultan Mohammed. He had spared it, of course, because he foresaw the need for storing vast amounts of material for the second wave of his invasion. Nearly all the warehouses were packed to bursting point with his supplies and equipment, some of which had overflowed into the narrow streets and alleyways.

The Medici Gunners had approached the quarter along the inside of the southern wall, their progress being somewhat akin to threading a maze. Rigo Leone had insisted that their three guns be carried dismantled, since even the creak of a wheel might have alerted a sentry on the wall top, thereby precipitating a battle for which they were not yet ready. That they would need to fight their way out of Otranto he had no doubt, and all of them were prepared to do so when the need arose. But for the present they crept through the dark byways like cats, intently and in dead silence.

By one o'clock in the morning Rigo and Leonardo lay prone on the roof of one of the smaller warehouses. Ten paces from them sprawled a dead janissary, upon whose unsuspecting back they had leaped from the gable of the adjoining building. Before he died the janissary had performed a notable service for them. and one which Leonardo had predicted: since he was the only guard they had seen on any roof, it followed that the warehouse he was protecting must be the powder magazine, or so Leonardo insisted. They lifted one edge of a skylight, and found that he was correct.

They peered over the edge of the parapet, and took note of the dozen or so guards who still patrolled the front, rear and sides of the building. Unless one of these were to call to the man on the roof, they presented no danger. Across the street, Tomasello Cennini lifted a hand from a neighbouring roof; he, in his turn, could be signalled by Balestraccio, who overlooked the wide main concourse running westwards to the central *piazza*.

Neither Rigo not Leonardo had any intention of being caught unawares; they had a ticklish job to perform, and they would achieve it more easily for knowing that their front and flanks were secure.

Leonardo hooted softly into his fists, and was answered from left and right below. Scudo and Giunta di Lenzo, then, were in position and their weapons were ready to fire. He could just make out the muzzle of Marco di Carona's gun, in the entrance to a workyard adjacent to the main street. Tactically, therefore, the gunners held the southern, western, and northern approaches to the quarter, and if they were not surprised by a watch patrol all would be well for the next quarter of an hour, at least.

Leonardo delved into the pouch at his waist and brought out a curious mechanism with an appearance somewhat like a clock. He had, indeed, built it in the main from the workings of just such an instrument, but now from one side of its case protruded a lever armed with flint, cocked against the pressure of a powerful spring. Below the flint was a spoon-shaped depression with a serrated edge, into which he now poured a tiny quantity of gunpowder from a leather flask.

'What is that?' Rigo asked.

'Our fuse,' replied Leonardo. At this Rigo reached into

his own pouch and produced three of the wrapped and measured charges normally used by the Medici Guns.

'I thought we would be laying a powder train,' he whispered.

'No,' said Leonardo. 'This is better than a powder train. Let me show you.'

As Shan Khara returned to his command post overlooking the main square of Otranto, Girolamo Riario rose from a chair and greeted him. He seemed drunk, and his eyes still glistened strangely; but he was calmer and more coherent.

'Well,' he said. 'I have found it.'

'Found what?' asked Shan Khara.

The Count held up a small triangle of heavy black silk, torn across two edges. From a brass eyelet in one corner of it a short length of wire dangled.

'*A pair of wings*,' Riario breathed. 'A machine that flies. Something like that, though I do not know what. I will take you to it.'

'What fantasy is this?' demanded Shan Khara angrily. 'Your dark wings have taken substance, have they? What rubbish is that in your hand?'

'It is a piece of . . . it is part of something—a device, a machine. Something as big as this room we stand in, or bigger. Will you come? His voice carried an undertone of pleading, and then slid towards madness again. 'Monsters,' Riario said. 'Huge monstrous *things*. There are three of them. Engines of the Devil? Who knows? Messengers of death . . . all broken, Turk, do you understand that? Twisted and lifeless. Empty. You have ghosts abroad in your city.' He flung the scrap of cloth violently away from him, as though it were a scorpion. 'Believe me or not, as you choose. It is all one to me. But they are here.'

He sat down again, clutching at his neck with nervous fingers. Shan Khara looked down at him, and then at the fallen piece of silk, frowning.

'I will come,' he said. 'Show me your monsters.'

Tesoro di Veluti prowled in near darkness, snapping his fingers and humming softly to himself. It had taken him more than an hour to examine every nook and cranny of the cathedral and to form an idea of its contents. For the first twenty minutes he had stumbled from chancel to sacristy, from choir to nave, before lighting one of the altar candles with a gunner's cheerful disregard for eternity.

It had been his sense of smell that first informed him that the great building was stacked with gunpowder. When he had lit the candle, his first moment of awe while crouched in the tower's oriel window was shown to be justified, and far, far more than justified. On every side of him, now, the orderly ranks and piles of barrels rose towards the vaulted roof of the nave and were lost in darkness overhead. Gunpowder packed the choir and transepts; powder hid the soaring pipes of the organ, crowded the altar steps, crunched loosely under his feet where it had escaped from occasional splits in the kegs that held it, and filled the air with the coarse fumes of sulphur and nitrates. Tesoro paced out the stacks of barrels, guessed their height, counted them, and did some mental arithmetic.

There were, he computed finally, about eight thousand tons of the stuff, give or take a ton or two.

Eight *thousand* tons?

He paced his way to the altar once more, and took the burning candle in hand. Somewhat belatedly, he began to move more cautiously. It was true that—particularly for a gunner who was familiar with it—gunpowder did not hold the terror its reputation lent it, and burned only when a flame was held directly to it. But Tesoro had heard somewhere that the occasional magazine exploded because of small quantities of powder suspended in the air, incautiously fired by an inspector's lantern. On the whole, he felt that if the cathedral of Otranto were to explode, it would be better if he himself were far from it at the time.

There was, of course, no doubt whatever in Tesoro di Veluti's mind that it must explode. After all, God, or Providence, or the wind had guided him here, and to waste his opportunity would be criminal.

Rigo Leone peered over the edge of the roof and scowled. 'A powder train is certain,' he said. 'This contrivance of yours—how certain is it?'

'I have tested it nearly sixty times,' said Leonardo, 'and it has never missed fire.'

'Then let us pray it does not misfire on the sixty-first attempt. Show me again.'

Obediently, Leonardo tipped another pinch of powder into the serrated steel pan, cocked the lever that held the flint, and wound the clockwork mechanism. Its time delay was necessarily imprecise, as Leonardo would have been the first to admit, but give or take a minute or so, it was a very deadly little thirty-minute fuse. Now, however, he tripped the spring-driven pawl with his finger for demonstration purposes; the flint descended with a sharp click, the flint scraped the steel serrations, and the pinch of powder flared briefly, shielded from any possible gaze by their extended cloaks.

'Sixty-one tests,' said Leonardo. 'In any case, a long powder train is far from infallible, particularly in our circumstances. Where would you propose to lay it? Around this roof? It would be seen at once from the top of the wall yonder, and a burning train can be made harmless with a single well-aimed kick. Moreover, this device will give us a far greater time to make our escape; you'd need a powder train several hundred paces long to give us anything like the delay this will provide.'

'Very well,' Rigo said. 'There is no need to argue the point for hours. Get on with it.'

'I have convinced you, then?'

'You will convince me when this building blows up, and not before. I am merely bowing before your enormous wisdom, as I always do, in order not to weary my tongue with discussion.'

'Is that so? One would think,' Leonardo said, 'that a man who has just taught the world how to fly might no longer be subjected to continual barrages of objections like yours.'

'Flying and suchlike nonsense is your province,' Rigo said calmly. 'Gunnery is mine, including all matters such as powder, shot, mines, fuses, slow-matches and powder-trains. I will accept your clockwork fuse when I have seen it work.'

Leonardo grinned and punched his stocky friend on the shoulder softly. Reaching across and retrieving the three gun-charges Rigo had been carrying, he then lashed some fishing line securely around the charges and fuse, afterwards tipping a larger quantity of powder into the steel priming pan than he had used thus far.

He packed more powder around the base of the clockwork itself, so that he now had what was in effect a serviceable incendiary bomb with a total charge of several pounds. To the top of this he tied one end of the hank of line.

He set the clockwork mechanism for about half of its total possible delay, wound it, and very carefully raised and cocked the flint.

'Ready,' he whispered.

Rigo lifted the edge of the skylight a little farther and looked down into the warehouse below. He then beckoned to Leonardo, who slowly lowered the time bomb through the opening of the skylight to the warehouse floor below.

'A lantern would be useful,' Rigo said. 'But one cannot think of everything, I suppose. Down a little more. Swing your line a fraction my way. That's it. It's sitting on top of a keg now.'

Leonardo poked his own head down through the skylight opening, confirming it. Satisfied, he dropped the remaining line beside him, and together he and Rigo sought a way off the roof. They were forced, in the end, to make a longer jump to the next roof than Rigo cared for; but a few minutes later they were alongside Scudo in the darkness of an alley, separated from the guards that patrolled the magazine by a distance of a hundred paces or more.

Shan Khara lifted the edge of a crumpled expanse of black silk, while Girolamo Riario looked on with an air of triumph.

'Well, Count,' the Turk said, 'you were right in part, it seems. Your dark wings exist, though they are not those of angels or devils. These are kites—and capable, I think, of carrying a man.' He looked up, scanning the night sky, before deciding that he was wasting time. He did not understand how it could be possible to fly such things without a cord, but he was far too practical a man to indulge in useless speculation.

'Kites?' Riario said.

'Are they not common in Italy?' said Shan Khara. 'Children play with them often in Persia and the Orient. And there are no ghosts in Otranto, Captain-General, unless your sick mind considers the men who have flown hither in these machines as ghosts. I can give names to them. They are Leonardo da Vinci, Captain Leone, and one Cipriano di Lucca, with all of whom I am familiar. You had better follow me.'

He strode off towards the main square, disregarding his companion's sharp and hissing intake of breath. Riario stared at a fold of silk, and felt the sudden sweep of a nameless panic seize him; rising in his gorge like fingers that choked off his very breath. He uttered a hoarse cry and set himself to follow Shan Khara, his chest labouring with every step.

In the square Shan Khara summoned one man after another, sending them upon the errands he saw as vital. He dispatched a party to the drain head, and another to the powder magazine, thus displaying an accuracy of thought which was commendable in the circumstances. To his Captain of Janissaries he gave orders to seal off the warehouse quarter from either side, and told him on no account to enter the area.

'We will take these men with their own weapons,' he said. 'Have the guns which we took from the Castello del Mar brought here to this square, and at once.'

'All of them. sir?'

'Every one of them,' said Shan Khara. 'By Allah, we will teach these clever infidels a lesson they will not soon forget!'

Tesoro di Veluti, with a keg of gunpowder under one arm, struggled to force open the small side door that led from the cathedral sacristy into the cloisters. After battering the lock to pieces with a crucifix—an act for which he begged the forgiveness of the Madonna, since he was a pious youth—he now kicked open the door itself. He turned, and removed the wooden bung that sealed his powder barrel, spilling a generous heap of black grains across the threshold. He was still humming softly, and occasionally broke into fragments of some tuneless song.

An impartial observer might have said that he lacked imagination, or simply that he did not know what he was doing. What would Rigo Leone tell me to do, he wondered? Do it quickly, do it right, light it correctly, and then—run like hell itself was on my heels. So be it.

Tesoro laid his train around the arcade surrounding the cloister lawn with the air of a man who is doing a sound job, and doing it well. *O dearest love,* sang Tesoro, who at twenty knew rather less of love than he did of gunpowder, *call to me from your window, and I will fly to you on the wings of the swan.* He turned a corner of the arcade, trailing black seeds of destruction tidily behind him. *For though I am far away from you, my heart is always listening for the sound of your gentle voice* . . . Here the contents of his powder keg ran out, and he crossed the lawn and entered the sacristy to choose another one.

He was not yet sure how long a train he intended to lay, but whatever its length he was determined that it should not be too narrow. A less determined man, of course, might have set the altar candle to burn down in its socket into an open barrel of gunpowder, but Tesoro di Velùti had no wish to wait around all night for the grand flowering of his handiwork.

He came out with a second keg and began to sing again at his task, tunelessly, as before.

Tomasello Cennini and Balestraccio appeared as shadows at the mouth of the lane, and approached on silent feet.

'They have us boxed,' Tomasello said. 'I cannot tell how many men there are, but they have sealed off our escape to the north and south.'

'Leaving us only the main square,' added Balestraccio. 'And it's ringed with cannon.'

'Rome's cannon?' asked Leonardo.

'All forty-seven of them,' Balestraccio said, grinning in the darkness. 'Rome's cannon.'

'Well, then,' grunted Rigo, 'what are we waiting for? We cannot stay here all night. Let us go up to the square and see what terms they have to offer us.'

The square, as they could see while they were still a considerable distance from it, had been illuminated with torches on every side.

'They are making a ceremony of it, are they?' said Marco di Carona, joining the other two gun crews from one side of the main street. 'Good luck to them, I say. How long until . . . you know?' He jerked his head over his shoulder.

'Not long,' replied Leonardo. 'But long enough for us to make ourselves heard, I trust.'

They strolled into the *piazza* two minutes later, twenty-eight men strong, with three cannon. Against them Shan Khara had drawn up every one of the guns he had taken from the Castello del Mar, ten on either hand and twenty-seven at the far side of the square. Their muzzles gleamed in the light of a hundred torches set in windows and on balustrades, or held aloft by the Janissaries and men-at-arms who thronged the covered walks all around. The Turkish commander himself was standing at the right of the square, beneath the window of his command post. Behind the line of guns ranked immediately opposite them the gunners could see one of the half-destroyed avenues that led towards the city's rear gates.

Leonardo, Rigo and Cipriano, together with Scudo's gun crew, proceeded straight to the redoubt in which was mounted the only Turkish cannon not pointing in their direction. This was, of course, one of those set in position to command the landward gates, and was of no tactical importance as things now stood. Its guards had deserted it, and were nowhere to be seen. None the less, Scudo climbed the redoubt and proceeded, with calculated insolence, to hammer a leaden spike into its touch-hole, thus removing it from any possible part in the action to come.

The gun crews of Giunta di Lenzo and Marco di Carona, meanwhile, wheeled to right and left of the group at the redoubt, and placed themselves to cover the sides of the square. They performed this manoeuvre with a casual and apparently ill-disciplined speed and grace; only a seasoned artilleryman would have recognised the months of practice that had gone into perfecting the flawless drill. Each of their guns were loaded with grapeshot, though this was a fact that mattered little. They aimed their guns—and relaxed.

To the assembled Turks, none of this was in any way comprehensible. The facts of the encounter were simple; forty-seven cannon were ranged against three; all were of about the same size and general design; and against twenty-eight Florentines was set a respectable portion of the entire garrison of Otranto. Of the Prophet's followers, therefore, only Shan Khara approached the situation with caution. These men were not fools, he knew, and appearances sometimes deceive.

He came towards the centre of the square, and raised his hand in the silence.

'Welcome, friends,' he said and acknowledged Leonardo's answering and gracious salute. 'I have been expecting you, though I confess I did not expect you to fly over my walls.'

Cipriano nudged Leonardo. 'Riario is behind him,' he murmured. 'Yonder, in the doorway. You see him?'

'I do,' said Leonardo, and raised his voice. 'Well met, indeed,' he called to Shan Khara. 'And what now?'

'That is plain enough,' answered the Turk. 'Your men are well drilled, and are managing a brave display; but I have you in the hollow of my palm, for all that. Come, now. What will it avail us to use our weapons upon each other? You will kill some ten or twenty of my men if I allow you one salvo. Then, you are—doomed. I would not care to see such a thing happen. Stand away from your guns and lay down your arms, and you have my word that I will treat you as honourable captives. Agreed?'

'Sir,' Leonardo replied with equal courtesy, 'we have been busy this night. I must warn you, in good faith. You cannot suppose, surely, that we are putting on a mere show of bravado?'

'Ah, but I can. I suppose it quite easily. Do I see my friend Cipriano di Lucca there beside you? Ah yes, I do. Now he is a man much given to displays of one sort and another, and an expert at not being what *he* seems, as I recall.' Shan Khara laughed. 'You play for time bravely,' he went on. 'Of *course* you have been busy this night. You have set a train to my powder magazine, and you are now waiting for it to explode. Correct?'

At this juncture two men appeared at a trot from the main street behind the gunners. One of them was holding aloft Leonardo's time fuse, now divested of its attached bags of powder. They came across the square and gave it to Shan Khara, bowing.

'But how subtle,' said the Turkish leader, examining the clockwork. 'How admirably conceived! Not a powder train after all. Your ingenuity knows no bounds, Leonardo da Vinci. And do you now admit that you have failed?'

'Yes,' said Leonardo. 'Our time-fuse *has* failed, it seems. Well, man proposes, but God disposes; and we will visit you again another day, perhaps.'

'Another day?' said Shan Khara.

'If God wills it. We request safe passage out of your city.'

'On what grounds?'

'On the grounds that if we are not granted it, we will wreak such carnage here as you have never before seen,' said Leonardo. 'I can give you no fairer warning.'

This brazen demand baffled Shan Khara and left him nearly speechless. For an instant he even wondered whether there might be more of his opponents in Otranto than those he could see before him; *had these Medici gunners set a deeply hidden ambush?* He dismissed the thought; had not his own troops combed the city, and were they not still doing so?

Still searching for words, he was thrust rudely aside by Girolamo Riario. With a look of madness in his eyes, the Count strode forward into the torchlight.

'Turk,' he screamed, 'why do you stand thus and argue with him? *Kill him!* Shoot him down like a dog, and have done! In the name of God and Satan, kill them all!'

Shan Khara caught at his arm, but Riario tore himself free and rushed towards the nearest Turkish cannon. He pushed through its crew and dragged its muzzle around to point directly at Leonardo da Vinci, some twenty-five paces away.

'You cannot kill me, Girolamo,' Leonardo said conversationally. 'Do you not know that?'

Behind Leonardo and unseen by him, a figure burst through the Turkish ranks and sprinted towards Rigo Leone.

'Go!' gasped Tesoro di Veluti. 'Run for your lives, all of you!'

Rigo took a firm grip on his junior gunner's doublet with his left hand and shook him, not unkindly. 'Yes, yes,' he said. 'Be quiet, infant. And where have you been all this time, in any case?'

'*For Christ's sake, run!*' Tesoro repeated wildly. 'We shall all be blown sky high!'

Rigo shook him harder, seeing clearly that Tesoro was close to hysteria. 'Calm yourself,' he said. 'The Turks have discovered our fuse. It is all over.' With this he nodded to Scudo, who came forward and enfolded Tesoro against his enormous chest, almost crushing the breath out of him and effectively stiffling his bellowed attempts at protest.

Leonardo was now within fifteen paces of Riario, and still walked calmly into the muzzle of the cannon aimed at his breast.

'Come, Girolamo,' he said, as though addressing a vicious and excitable hound. 'Come now. You understand me, Girolamo. I cannot be killed. Not here. Not now. Not by you.'

Count Girolamo Riario drew back his lips in a dreadful grin, and plunged the glowing end of a slow-match into the cannon's breech.

'Die!' he howled. He threw his head back and bayed again like some wild animal. '*Die!*'

Powder spurted into flame at the touch-hole. There was an ear-splitting, metallic detonation, and smoke billowed in the torchlight. As it drifted and cleared, every man present could see at once the gaping rent that ran the entire length of the barrel, and the torn muzzle curled outwards in segments like the petals of a bronze flower. Leonardo stood still, unharmed. Beside the tilted carriage of the ruined gun Riario was crawling, shaking his head from side to side, while somewhere at the far side of the square a fragment of metal, or it may have been the cannon ball itself, hummed away into the darkness.

Leonardo addressed Shan Khara.

'Mining powder,' he explained. 'It is too powerful and explosive for gunnery, and we filled all your charges with it many days ago. Fire any of your guns, and they will burst

197

even as this one. Do you wish to try?'

Shan Khara looked at the wrecked cannon and the crawling man beside it.

'No,' said, and managed a wry smile. 'I believe you, Florentine. It is a mercy, perhaps, that I have a great deal more powder of my own.'

Half a mile away, fire crept across the tiled floor of the cathedral cloisters, eating its way daintily along the last few inches of Tesoro di Veluti's carefully laid powder train. It seemed to pause at the threshhold of the sacristy, flaring up into whitehot brilliance as it found more nourishment there. It entered the cathedral like a thief, and grew in a fraction of a second to a stature and power beyond imagination.

The cathedral of Otranto inhaled, and held its breath.

Then its walls, its roof, its pinnacles and its tower erupted up into the night, a fountain of masonry and timber hurled into destruction by eight thousand tons of gunpowder; of sulphur, saltpetre and charcoal coverted in an eye-blink to ash and incandescence. A wave of heat and pressure leaped outwards, devouring all before it, fusing stained glass into droplets of coloured moisture and plucking asunder arch and buttress like straws caught in a whirlwind.

The men in the square, Turk and Florentine, saw for an astonished moment the shapes of buildings outlined as black silhouettes against a dazzling and soundless background of light. Then the immense concussion washed over all of them, bursting eardrums and scattering their senses while they strove to understand what had happened, while the remains of the city about them turned to scorched and tumbled ruins beneath a smoking sky from which rained missiles, great and small.

Then, slowly, man by man, those who were able to do so began to pick themselves up. All were deaf except for the gunners of both sides, whose trained reflexes had protected their ears. Many were stunned by the gigantic shock itself, and here and there a man lay still, crushed by a piece of falling brickwork or pinned by a toppled column.

Of the previously blazing torches only a dozen or so

remained alight, the rest having been snuffed out by the suction that followed on the heels of the blast; but the havoc all around was visible in the orange glow of fire that lit the base of a spreading and mushroom-shaped cloud overhead. At the far end of the main concourse the seaward gates, each thirty feet high, hung askew from their shattered pillars. Beside them a breach in the fabric of the massive outer wall clasped the remnant of the great cathedral tower, thrown intact and toy-like across the entire heart of the town.

On the cobbles of the square, shards of glass were scattered everywhere, and many who now staggered to their feet were surprised to discover themselves bleeding from gashes ripped by flying splinters. Leonardo examined himself superficially for injuries of this nature, found none, and walked across to where Girolamo Riario lay amid a welter of broken gun-carriages and canted bronze barrels.

The Count lay on his side, his knees drawn part way to his chin. At first Leonardo thought he was dead, but then he took hold of Riario's shoulder, turned the man's face upward, and sighed. Girolamo Riario had made that long and final retreat from the world reached only by those whose minds have given way entirely; he was sucking at his thumb like an infant, his eyes were empty of rage or recognition. Leonardo allowed his body to slump again, and walked across to Rigo, Tesoro, and Scudo.

He found the Captain-Gunner engaged in gentle reprimand.

'Tesoro,' said Rigo Leone, 'will you in the future remember that when making a report, you should speak plainly and not yell at me like a savage? Will you do that? Say, "I have laid a fuse to a great deal of powder that you don't know about." Something of that sort. Eh? Do you see, infant? It's more helpful.'

'Hah?' said Tesoro.

'Just as a favour to me,' Rigo added.

'I can't hear you,' said Tesoro di Veluti. 'I'm sorry. There seems to be something the matter with my damned ears. *What* did you say?'

'Nothing of importance,' said Rigo Leone.

Eighteen

'IT WAS, WHEN all is said and done, an unimportant Christian city on Italian soil,' observed Sultan Mohammed II with a touch of amusement. 'Its loss, therefore, will hardly weaken our Empire. And since I did not have you killed when you were brought here to my ship—which may have been foolish of me—I now offer you such poor hospitality as my household may afford, in the hope that we may continue to be friends . . . of a sort.'

The hospitality he spoke of was far from poor; rather, it was opulent in the extreme. The galley's awnings were festooned with glowing lanterns, for the early summer afternoon was drawing to a close. It was well-nigh impossible to walk more than a pace in any direction without stumbling over one low table or another, laden with food and drink.

Across the harbour could be seen the breached outer wall of Otranto, its seaward gateway still open and unrepaired and the battlements which topped it gaping like broken teeth. Behind that wall, Leonardo knew, hardly a building remained standing. The towers and roofs which had formerly shown proudly above its castellations were gone, dissolved into pathetic heaps of debris from which protruded here and there the broken columns of an arcade or the corner of a civic palace.

He turned from the cabin door and came back to take his seat at the Sultan's right hand. Bianca was at his left, while Rigo, Scudo, Cipriano and Tesoro reclined in varying degrees of comfort upon cushions round about. Shan Khara, though somewhat subdued, was none the less amiable, plying the assembled company with delicacies.

'And why did you spare us?' Leonardo asked disarmingly. 'You must have been considerably provoked at the time, my lord.'

'Provoked indeed,' said Sultan Mohammed drily. 'I was enraged beyond measure. Yet it seemed to me, even then, that to take vengeance upon such brave and resourceful men as yourselves over the loss of a trifle such as two hundred thousand barrels of gunpowder would be the act of a revengeful child. On the other hand, to execute you for the loss of my entire campaign in Europe would be inadequate punishment. So I reasoned. It may be that Allah stayed my hand. Who can tell?'

'Are you saying to us plainly, my lord, that your Italian campaign is ended?' Leonardo asked him.

The Sultan regarded him for a minute in silence, and then rose to his feet. 'Will you forgive us, little Vizier?' he said to Bianca, and took Leonardo's arm. Together they walked to the ship's rail.

'This is no secret,' Sultan Mohammed said, 'yet it is something to be said privately between us. Yes, Leonardo da Vinci, I am finished for the time being with your country—and with Europe. The Ottoman Empire will seek expansion to the east rather than to the west, though I have little doubt that we shall skirmish in the Adriatic as we have always done. But you have, as you intended, destroyed my supply of gunpowder for this year's war. I cannot readily replace it. Well, as you see, it is a thing past and done now, and I am a philosophical man. Also a practical one, I think. Two men were to have smoothed my path across Italy by their corruption. One is dead and the other mad beyond recovery—two more matters that I can lay at your door, my friend. I console myself that although your flying machines have deflected Islam from Italy, Italians will not believe you, nor Rome thank you.'

'Quite true,' said Leonardo.

'And you?' Sultan Mohammed said. 'Now that you can fly through the air, will you teach others to follow you?'

'No,' replied Leonardo. 'Your little Vizier, the lady Bianca, compels me to see that my flying machines will be used for killing and for war. If four Medici gunners borrow wings and soar like hawks, that is one thing. But ambitious and savage men will propose flying armies, and that is quite another. I will not assist them towards their ambitions. Oh, I will lay out the principles of flight so that men with eyes to see them can rediscover its secrets for themselves. I had thought, for instance, of writing a small treatise on the flight of birds. But farther than that I will not go. My flying machines themselves lie buried beneath Otranto's ruins, do they not? Let them lie.'

'There speaks wisdom,' said Sultan Mohammed. 'I believe that indeed Allah has you in his care. Well, you are welcome at my court whenever you choose to come there, and perhaps one day you may even enable me to reap the profits of my own forbearance. Who can tell?' He glanced at Leonardo with shrewd irony. 'And meanwhile I wish you happiness, both for yourself and for my little Vizier, until that day when we stand for judgement at the feet of the One God.'

'It is all very well,' said Bianca some time later, when they had returned to the hills beyond Otranto, 'but something has been troubling me for a long while now.'

'And what is that, my heart?' said Leonardo, his arm about her waist.

'Your taste for the dramatic,' Bianca replied. 'Everyone has told me how you stood before the muzzle of Girolamo Riario's cannon, and dared him to fire it. *Was* it drama, Leonardo? Or did you guess that Riario would not fire?'

'I was not guessing my love, I assure you.'

'Oh yes, you were. Supposing Shan Khara had taken the trouble to test Rome's cannon and their powder-charges before bringing them to the square? You would not be here now. Perhaps the odds were in your favour, but it was guesswork.'

'Nothing of the kind,' Leonardo said, and kissed her. 'I knew as soon as we entered the *piazza* that he had *not* tested them. He took forty-seven from the Castello del Mar, and he brought forty-seven to the square. If he had tried his powder beforehand, he would only have been able to muster forty-six. One of them would have already burst.'

'Ah-ha,' laughed Bianca. 'I *see*. And do you know what I think? You *are* clever, Leonardo. Very clever. But one of these days . . . my dearest Leonardo . . . *one of these days . . .*'